MW01491237

DIRTY SECRETS

SPECIAL WEAPONS & TACTICS 7

PEYTON BANKS

ENB PUBLISHING

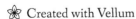

BLURB

A forbidden night of passion. She's his weakness, but he'll risk it all when it comes to her safety.

Zain Roman had sworn off women. Now a bitter divorcé, he no longer believed in the sanctity of marriage. Zain was only interested in having fun, with no strings attached. He was committed to his job in policing the streets and taking down bad guys as a member of the finest SWAT team in the state.

He loved his team, and when he lost a bet, he was man enough to pay up.

Salon owner Omara Knight knew she was playing with fire. One look at the officer sitting in her chair, and she knew she was intrigued. Omara had no time for a love life. She had a business to run and a son to raise.

Zain was a temptation she should avoid. Her sister warned her about him, but Omara never did as she was told.

There was something about a man in uniform that had her wanting to indulge in the sexy pleasures his eyes promised. One night was all she needed.

At least that's what she tried to tell herself.

Zain sensed Omara was hiding something, and when her past came back for her, he's willing to do everything in his power to keep her safe—even give her his heart, but will it be too late?

If you're lucky enough to get a second chance at something, don't waste it.

UNKNOWN

1

"Who the hell brought this here?" Zain Roman chuckled. He wiped the tears from his face as he laughed at the antics of his team.

Someone, they were not sure who, had set up a dartboard in the precinct's bullpen. Competitions had been kicking off for weeks amongst the staff.

This was one thing he loved about his team, they were stubborn and extremely competitive.

"No one has admitted to it yet," Ash replied. He leaned against the desk of one of the detectives.

They were drawing a crowd. It was late afternoon, but everyone wanted to watch the members of Columbia's finest SWAT team go against each other in a heated game of darts.

"All right, Iker. Don't let her beat you." Zain ran a hand along his bearded jaw. He hadn't been one to wear hair on his face until a few years ago when his life had been turned upside down.

"Don't you worry. I got this." Iker strode forward and tossed him a wink.

Zain held out his fist that Iker met with his own. They were close friends. He and Iker had pretty much joined the Columbia police department at the same time.

Fresh cadets from the academy, they had both been inexperienced and wanted to make a change. From the first day they had met, Zain knew Iker would be a trusted officer he could count on and a good friend.

Fast forward years, and he had been right.

They had been there for each other for their ups and downs. Zain had supported Iker when he had walked away from the love of his life. Zain had thought Iker crazy, but then he had to let the man live his own life. It wasn't until recently where Iker realized the error of his ways and fought to get his woman, Jessica, back.

Zain was there to watch his friend grovel and practically stalk her to win her back.

Now all was right in the world.

Zain glanced around at his team. In the past few years, everything had changed for them. They had been a grouchy group of men who were focused on their careers.

Mac was now married to Sarena and had a daughter named Nia. Declan was married to Aspen. Ash was married to Deana with their son, Evan. Myles, of all people, had settled down with Roxxy, a woman who was a saint to put up with the big guy. Brodie was engaged to Ronnie, and they had welcomed their new bundle of joy.

Everyone was happy.

Including him—just being single.

He was done with relationships. His failed marriage had taught him a very valuable lesson.

Love wasn't real.

"You ain't got nothing," Jordan muttered, breaking into his thoughts.

Laughter filled the air at her cockiness. Jordan had every right to be full of herself. She was a damn good police officer and she was more vicious than any of the guys. She could hold her own and would certainly rip any of their balls off if they tried to help her.

"Don't try to cash a check your mouth can't pay out." Zain smirked.

"Oh, is that a wager I hear?" She faced him, her eyebrows raised. Jordan folded her arms and took him in.

"Here we go." Myles clapped.

Everyone knew Jordan couldn't turn down a bet. She easily bested most of them in friendly competitions.

"My money's on Jordan." Brodie snickered.

"Mine, too." Dec tittered.

"I got Zain." Mac sniffed. The SWAT sergeant walked over to Zain and slapped him on the back. "Lose and you'll answer to me."

Zain paused and watched Mac head over to where Dec was standing.

"We doing this or not?" Jordan challenged. "We're both warmed up. One shot."

"I'll bite. I win, you put Curt out of his misery and go out with him." Zain grinned.

The entire precinct knew Curt had tried to shoot his shot with Jordan, but she had turned him down at least ten times. Zain had to give it to the dude, he was determined.

Jordan rolled her eyes as howls and laughter filled the air.

"Where is dear ol' Curt?" Zain glanced around and didn't see the beat cop.

"He's out on patrol," someone shouted back.

"Okay, okay." Jordan held a hand up. Silence fell while everyone waited. "Fine. I'm woman enough to take that wager. If I win, you get a hair and beard cut."

The room exploded.

Zain swept his fingers through his unruly mop. He had been letting it go, not really caring about it. The length was much longer, and his mother had been complaining about it, too.

"Sure, you win, I'll—"

"Nope. I pick the barber," Jordan interjected.

Zain paused. He knew he looked unkempt, but he didn't just let anyone cut his hair.

"Who?" he asked.

"Not telling." She barked a laugh and pointed at him. "Worried?"

"Not at all." He strode forward and stopped in front of her. "Just want to make sure you choose someone worthy of putting their hands on this." He motioned to his face.

She threw her head back and roared laughing.

"Deal?" She wiped the tears from her face before holding out a hand.

He took her smaller one in his with a firm grip. "Deal."

"All right. Looks like we have an official challenge." Ash walked over to the board and snagged two darts and brought them over to them.

The chatter around them increased. Bets and wagers were placed. It was easy to see the females standing around watching were rooting for Jordan.

He didn't care.

He was used to being the underdog.

"I hope you got a sexy outfit planned for Curt," he teased.

"Don't get your hopes up."

They stood back as Ash began going over the wager for those who joined. The crowd was getting bigger. The next shift was coming on, but word had made it through the precinct.

Zain rotated his head and stretched his arms out for show.

"Don't let me down," Iker said and gave Zain a salute.

"Who's going first?" Ash asked.

"Ladies first." Zain nodded.

"Not today. You're up, Roman." Jordan gestured to the board.

"Fine. Let me show you how it's really done." Zain walked over to the piece of tape on the floor.

Jordan moved to stand a few feet away from him.

"The mighty Zain is trying to teach me a lesson." She rested the back of her hand against her forehead dramatically. "Whatever shall I do?"

"Just watch."

The room fell quiet. He zoned in and focused on the red bullseye. He could hit it, no problem. He raised his arm and kept his elbow up and his eyes on the target. Holding his arm still, he tossed the dart, launching it in the air.

He held his breath, watching it land in the green ring around the bullseye.

"Yes." He spun around and met Jordan's gaze.

Cheers and whistles sounded. It wasn't a bullseye, but he would take it. Close enough.

"Cute." She smirked. She motioned for him to budge out of the way.

The crowd settled, and all eyes were on them.

"Let me show you how it's done."

Zain chuckled. This was one of the reasons he loved his team so much. They were close-knit, and everything was fun and games until they were in a heated situation.

On duty, he knew he could count on every member of the SWAT team. They were called into situations where lives were at stake, and he had to trust that someone would have his back.

"Get him, sis!" a voice called out.

Zain grinned.

Of course she would have the women backing her.

Zain stood by Iker and folded his arms.

"Nice throw." Iker elbowed him.

"I'm sure Curt is going to appreciate this favor," Zain called out.

Jordan gave him the bird and faced the board.

The room fell silent again. Tension filled the air, but Zain wasn't worried about this little competition.

Jordan raised her arm and tossed her dart.

Zain's smile disappeared.

Bullseye.

Jordan screamed and jumped up and down in place. The room exploded in cheers and laughter.

"Holy hell," Zain muttered.

"Well, man, it will be you paying up this time." Iker cracked up.

Zain batted away Iker's attempt to tousle his hair.

Jordan turned to him with a devilish glint in her eyes.

Shit.

Their team converged on them while the other bystanders dispersed.

"Looks like it's your turn to pay up to Jordan."
Brodie laughed.

"Damn, man. You lost to a—" Myles was cut off
by Jordan slamming the back of her hand into his
stomach.

"Don't you dare say it." Jordan gave him the
side-eye.

"You know I'm just playing." Myles grinned. He
patted his rock-hard abs, not bothered at all by
her hit.

"I have just the place, and we can go right now."
Jordan eyed her watch.

"Tonight?" Zain raised his eyebrows. He shoved
a hand through his hair.

"Yup. Wouldn't want you to back out of the
deal."

"Never that. I'm always a man of my word."

"We're going to make damn sure he's getting a
cut." Brodie snickered.

His hair had been the talk of the group. Zain
didn't see what the issue was, but he would honor
their bet.

"Pretty soon, he'll be putting it in a bun." Declan
smiled.

Zain held up his hands. He knew when he was

outnumbered. He had a suspicion the fellas had put Jordan up to it.

"I'll do it. She won fair and square."

"Good. We're going now." Jordan folded her arms.

"I think I'll even tag along for this," Mac said. His lips curled up in the infamous Mac smirk.

"Let's go." Iker wrapped an arm around his shoulders.

They followed Jordan out of the precinct after grabbing their gear. They arrived outside to the parking lot, and Zain paused. His gaze landed on her little car.

"We are not riding in that."

She had a tiny sedan that was a four-door, but he didn't see why. All of the guys were over six feet tall and would be crammed.

"What is wrong with my car?" She gasped. She spun around and leveled her gaze on him.

"It's too damn small," Zain muttered.

"None of us can fit in there." Iker snorted. "We can take my truck."

"Yeah, we'll follow y'all there."

Brodie and Myles headed toward his SUV.

"Seriously? None of you want to ride with me?" Jordan hefted her bag up on her shoulder.

Everyone was dispersing to their oversized vehicles.

"None of us can fit in your car," Myles shouted over his shoulder.

"Come on. We'll take my truck, and I'll bring you back here later." Iker walked over to her and draped his arm around her shoulder.

Zain laughed at Jordan's pout.

"Fine."

They piled into Iker's vehicle. Zain sat in the back to allow Jordan to be up front. He had plenty of legroom and cringed at the thought of Jordan's ride. He's knees would have been to his chest.

Iker pulled out of the parking space and headed toward the street.

"Where are we going?" Zain shoved Jordan's shoulder. "And who will be cutting my hair? Do you even know him? Is he any good? A professional?"

She turned around and grinned at him.

"We're going to my sister's shop, and she'll be giving you a fresh cut."

———

"ARE you sure your sister will be up for this?" Zain sighed, strolling along the sidewalk with Jordan.

The rest of the team was behind them, joking and already taking bets if he would chicken out.

He wasn't too sure about a woman cutting his hair. He had a barber he had been going to for years.

He'd just stopped going recently.

His unruly hair hadn't kept him from enjoying life. Women loved to run their hands through his dark curls. It was a conversation starter when he hit the bars.

"She'll do it." Jordan grinned. She glanced over at him with her eyebrows raised. "Don't tell me you're nervous about my sister cutting your hair."

"Hell yeah, I'm nervous. I don't know your sister, nor do I know if she's any good. This is a master-piece, and I need to make sure she can handle this." He tunneled his fingers through his hair. He shuddered at a thought that appeared in his head. "I won't be the first man she's cut, right?"

He didn't want to be a guinea pig. It would be his luck, he'd have a horrible haircut and would have to live with it until it grew out.

"Just watch. She'll have you looking like a human again." She snorted.

They arrived at Fly Styles, and it appeared as if they were closing up for the night. The main window revealed a single female sweeping up around her chair.

Zain's gaze narrowed on her. She was unaware of them standing outside. Her long dark hair was pulled back into a high ponytail. He paused in front of the window and took in the salon. She glanced up and caught sight of them.

Their eyes connected for a brief moment.

The air in his lungs escaped him as he took in her beauty.

Jesus.

"I have a set of handcuffs if we need them," Myles announced, breaking into Zain's thoughts. He slapped Zain on the shoulder, coming up behind him.

Zain blinked and turned to his teammates. He'd seen Jordan's sister once or twice at a few of their functions. He couldn't remember her name but recalled hearing she had a son. Jordan talked nonstop about her nephew. Now he was ashamed he had never paid close attention.

"Not even going to ask why you just have them randomly in your bag." Ash snorted.

"Roxxy called and said—"

"I really don't want to know," Mac grumbled. The sergeant brushed past Myles and stopped by

Zain. "But keep them out just in case we need them."

Laughter went around.

"Come on in." Jordan waved for them to follow her in.

They piled into the salon after her.

Zain's gaze landed on the woman who looked slightly similar to Jordan.

"What is going on here?" Jordan's sister's eyes widened.

"This is Zain." Jordan reached back and pulled him forward.

He stopped next to Jordan, suddenly tongue-tied. She was even more gorgeous close up. Her big brown eyes connected with his. His palms grew sweaty. He wiped his hands on his jeans.

"Hey." It was all he could muster.

What the hell was wrong with him?

This was not him. He never grew nervous around a beautiful woman.

Normally, he thrived in the presence of someone as drop-dead gorgeous as she was, but for some strange reason, he froze.

"Hello. I'm Omara." She reached out her hand to him.

He enclosed his larger one around hers. His breath caught at the softness of her skin.

"Nice to meet you," she said.

"You as well." He cleared his throat.

Jordan moved on and rattled off the rest of the team's names. He kept his attention on Omara. It was a beautiful name. Her luscious lips tipped up into a smile.

Her curvy frame was definitely that of a woman who piqued his interest. She was thick in all the right places.

"Um, Zain?" Omara chuckled.

"Yeah?" He blinked and met her gaze.

"Can I have my hand back?"

He jerked back and snatched his hand from hers.

"Awww...don't tell me Zain is smitten." Iker barked a hefty laugh.

Zain's cheeks warmed at the joke.

"Ha, ha, ha." Zain tried to play it off, but his team was in the mood for busting his balls.

Jordan quickly continued the introductions until Omara had waved and greeted everyone.

"So, what is going on?" Omara asked.

"Zain lost a bet, and the agreement was for him to get a haircut." Jordan folded her arms. She smirked and motioned to him. "Think you can fix him?"

"I think a Mohawk would look great on him," Mac proposed.

"Fuck no." Zain ran a hand through his hair. That would be ridiculous, and he would never live that down at work if he showed up with a damn mohawk. He glared at Mac for even suggesting such a thing.

"Well, can you fix him?" Jordan asked again.

Zain didn't miss the way Omara's gaze cruised along his body. He stood straighter, recognizing the look. She did a little thing where she bit her lip, and he hardened.

Her gaze flicked to his, and he was a goner.

"Let's see, shall we? Come have a seat in my chair."

2

Omara didn't know what she was thinking. She slid her fingers through the thick locks of Zain's hair.

She'd never felt arousal when washing a client's hair, and at the moment, she was turned completely on.

Zain was sexy as hell. She'd noticed him at a function she had attended with Jordan one night. He had a swagger to him that had caught her eye. His hair was thick and beautiful. When she had done a quick assessment, she'd discovered some split ends, but that would be fine. She'd cut it, then trim his beard, and the man would be sex on a stick.

The shampoo was lathering perfectly in his hair. She bit back a giggle, looking at his oversized frame trying to fit in her shampoo chair. It was almost comical to see a big police officer decked out in the salon's black cape. It had been a while since she had cut a non-African-American man's hair, but she was confident she would do well.

Jordan always had her back.

If Jordan was sure she would do fine, then she would believe in her.

Omara glanced over at Jordan, seeing her joking around with one of the guys. She had been worried Jordan would resent her after she had moved to Columbia. Her sister had given up everything back in Atlanta to be closer to Omara and her son.

Omara's heart did a little pitter-patter at the thought of her child. Jason was the light of her life. She couldn't believe he was already eight. It seemed just like yesterday she had brought him home from the hospital.

She could never repay Jordan for everything she had done for her.

A sigh escaped Zain, bringing Omara's attention back to her new client.

"Are you comfy?" she murmured. She grabbed her comb and pulled it through his hair.

He opened his eyes, and she was hit with the sexiest eyes she'd ever seen. They were hazel with big flecks of gold. His lips curled up into a grin that had her core clenching.

"Yeah. Your fingers are magical."

She bit her lip to keep from making a smart-ass remark. She didn't know him to joke with him in certain ways.

"I don't like that smirk." He laughed.

"I don't know what you are talking about." Omara shrugged. The smile wouldn't leave her lips. It had been a while since she had held the attention of man. Not that she didn't have men attempting to get with her.

It was always the ones who were up to no good.

She was done with that life. If remaining single meant she didn't have to deal with a man in and out of jail, drama, and abuse, then she'd get a dog when Jason left for college.

She dropped the comb in the sink and turned the water back on.

"You do. What's going on in that pretty little head of yours?"

Her heart fluttered at the compliment. Her gaze flicked to Jordan who wasn't paying her any mind. Her sister would probably kill her if she knew she was flirting with one of her coworkers.

Omara grabbed the nozzle and rinsed his hair.

"I've been told that before, and I'd have to say it's a gift." Her grin grew wider at the sight of his eyebrows jumping up high. "They always come back wanting more."

"Is that so?" He closed his eyes, relaxing in the chair.

She glided her fingers through his hair easily. She took advantage of the moment and studied his features. His beard definitely needed trimmed.

His lips.

They were made for kissing. She wouldn't be opposed to them running along her entire naked body.

Just the fantasy of seeing them wrapped around her nipple had her holding back a moan.

Omara shut that train of thought down. She glanced down at Zain and found him watching her.

"I'd love to know what was going through your head just now," he murmured. Those eyes of his had a way of looking right through her.

"What are you talking about?" A nervous giggle escaped her.

"The way you gripped my hair while you were lost in thought must mean it was good," he teased. That crooked grin of his was dangerous. "I liked it."

How the hell did Jordan work with these guys

day in and day out? Each of them were drool-worthy. Tall, muscular, and sexy as sin. Her sister spoke of her team as the brothers she didn't have.

It had only been Jordan and Omara growing up. They were extremely close. Jordan had always been her protector. When they were younger, no one dared mess with Omara or they would have to answer to her older sister. Jordan had always been the one getting into fights, so their father had put her in karate to help channel her need to expel her frustrations and anger.

It was a wonder Jordan had grown up to become a police officer. She was tough, unlike Omara, who had a bad habit of letting people run all over her.

"Honey, I don't think you could handle what runs through this mind of mine." Omara grinned, trying to avoid telling him that she was thinking of them in different sexual positions. It had been a while since she'd had any sexual encounters with a member of the opposite sex.

"I definitely like you," he said, closing his eyes again.

She finished rinsing Zain's hair. She took a few moments to make sure it was completely clean and no suds left before wrapping a towel around his head. She sat the chair up and motioned for him to follow her over to her styling chair.

Omara felt his eyes on her. His gaze was like a heated caress. How could this man have turned her on and hadn't even touched her? That's how Omara knew she needed to get laid.

She was never one for one-night stands, but if it was Zain, she'd take that opportunity without thinking twice.

He took a seat in her chair while she gathered what she'd need to cut his hair and style it. Once she was ready, she released the towel and ran it along his hair, trying to get as much moisture out as she could before she started the trim.

"How much do you want taken off?" she asked. She dropped the top along his shoulder and reached for her comb. She slid it through his thick locks that were dark and silky smooth.

"Enough to where he resembles a human again," Iker shouted out.

Laughter went around. Jordan and her coworkers were sprawled around the waiting area. They all were patiently waiting for Zain's reveal.

"You fuckers are just jealous." Zain snorted. He twirled the chair around to face the mirror. He took himself in while thinking. His hair was touching his shoulders, and he could easily put it in a small man bun if he wanted. He settled back and blew out a deep breath. "How about a few inches to shut them up."

"Okay." Omara laughed. She lifted her shears and comb but paused when he rotated to her.

"You are a professional, right?" he asked.

"Um, yeah. Of course I am." She motioned around the shop. What the hell was his problem? He was clearly sitting in a salon. Jordan had shared with her how he and Iker were the craziest of the bunch. How many screws loose did he have?

"Your sister didn't put you up to giving me a bad cut, because if she did, I'll pay you double whatever she's paying you." He was dead serious as he stared at her.

She fell into a fit of laughter. She glanced over at her sister who lifted an eyebrow. She shook her head and turned back to Zain.

"I promise my sister has not paid me off to give you a wack job. I didn't know y'all were coming until you showed up here. I was supposed to close up this shop and head home." She gently turned his chair around and met his eyes in the mirror. "And I promise that your haircut will be fire. No woman would be able to keep her hands off your hair."

"Never had that problem before," he grumbled.

Omara rolled her eyes. She pushed down the hint of jealousy that reared up inside her. How could she feel this way when today was the first time they'd actually spoken to each other?

She began doing what she did best. She loved her job. There was something about helping a person gain confidence by making them look good. Ignoring the conversations from the reception area, she concentrated on trimming and styling Zain's hair.

"Jordan tells us you have a son," Zain said. He sat still, his eyes closed.

"I do. An eight-year-old who keeps me busy." She chuckled. Jason was the light of her life, and she was proud of the little man. With everything they'd been through, he was growing into a good young man. He was intelligent, kind, and caring.

"Jason, right?"

"Yeah." Omara wasn't surprised that Jordan spoke of Jason. The two of them were thick as thieves. Jordan was the doting auntie who loved spoiling her nephew.

"Is he into any sports?"

"He is. He's into football, and Jordan recently signed him up for karate." She bumped the chair to make Zain face her. He opened his legs to allow her to stand in front of him. She didn't want to think what this could look like. Her breath caught in her throat at the thought of sitting on his lap.

Then she remembered how much of a player Zain was. When Jordan came over to her house, she shared stories of her teammates, and Omara hazily remembered hearing that Zain was divorced.

"You have any children?" she asked.

"None that I'm aware of." That sexy grin of his spread across his face.

"What do you mean none that you're aware of? You just out there, huh?" she asked dryly.

His eyes popped, opening. He must have heard something in her tone because he grew serious.

"My ex-wife wasn't ready for children. Every time I wanted to try, she came up with some excuse. By the time we separated, I was actually thankful we hadn't had kids." His voice trailed off, and he stared off at something in the distance.

Omara's heart ached at the thought of this big, sexy man wanting to have a child of his own and being denied the joys of parenthood.

She blew out a shaky breath.

Shady exes were her specialty. She knew all too

well about being deceived by someone who she'd thought loved her.

"I'm sorry," she whispered. Omara didn't know what else to say. Studying him, she sensed there was more to the story, but she wasn't going to push him to share.

He blinked at her words. The distant expression on his face disappeared, and that smile of his came back. Zain seemed to be a master of trying to disguise his feelings, but Omara sensed he had been hurt by his wife's actions. Omara had become really good at speaking with her clients. Part of her job may be to make someone look good by the time they left her chair, but truthfully, the majority was listening to people's troubles and talking with them about them. Who would have thought hair stylists were also therapists?

"Don't worry about it. Honestly, not having kids with her turned out for the best."

"Having a crazy baby daddy is enough. Chicks can be deranged, so maybe you did dodge a bullet if she's as bad as you describe," she murmured. She held back a shiver that threatened to overtake her. Omara was very experienced with having a lunatic of an ex.

She had fallen in love hard when she was

younger. Derrick Allen was handsome, a smooth-talker, and had set his eyes on her. Omara had been just nineteen years old, attending the local community college back in Atlanta. Her family had been poor, and she'd grown up in a low-income area of the city. She'd set her sights on going to college and making something of herself. Both she and Jordan were determined to do well for themselves. Their parents had been right behind them, wanting them to succeed. Every resource they had, they directed toward Omara and Jordan. Whatever Jordan had needed to get into the police academy, they'd helped. What Omara had needed for college and beauty school, they'd given. Cecil and Irene Knight sacrificed so their girls could have a better life.

She'd been in the cafeteria one day at school. She'd been eating her lunch while waiting for her next class to start. There were a group of guys sitting not too far from her, laughing and joking around. They were acting silly, and she couldn't help but laugh at their antics. One of them caught her eye. He'd been tall, dark, and handsome with a bright smile. He'd stood from the table and made his way over to hers.

"Is this seat taken?" he asked.

"No, it's not."

"Mind if I sit here with you?" His grin widened as she acted as if she had a hard decision to make.

"Hmmm...I guess I don't," she replied, a soft smile spreading across her lips.

He barked a laugh and took the chair. He spun it around and sat on it backwards.

"My name is Derrick." He held his hand out to hers.

She slid her smaller one into his and shook it.

"Omara."

And that was how it had started. Derrick had swept into her life and buried his way into it. He had been like a virus. Snuck in and then destroyed everything to the point where she needed to reboot.

Start her life over.

Just her and her young baby.

She glanced down at Zain and found him watching her. The intensity in those light-hazel eyes left her clamping her thighs together. His gaze trailed down her form, and suddenly she was very self-conscious. She wasn't as thin as she used to be. Having a child had added on permanent thickness to her hips, thighs, and ass. She still had a fairly flat stomach and oversized breasts—she was proud of her girls. They'd gotten her a fair share of free drinks when she went out.

She didn't consider herself gorgeous but knew she was pretty.

She finished his hair and moved over to his beard. She'd forgotten how close she'd have to be to a man to trim his beard. She was able to take the time to study Zain. There were flecks of gold in his irises. His skin was smooth, and there was a tiny scar on top of his lip. She wondered where he had gotten it from. His lips—God—were so damn kissable.

This was torture.

She tried to think of him as a regular paying client, but there was nothing regular about Zain.

"So this baby daddy, he giving you trouble?" Zain asked.

His voice was soft, but she caught the slight hardness that was hidden underneath it.

"Nothing I can't handle," she replied automatically. There was no way she was spilling her guts to this man about the hell Derrick had put her through. "Now hold still."

She turned on the liners and began cleaning up his beard and shaping it. She took her time to ensure it was clean-cut. A few minutes later, and she was done.

"Voila. All done." She backed away from him and dropped her clippers on her workspace. She removed the black cape from around him and shook the hair off onto the floor. She'd sweep it up in a moment.

Zain stood from the chair and assessed his new look in the mirror. Her breath hitched at the size of him. He towered over her, making her feel small and dainty. His dark t-shirt clung to his form, showcasing his hard muscles. She was a sucker for a man with toned abs and a hard butt, which Zain had both. Her gaze dropped down to his backside in his jeans. She bit her lip, wondering if he was a boxer brief man or boxers. She doubted he was a tighty-whitey man.

"Damn. I barely recognize Zain's ugly mug." Jordan walked over to stand beside Omara.

She blinked and glanced up, meeting Zain's eyes in the mirror. His lips curled up in the corner in a sneaky grin.

She was busted.

He'd caught her checking him out. Omara's face warmed in embarrassment. She turned to her sister and beamed.

"You like?" she asked.

Their teammates arrived near them, laughing and teasing Zain. Even the hardened sergeant, Mac, cracked a smile and landed a soft jab on Zain's shoulder.

"Welcome back to civilization," Mac said.

Omara had met Mac a few times since her sister had joined their precinct and the SWAT team. Omara was so proud of Jordan for sticking with her dreams. She'd wanted to become a member of a great team that she felt comfortable and safe to work with. According to Jordan, she could count on these meant to always have her back.

"Shit, like we need Zain to have an even bigger ego." The one named Iker snickered. He folded his arms and stared at Zain.

"Don't you go worrying about my ego. I'll find someone pretty enough to stroke it," Zain joked.

Even Omara had to roll her eyes at the bad joke.

"Why don't we go out and get a drink," Brodie offered.

"Someone get a pass tonight?" Myles asked, wrapping an arm around Brodie's neck.

"Ronnie doesn't control me." Brodie grinned.

Laughter went around the room. Omara was fascinated by the camaraderie in the team. It was no wonder Jordan loved the guys so much. They were tough-as-nails cops but had a love for each other they didn't hesitate to show.

"She did tell me not to be out all night," he admitted sheepishly.

The gang groaned, but Omara had a feeling they were all basically in the same boat.

"That's why I'm still single," Jordan announced.

"Hell yeah." Zain bumped fists with her.

Omara chuckled. It was good to see her sister happy for once. She hadn't had luck in the men department either. Her last boyfriend who she'd been with for a few years couldn't keep his dick in his pants. Jordan, being the big strong woman she was, had handled him. Omara wished she had half the strength of her sister.

"Me and Omara will come." Jordan threw an arm around Omara's shoulders.

"I will?" Omara sputtered.

"Of course. You have to come." Zain leveled her with his gaze.

That crooked grin of his had her core clenching. Well, if he wanted her to go out with them, then she guessed she could. It'd been a while since she had gone out and had some fun.

"I guess I could. I just have to pick Jason up and I'm sure I can have him spend the night over at a friend's house." Omara looked at her sister.

"You know he will be dying to go over to Ricky's house. Call Ricky's mom. I'm sure they won't have a problem with him staying the night." Jordan gave her a squeeze. "Plus, you need to get out the house. You are the youngest old person I know."

"Fine." Omara grinned. She turned back to the group, and her heart did a funny beat when her gaze met Zain's. "Count me in."

3

"This round is on me," Zain announced.

He walked behind the waitress who carried their frosty beers. It felt good to be out with his teammates. It was getting harder for them to all meet up for drinks as they once had. His brothers were all getting hitched and settling down and starting families. Zain was proud of them. He'd done the marriage thing before, and it hadn't worked out for him.

The sanctity of the institute of marriage wasn't for him. He'd done that. Got the t-shirt.

Zain would enjoy his life as a single bachelor.

It was the best life.

No commitments. No one to worry about where he was and why he was late coming home.

No one to sit and worry when he went out on missions when SWAT was called in.

He and his team were dangerous motherfuckers. They faced bad guys who no one else was equipped or trained to handle.

That was his job.

Run into hell with his brothers and sister in blue to save the day.

"It's about time you paid for something," Declan grumbled, picking up his glass.

Almost everyone was there, except for Jordan and Omara. Zain sat and grabbed his mug. He took a healthy sip and eyed the door of the Pub. He wondered if maybe Omara and Jordan had changed their minds. Jordan he was sure would come, she never missed a night out with the team.

Ever since joining SWAT, Jordan had fit right in. She was their little sister, and they'd do anything to protect her. The woman was downright fierce and could probably kick any one of their asses. She could hold her own out on missions and didn't take any shit from anyone.

"How's Jess doing?" Zain asked. He leaned back in his chair and turned his focus on his best friend, Iker.

The past couple of years had been rough for his

buddy. He had walked away from the love of his life in order to protect her. Iker had been in his own hell since. He'd taken to drinking and whoring around. It was Zain who'd hauled his sorry ass out of some sleazy bar. Iker had been on a two-week binge.

No one knew about this but Zain.

And Mac.

Mac was like the older brother of the group. He knew everything about everyone. That was why he was in charge. Iker was a vital member of their team, and they couldn't afford to lose him.

Zain had dragged him back to his place, sobered him up, kicked his ass, then pushed him back out in the world. The two of them took dangerous missions assigned to SWAT. They entered buildings first. Zain helped Iker channel his focus on catching bad guys.

Zain would do anything for his brother.

Helping him during his days in hell was only payback from when Freya had left Zain.

He had been in love with his wife. She had been his entire world, but the bitch clearly hadn't returned the love he had for her.

Freya Roman—she still had his last name— wanted more out of life than being the wife of a cop. She had strived for more. She had wanted him to push and move up the ranks. Her dream for him would have been captain.

But that wasn't Zain's dream.

He loved what he did.

SWAT was his calling, and he was damn good at it. Patrolling the streets and ensuring their town was safe was what he did best. He didn't want to deal with the bureaucracy or the politics that came with a higher-up position. Hell, he didn't even know how Mac and Declan handled it. As the two sergeants of their team, they were in charge and had to kiss ass, deal with the captain and the mayor's office.

Put a badge on his chest and a gun in his hand, and that's where Zain belonged.

"She's good. She should be finishing up at the museum. They have another big event coming up, and she's been practically living there lately." Iker grinned.

This was the happiest Zain had seen Iker in years. Zain was glad they were back together. The two of them were made for each other. He had tried to talk him out of the stupid move, but Iker was convinced it was what was best for them. What was best to keep her safe.

"When is the next cookout?" Ash asked. He leaned his chair back to balance on the two legs.

"Soon," Mac said.

The entire team met quarterly at Mac's house for a gathering of good food, drinks, and hanging out. Over the past few years, the group had grown. It had started off just the SWAT members, but now it included their families. Mac and Sarena with their daughter, Nia, Ash and Deana with their son, Evan, Brodie and Ronnie with their son, Xander. Myles and Roxxy, Declan and Aspen, Iker and Jessica. Only Zain and Jordan remained unattached.

But the more the merrier. Their family as growing, and Zain looked forward to his role as uncle to all of the children being born of the healthy relationships.

He took another swig of his beer. At one point in his life, he had wanted what his teammates had. A secure, steady relationship with the woman he loved. A few kids. He'd thought he'd had that with Freya.

But it wasn't meant to be.

She was so career-focused, and he didn't know when she fell out of love with him or if she ever loved him in the first place. He would guess the moment she'd figured out he couldn't be manipulated to become what she wanted, she'd checked out of their marriage.

He'd discovered that she had been sleeping with

her boss with the idea of moving up in her company. Hell, he'd found out she'd slept with a few of the bigwigs at her job. She'd taken money from one of them, becoming his mistress. In the divorce, he'd learned of a bank account with over two hundred thousand dollars in it that she'd hid from him. Her suitors were generous with money for her.

Their divorce had been bitter.

He'd taken her for half of everything she'd had.

That little dirty money she'd saved from the men she'd slept with—half had become his.

He considered it payment for all of her lies and deceit. She had made him think they were going start a family. Got his hopes up. What man wouldn't want a little version of himself running around? He and his brother, Luca, had a great upbringing, and he would have loved to make his parents grandparents. They were patiently waiting for the day.

Luca, a football coach and teacher at the local high school, was still single with no children. He was open to marriage and children, but just hadn't found that special one. Their mother made sure they both knew she was still waiting for the news she'd be getting a grandbaby.

Freya had made a big show of no longer needing to take her birth control pills, when in reality, she'd gone and got an IUD. She'd never had any intention of having children anytime soon.

"It's about time your lazy ass showed up," Myles rumbled.

Zain blinked and looked up to see Jordan standing by one of the open seats. There was no sign of Omara. Disappointment filled Zain at the thought of not seeing her again.

Why would he be disappointed?

The woman was downright beautiful. Her hands gliding through his hair had him harder than he'd ever been. He was thankful for the black thing she'd put on him when he'd first sat in her chair. It hid the evidence of his reaction to her.

Hell, maybe it was best she didn't come. Jordan would have his balls if she found out he was sniffing around her sister.

"Sorry we're late. Omara had to drop her son off at his friend's house," Jordan said. She rested the strap of her purse along the back of the chair.

Zain peeked up at the word 'we're.'

He quickly scanned the bar that was full. It was late, and plenty of people were in the Pub to have a good time. This was one of their favorite hangout spots to grab a drink. The Pub had great food and didn't skim on the alcohol. There was nothing watered down here, and they always ensured the SWAT team had a table.

"Glad she could make it," Mac said. He motioned for her to take the seat. "Where is she?"

"Over at the bar. She saw someone she knew." Jordan pulled the chair back and sat.

Zain tried to remain inconspicuous as he scanned the bar. He pushed his chair back and finished off his beer, slamming the empty mug on the table.

"Be right back," he announced to Iker.

His friend raised his eyebrows at him but didn't say a word. Zain ignored the glances from his other teammates and disappeared into the crowd.

Music was pumping from the speakers, but everyone's attention was on the televisions. Tonight they had NASCAR on. A popular race was on all of the screens around the bar.

But that wasn't what captured Zain's attention. He caught sight of Omara and just about stopped dead in his tracks.

Her hair pulled up in an immaculate high pony-tail exposed the perfect column of her neck. Her shirt didn't leave much to the imagination. Her back was left bare; her silky olive shirt had two thin straps that crossed along her skin. Her legs were encased in black leather leggings and showcased her curvy hips and plump ass, and her feet—Zain swallowed hard.

Heels.

Open-toed, heeled boots that added about three to four inches to her height.

Zain's gaze narrowed in on the two males standing next to her. His feet moved before he even knew it. He arrived behind her. The sound of her laughter tickled his hearing. It was something he already knew he loved hearing. The only problem was that he wanted to be the one to make her laugh, not some other asshat.

"Omara," he called her.

She turned around, and he froze in place. The woman had light makeup and ruby-red lips. Her mouth was highlighted in one of his favorite colors. He would love to see what those red lips would look like stretched around his cock, taking it deep in her throat.

She finished off her shot and sat the empty glass on the counter. She glanced at her friend and smiled. Zain sized up the dark-skinned man. His hair was kept cut close to his head, and he was a few inches shorter than Zain. His friend had clipped locks and was around Omara's height.

"It's nice seeing you guys. We'll have to meet up

some other time." She rested a hand on the guy's arm, and Zain had to bite back a growl.

"No doubt. Call me, and we'll figure out when we can get together."

Zain impatiently watched her hug both men and share last-minutes jokes and laughs. He folded his arms in front of his chest and waited. Once they were gone, she focused her attention on him and rested back against the bar. He moved to stand next to her.

He didn't know why, but he needed to be close to her. He caught the eye of a man a few spots away who had been checking her out. Zain glared at him. Most men couldn't meet his gaze, and this one was no different. He turned, putting his back to Zain.

"How you going to come over here acting like you're my man or something?" She smirked.

The twinkle in her eye and the slight tilt of her lips captivated him. The crowd's chatter around them grew louder. He leaned in, his lips brushing her earlobe.

"Baby, if I were your man, those fuckers wouldn't have gotten that close to you with what you have on."

He pulled back slightly and stared down at her. Omara's lips parted a little. He was crazy. Jordan would have his balls, but this woman right here would be worth it.

She rested her forearms on the counter. He shifted closer to allow someone else to fit in behind him. His cock was fully erect and straining against his jeans. Omara eyed him. There was no hiding the fact he was hard for her. She stood on her toes to reach him. He bent down so she could get nearer to his ear.

"You talk big words for a man who doesn't do attachments."

His eyebrows jerked up high. Apparently, her sister had told her about him. He slid a hand along her waist. It was an intimate gesture, but if anyone from the team questioned him, he'd lie and say they couldn't hear each other and it was crowded.

"My words aren't the only big things I'm carrying around."

She jerked back from him with saucer eyes. Her lips spread into a wide grin, then she fell into fit of laughter.

"You are so corny." She rested a hand on his chest while trying to catch her breath but continued laughing.

He grinned and knew it was stupid, but it was true. He was blessed with a big cock and a big gun.

Both, he never left home without them.

"What are you drinking? I got your next one." He waved down the bartender, keeping an arm around her waist.

"I can buy my own, Zain," she grumbled.

He drew her close and didn't miss the way she bit her lip. It was a sexy one that had him growing even harder.

"Not while I'm here, you won't," he growled. Hell no, she wouldn't be paying for her drink. What kind of man did he look like? He'd never let Jordan pay for anything when the team was out, and he'd be damned if her sister paid for something.

The bartender made his way to them and took their order before stepping away.

Omara faced him and leaned into him, a sensual grin on her lips.

"Now I did warn you earlier," she breathed. She eyed him playfully.

He thought back to what she could have warned him about but drew a blank.

"About what?"

"My magical fingers," she quipped.

They always come back wanting more.

Oh, he remembered all right. Those hands of hers needed to be on him.

The bartender came back with their drinks. Zain took care of the bill and turned back to Omara, finding her with her glass raised. She had ordered something called a Weekender. He picked up his bourbon and held his glass up near hers.

"And what are we toasting to?" he asked.

"Whatever may be." She pressed her glass to his.

"That I can agree on," he murmured. He took a sip of the strong drink, welcoming the burning sensation as it slid down his throat. Zain hid his shock. Was she suggesting what he thought she was?

Omara didn't appear to be a woman who had one-night stands or hookups, but if that was what she was offering, he'd be down.

She sipped her drink and stared at him. He glanced down at her and couldn't tell if she had a bra on. Her heavy mounds were a good size, and he was sure they would fill his hands completely. When he was behind her, he hadn't seen any straps.

Now that he was thinking about it, his cock twitched.

He cleared his throat, needing to think of something else.

"There you two are," Iker said, sliding up next to Zain.

His intense look spoke volumes. Zain knew without even asking what his friend was thinking.

Are you fucking insane? This is Jordan's sister.

Maybe he was, but there was something about her that drew him to her.

"I was chatting with some friends, and then Zain found me," Omara replied, not even batting an eye. She smiled up at Iker. "We were just about to come join everyone."

Iker also didn't miss how close Zain and Omara were standing. His eyebrows rose even higher. Zain just grinned at him and slid his arm around Omara's waist.

"Come on. Let's go join the group before they all come looking for us," Zain said. His hand met the smooth skin of her back, and he bit back a groan.

"Omara, go ahead without us. Everyone is over in that corner over there," Iker pointed out.

She stepped away from Zain with a curious expression but gave a nod. She waved and walked away. Zain couldn't take his eyes off her leather-encased ass if he tried.

"No." Iker's firm word broke through his lust-filled fog.

"What?" Zain blinked.

"I already know what you are thinking. No. Not

going to happen. Find someone else." Iker shook his head.

"I don't know what you're talking about." Zain lifted his glass and took another sip.

"Don't give me that bullshit. I know you and know what's going through that thick head of yours. That is Jordan's little sister."

"And?" Zain didn't appreciate his friend coming over to warn him. He knew who Omara was and what he'd be getting into.

"Seriously. You just going stand there and not say you didn't think that Jordan wouldn't want you sniffing around her sister?"

"I mean, I've thought about it." Zain sipped again then stood to his full height. Omara was a grown woman and could do what she wanted, and if that included fucking him, then he was all for it. "I'm not afraid of Jordan."

"Final words of a dead man if she finds out you were practically humping her sister at the bar," Iker scoffed. He threw an arm around Zain's shoulder and guided him through the crowd. "It was nice knowing you, man."

4

"Is that even legal?' Omara exclaimed. She couldn't even remember the last time she had laughed this hard. The SWAT team was very competitive. The Pub had pool tables, and the guys wanted to show off.

Omara was unable to keep her eyes off Zain. It was getting harder to do it with her sister sitting beside her. She glanced over at Jordan and found her preoccupied with her phone again for the millionth time.

"Who are you talking to?" Omara asked. She was being nosy, since her sister had talked her into joining them.

"None of your business," Jordan replied with a sly grin.

Omara stared at her. She was officially intrigued. It wasn't like Jordan to be glued to her device. It was always Jordan who complained Jason was on his too much. This was suspicions. Her older sister was up to something.

"Really? That's your response? And here I thought we were close." Omara leaned into Jordan and gave her a little nudge. Omara had no room to speak. She was keeping a big secret from her.

Her crush on Zain.

At the bar, she was sure her panties had melted off her body. The man was downright dripping sex appeal. Little did he know that her friend and his partner were gay and very happy with their relationship.

The jealousy had rolled off Zain in waves. He'd acted like a kid whose toy was being taken. That display had her instantly wet. Any other day she would die before admitting that, but it was the God's honest truth. There was something about that man that had her wanting to thank his mother and father for having him.

"A girl has to have some secrets." Jordan winked at her.

Omara's mouth dropped open in shock. It had to

do with a man. Omara was so sure of it. Well, it looked like two would be playing this game.

Omara turned back to the table. Zain and Iker were going against each other in a very intense game of crazy eights. There was plenty of shit-talking flying through the air, and the other teammates were right in the thick of things.

"You better be ready to put your money where your mouth is." Zain chuckled.

"Don't worry, my money is always safe." Iker grinned. He lined up for his hit and sank his target back. He tossed a wink to Zain. "It's going to stay safe in my damn wallet."

Laughter filtered through the air. Omara couldn't stop laughing. She glanced down at her empty Coke glass. She had switched from alcohol a while ago. She didn't go out and drink like she used to. A few drinks, and she was done. Even though Jason was staying at a friend's house, she didn't want to go home drunk. Omara was now considered a lightweight.

Zain's eyes met hers. He did a little flex of his muscles, walking over to the table. She couldn't help but appreciate his lithe form. His short-sleeved shirt revealed his muscular forearms. The sight of them sent a pulse through her. A small crowd had gathered around the team, but they ignored it. SWAT obviously had its groupies. None of the guys even looked in the direction of the females watching them.

"Don't be too sure, my friend." Zain snickered. He stalked around the table, his movements that of a hunter. He stopped in front of Omara and Jordan with his back facing them.

Her gaze slid along his form then locked on his jean-clad ass, and she had to hold back a sigh.

His body was perfection.

"Here we go," Declan said, taking a pull on his longneck beer.

The sergeant whispered something in Mac's ear. The grin that spread across his face was cynical and downright scary. Not that they had anything to worry about, but for some reason she could tell the two were up to something. Omara almost pitied the team.

Brodie took notice and shoved Myles. He eyed the two sergeants and scowled. Omara's assumption was correct. They were scheming.

Zain lined up his shot. The muscles in his back flexed as he drew back and thrust the stick forward. The sound of the cue ball hitting his target pierced the air. Everyone went wild. Omara couldn't see the pool table, but Zain must have successfully sunk his balls. He threw up his hands and sent his stick flying onto the table. Omara shifted on her stool and grinned. It didn't matter that these men were the baddest SWAT team, they were still competitive like boys. They all had bets riding on the game and were making each other pay up. Brodie was at the center with a wad of cash in his hands. Not much. They'd each placed five-dollar bets.

Omara looked to Jordan, surprised she didn't join the melee.

Jordan's focus was on her phone.

Again.

Yeah, there was something up with her, and Omara was quite certain it was a man. There was a small smile on Jordan's lips that Omara hadn't seen in a while. She'd wait and see if Jordan would come clean.

"Hey, sis. Would you be opposed to one of the guys taking you home?" Jordan turned to her.

Oh, this was definitely about a man.

Omara stared at Jordan for a second. They had ridden together. Had she known her sister was going to be ditching her for a booty call, she would have driven her car.

"Sure, but you are going to explain yourself, young lady," Omar murmured.

Jordan grinned. She looked like the cat who'd just caught the canary.

"You're the best sister ever." Jordan hopped down from her chair and wrapped Omara into a tight hug. Her lips brushed Omara's ear. "I promise I'll tell you later."

Omara shook her head. She wasn't even mad at her. She had sacrificed much to more to come to Columbia; she worked hard and helped with Jason. She rarely did anything for herself, so Omara would leave her be. If none of the guys could take her home, she'd call for a car on the popular shared ride app.

Jordan walked over to the guys and spoke with them briefly. Without hearing the conversation, Omara already knew who'd volunteered for the job.

Zain casually glanced at her.

The look said everything.

And it was everything she was hoping for

Her heart skipped a beat at the thought of being alone with him. The guys must have questioned Jordan on where she was going. They knew her sister well, too, and apparently, she didn't give them any more than she'd given Omara.

Omara stood and went over to join the conversation.

"Stop trying to be in grown folks' business," Jordan was telling Brodie, "there is something I have to handle."

Omara would have believed her if the grin on her lips hadn't been so devious. Omara had seen that expression plenty of times when Jordan was younger and about do something crazy.

"It's not a problem. Someone will make sure Omara gets home safely," Mac said. It was clear he didn't believe Jordan either.

"Thanks. I'll owe whoever." Jordan looked down at her phone again before giving Omara a quick hug, and she scurried off, disappearing into the crowd.

"I'll take her. It's on the way to my house," Zain said. He slid his hands into his jeans pocket. He didn't meet her gaze.

"You sure?" Iker questioned.

Something unspoken passed between them.

"Of course, having Jordan in my debt is a dream come true." Zain rubbed his hands together.

"I appreciate it," Omara said. She moved closer to him, unable to stay away any longer.

"If that's the case, I'm about to head out," Myles announced.

"Me, too," Ash said.

"Omara, Zain will take good care of you," Declan said. He gave a salute to them. "Y'all have a good night."

Omara watched their little party dribble down to just her, Zain, and Iker. Omara felt as if she were almost one of the team. Everyone had been welcoming, and she had learned a lot about her sister on the force. Jordan was a badass and had made a good reputation for herself. Omara was proud of her. She hadn't been happy with her precinct in Atlanta. There had been a lot of conniving and backstabbing at her old job. The girl had been completely miserable there even though she loved working in the city. This made Omara feel so much better about her moving to Columbia to be near her.

"You want to hang around a little more?" Zain asked. He racked up the balls on the pool table. He glanced over at Iker.

Omara wasn't sure what was going on between the two. Iker shot Zain a glare.

"I'm trying to decide of I should stay around and make sure you don't do something you will regret or sit back and watch Jordan hand you your ass."

Ah, it was about her.

Iker must have seen them at the bar. The two entered a silent staring contest. Zain stood to his full height, not backing down from his friend. Iker was right. Jordan would be pissed, but Omara was a grown woman who was very capable of making her own decisions.

"Excuse me, gentlemen." She leaned against the table.

They both swung their attention to her.

She offered a small smile to try to defuse the situation. "As much as I love my sister, she doesn't rule me. And if I ask Zain to teach me how to play pool, then that is my business."

Iker scowled then glanced away from her.

"Fine, but don't say I didn't try to stop whatever this is." He motioned to them. "I'm not answering to Jordan."

"Don't worry, Iker. I'm a big boy. I can handle myself." Zain was talking to his friend but watching her.

All Omara heard were the words "big boy," and plenty came to mind.

Like the bulge she had felt when he'd pressed against her.

She immediately heated at the thought of seeing his naked cock.

"I'm sure Zain appreciates you looking out for him," she said, trying to smooth things out.

Iker ran a hand along his face. "Yeah, whatever. I'm going to head home. I'm sure Jess is waiting for me."

He walked over to Zain who stiffened at first. They did the manly hug thing with Iker whispering something in his ear. They separated with Iker issuing a wave and spinning around on his heel and walking away. The bar still had plenty of patrons hanging around. The music appeared to be louder. The other pool tables were occupied with groups of people having fun.

Omara's muscles tensed at the sudden presence of a warm figure standing next to her.

Zain.

She swallowed hard. Tilting her head back, she found his gaze on her. The heat in his stare had her pulse racing. He really towered over her. Everything about him had her almost salivating. From the way he walked, his smile, the feeling of his hardness against her softness.

She didn't know where this was going, but she was down for the ride.

"You ready?"

Zain's deep voice sent a wave of desire through

Omara, and she jerked her head in a nod. She was ready to follow this man anywhere. He lifted his hand that gripped a pool stick.

That's right. She'd said she wanted Zain to teach her pool. She took it from him, slightly disappointed. He walked backward to the table, and a sexy grin appeared as if he read her thoughts.

"What's the look for?" His eyes twinkled. He knew exactly what she was thinking.

"Nothing." She sniffed and studied the stick, trying to ignore that smile of his. She had watched how they held the sticks and tried to mimic it. She bent over the table to test it out. She glanced over her shoulder, finding Zain staring at her ass. She gave a cute wiggle. She knew what she looked like. She and Jordan were blessed with nice figures. "See something you like?"

His gaze flicked to hers. She didn't know where she'd got this boldness from but she was having fun with it. Did she really have time to date? No, she didn't. She had a salon to run and a son to raise, but it didn't mean she couldn't have a little fun.

And from the way Zain was eyeing her ass, she would be able to get what she wanted tonight.

She straightened as he came to stand next to her.

There was little to no room between them. His hand settled on her waist, his mouth near her ear.

"Let me show you how to hold that properly." His lips brushed the shell of her ear.

A shiver rippled through her.

He positioned her hand around the stick with his on top of hers. "You wrap your hand around it like this and make sure you grip it tight."

Her breath stalled. The feel of him had her core clenching. The slickness of her pussy seeped from her slit. The man knew what he was doing. She met his heated gaze.

"Am I to hold it with both of my hands?" she breathed. It was a solid question, but she wasn't talking about the stick, and by the flaring of his nostrils, neither was he.

"It's long enough, you'll need two hands to control it."

A whimper escaped her. She bit her lip at the image coming to mind. What would his cock look like? Would it be thick and long? Did it curve? Would it be angry red? What would he taste like? She'd never been with a white guy so she was definitely curious.

Suddenly, she didn't want to be at the bar anymore. She dropped the cue on the table and turned around in Zain's arms. She was playing with fire, she knew, but what she wanted was for one night to be the focus of a sexy man's attention. The need to be fucked so thoroughly she wouldn't remember her own name come morning.

That was what she wanted.

And Zain would be the man to do it.

She'd never thrown caution to the wind like this before. She'd always had to put her child first because he was the most important thing in her life. His needs mattered.

Not hers.

But tonight, she wanted to be selfish.

She wanted to take advantage of him being away at a friend's and indulge in something—or someone —tonight.

"There's no one at my place." She leaned into Zain, pressing her breasts to his hard chest.

His hands came down to sit on the curve of her ass. She offered what she hoped was a sexy grin and stood on her tiptoes. Even with her heels on, he still towered over her. He bent down, his focus on her.

She brushed her lips against his softly, then nipped at his bottom lip. "Why don't you come home with me?"

Her heart pounded.

She'd had sexual partners outside of her son's father. But all of those had been short relationships, never a one-nighter where she invited someone to her home. She felt it would be safe to invite Zain since he worked with her sister. If Jordan trusted him to back her up out in the field, when their lives were at risk, then she could at least trust he'd be safe to take to her home.

He reached up and cupped her cheek. She leaned into his large palm.

"I don't do relationships, Omara. I want to be clear," he murmured.

Even over the loud thump of music, she'd heard him. The hard bulge nudging into her stomach was a distraction. Omara rubbed herself against it, wanting to feel more of it. She actually ached to have him thrust inside her. She wanted to feel him stretch her out and go as deep as humanly possible.

"If I go home with you, it will only be for fucking."

"That's exactly what I want," she replied.

His eyes widened in shock, and he swooped down and claimed her lips.

The kiss was explosive. Omara moved close, wrapping her arms around his waist. She was taken aback by the sheer power of him. His hand held her face in place while he plundered her mouth. His tongue was bold as it pushed forward and stroked hers.

Omara gasped and held on tight. He nipped her lip, soothing it with his tongue. Desire raced through her body. Her knees were growing weak, and she had to fight to keep from falling to the floor.

Zain drew back and stared at her with his hooded gaze. Her lips felt swollen and tingled. She couldn't remember ever being kissed that way. She bit her lip and felt a groan rumble through his chest.

"Let's go." He took her hand and towed her behind him through the crowd.

There was nothing else he needed to say. She held on to him tight and stayed close to his back. There was a hard form underneath his shirt.

His gun.

Another surge of desire ripped through her at the feeling of his weapon.

The crowd parted for him as if sensing it would be best for them.

These were very smart people.

5

Zain lost count at the amount of red lights he blew through. Omara's perfume filled his truck and played with his senses. It had taken everything he had to not find a little dark corner of the Pub and take her up against it.

But Omara wasn't that type of woman.

Hell, it was bad enough she was Jordan's little sister.

His cock had been hard from the moment he'd met Omara over at the bar. Everything about her kept him on edge.

Her smile.

Her laugh.

Those damn leather leggings.

Just the image of her bent over that fucking pool table would be forever burned in his mind.

His cock grew impossibly hard, straining against his jeans, demanding to be let out.

"Turn left at the intersection." Omara's husky voice broke through his thoughts.

He jerked his head in a nod, too afraid to look at her. If he did, he wouldn't be responsible for his actions. Like pulling into one of the hotels and booking a room. All he needed was a massive bed and Omara spread out naked on it.

He tightened his grip on the steering wheel and followed her instructions. He hadn't been lying when he'd said her place was on his way home. He didn't live too far from her. Omara quietly directed him to her pace.

The air in the cab was filed with sexual tension. He made the mistake of glancing at Omara and finding her watching him.

"What is it?" He smirked. He coasted to a halt at the stop sign. "Are you having doubts?"

He had to ask. Things had gotten heated at the bar, and if she'd changed her mind, then he would drop her off and head home.

"Not at all." She paused for a second and stared down at her hands.

He continued on; they were less than a minute from her place.

"I'm just trying to decide if I'm sucking your cock first or if you want to eat my pussy first."

Zain jerked his head around, unable to believe the words that had just escaped her mouth. A sensual, wide grin spread across her face. A car horn sounded. He focused back on the road, the truck swerving. He righted the vehicle and brought it back onto the right side of the road. Omara fell into a fit of laughter.

He grinned and put both hands back on the wheel.

"That's funny, huh? You almost made me wreck this truck." He snickered.

"I'm sorry." She exhaled. Her hand waved at her face. "You should have seen the look on your face."

She pointed out her house when he veered onto her street. He pulled into her driveway and killed the engine. Zain scrubbed a hand along his face. Her fucking words rattled him to the core. It was like she had read his mind. He had been fantasizing about those plump lips of hers being wrapped around his cock.

"I just wasn't expecting it." He shook his head and grinned at her.

"You do know women have very dirty minds, right?" She bit her lip and leaned forward, trailing her fingernails along his thigh.

His smile disappeared at her touch. His gaze dropped down to her lips that were still swollen from his kiss. Her hand arrived at the bulge in his jeans and gripped it.

"Especially when this thing right here keeps teasing me."

He growled and reached for her, bringing her face to him. He put his mouth to hers, taking her lips in a brutal kiss. The woman was driving him crazy. He couldn't even remember being so affected by any female before.

Not even his ex-wife.

Omara wasn't shy and kissed him back with just as much fire as he had burning in him. She drew back and stared at him.

"There is just one thing," she said.

He couldn't take his eyes off her lips. They were so fucking tasty, and he couldn't wait to have them wrapped around his cock. Since she was thinking about it, he didn't want her to miss out on it.

"What is that?" he rasped. His fingers were on the door handle. It was time he got her in the house before he dragged her over onto his lap.

"You have to be gone before my son comes home." Her eyes grew wide with worry.

He got it. She didn't want her son to come home to find a strange man in his mother's bed. He could completely respect that. It just went to show how good of a mother she was, thinking of her child.

"Not a problem," he murmured.

He leaned forward and pressed a hard kiss to her lips before getting out of the vehicle. He stalked around the front and arrived at her door. He opened it and held out his hand for her. She placed her smaller one in it and hopped down to stand in front of him. She was small with curves. Those heels brought the top of her head to his chin. She tilted her head back to meet his gaze. He couldn't resist another kiss.

He backed her up and took command of her mouth again. He captured her moan as she leaned into him. He pushed his tongue into her mouth, seeking hers out. She tasted so sweet, and he was sure her pussy would be even better.

He tore his lips from her.

"Dammit, I can't stop touching you." He grunted.

"Come inside and you won't have to," Omara purred, running a hand down his pectoral muscles.

Her curvy frame lay flush against him, making him step back. He shut the door and took her hand, escorting her to the front door.

They entered her home. Zain scanned the front room and immediately recognized the homey feeling. It was Omara and her son, and it was filled with love.

"Don't mind the mess. Jason didn't have time to clean up his stuff before he left. I promised him it would be waiting for him when he returned." She smirked.

The living room wasn't really messy. There were a pair of small tennis shoes on the carpet near the couch, video games and a controller were on the floor, and a blanket was strewn on the ottoman.

He smiled, remembering when he was a child and his gaming system he and his brother shared. There had been plenty competing between them, and fighting, when one was caught cheating.

Zain turned around and found Omara watching him. His gaze trailed down her body, and the desire he had for her came slamming back into him. Her wide eyes were locked on him. Her breasts rose and fell swiftly. He stalked toward her, intent to take what she was offering.

He gathered her into his arms. She immediately

stepped into his embrace. He leaned down and captured her lips with his. Zain loved how responsive she was. How her body complemented his and her curves were meant to be next to him. He plundered her mouth with his tongue. She tasted of Coke.

"Where is your bedroom?" Zain tore his lips away from hers. He could spend all day kissing her, but there was another set of lips he was determined to devour.

Omara blinked, her eyes coming back into focus. She gave him a sensual smile and took his hand in hers. She led him down the hallway and playfully spun around and pulled her shirt over her head, leaving her in leather leggings and black pasties covering her nipples. Zain's control snapped. A growl escaped her. He backed her up until the wall trapped her. Omara gasped when he pressed his hard cock to her stomach.

"Want to pay games?" he murmured. He stared down into her big brown eyes.

That sly smile of hers returned. She raised her eyebrows.

"Games? I already told you what I was contemplating." Her hand went to his jeans and undid the button.

Zain rested his hands on the wall on both sides of her head.

"And what did you decide?" he said.

He couldn't wait to get his hands and mouth on her. But if she needed to have his cock in her mouth then he would only be too happy to oblige her. Zain was all about putting the needs of his woman first.

His woman?

No. She wasn't his.

There would be no claiming Omara, they had an agreement. Tonight was just fucking.

Two adults needing to expel some pent-up tension.

The sneaky woman had his jeans open within seconds, and she pushed them down.

"Your dick, I want to taste it," she said.

The air in his lungs rushed out. She grinned and knelt on the floor before him, guiding his jeans to his ankles. He swiftly kicked them away. Her small hands wrapped around him. Her eyes widened, and she glanced up at him.

"I wasn't lying, sweetheart." He chuckled. His smile disappeared the second her tongue wet the tip of his cock. The sight of her on her knees was almost enough to do him in.

"Good thing you weren't lying or you would

have been sent home."

His cock twitched at her giggle. His eyes widened at her little remark.

Thankfully, Zain never had to lie about his dick size.

He pitied any man Omara would send home without the pleasure of getting to know her physically. His hands balled into fists at the thought of another man sampling her goods. A groan escaped him at the sensation of her hot little mouth closing around the head. Her hands gripped him tight and guided him farther.

Omara's moan sent a shockwave of heat through him. He couldn't take his eyes off the picture of her lips wrapped around him. Her hooded gaze was on him as she pulled back. The woman was a goddess. Her mouth and tongue and everything was perfect.

Her tongue worked wonders, encircling his mushroom tip and trailing along his shaft. Her confident hands slid along him, teasing him, before directing him back between her lips.

Unable to resist any longer, he reached down and slipped his hand to the base of her neck. It took everything he had not to push forward, completely sinking into her throat. He didn't want to hurt her.

He slowly thrust his hips forward until he met

the back of her throat. She swallowed without having to be told.

"Fuck," he breathed. If he died right now, he would already be in Heaven.

She set a steady rhythm at first. His basic instinct was to pound away into her mouth until he exploded like a barbarian.

What the fuck?

He'd gotten plenty of blow jobs in the past, but none of them could hold a candle to the way Omaha was sucking the soul out of him. He tightened the grip on her neck as her pace increase. He closed his eyes, basking in the sensation of her mouth, tongue, and hands on him, but it didn't help. The sounds of her throaty moans and an occasional gag had him unable to catch his breath, his hips moving of their own accord.

The power of a woman on her knees was enough to do any man in.

At that moment, she could have asked him for anything and he would give it to her.

A shudder rippled through his body. He slid his hand up the nape of her neck to bury his fingers in her soft hair. His orgasm was fast approaching, and as much as he wanted to spill himself deep in her, he needed to ensure she was receptive to it.

"You love sucking my cock, huh?" he rasped.

Her big brown eyes met his gaze. She pulled back away from him, leaving the tip resting against her lips. He wasn't sure if she was aware of how she slowly rubbed her lips continuously along him while she gazed up at him. It must be an unconscious move. Her hand kept a possessive hold on him as if she'd claimed his cock.

She was the most beautiful woman in the world. Her skin was flushed, her hair was in disarray, and her mouth and chin were slick with her saliva.

This was dangerous.

This was to be a night of fun with no feelings, and here he was, gazing down at this woman, thinking about starting a possible future with her.

A small drop of his seed appeared on the tip of his cock. Her gaze flicked to it, and he watched with bated breath her tongue sneaking out and cleaning it off.

He forgot what they'd been talking about.

What had he asked her?

"If you have to ask me if I'm enjoying sucking on this dick then I must not be doing it right." Omara stroked the length of him with a devilish grin. She knew exactly what she was doing to him. "Now stop holding back, Zain."

A growl ripped out of him. Something exploded in his chest. Zain took hold of her head and pushed his cock into her mouth. He moved as if he no longer controlled his body. Long steady strokes sent him deep. Her moans fueled him. He kept going, his hips quickening.

She rested her hands on his waist, opening her mouth even wider. Zain couldn't tear his gaze from Omara's if he tried. His skin grew hot, his breaths were coming fast, and sweat spilled down the side of his face.

A pulse of pleasure soared from the tips of his toes to his balls.

"Fuck, I'm about to come," he ground out.

This was her one and only warning. The storm brewing inside him was demanding to be let out. Omara's small hand wrapping around his shaft and the pleading look in her eyes for his seed was all he needed. His cock swelled, sending thick streams of release into her waiting mouth.

A roar escaped Zain as bolts of lightning raced through him. Omara swallowed every ounce he fed her. Once his body stopped spasming, he pulled out of her mouth. He released a curse, seeing he was still semi-hard.

How was that even possible?

What had Omara done to him?

He glanced down at her, finding a smile on her lips. She licked them with that dangerous tongue of hers.

Zain hefted her to her feet without a word. He bent down and tossed her over his shoulder.

"Zain!" Her giggles filled the air.

"Which room is yours?' he growled.

She'd had her taste of him, now he needed his. The little hellion nipped him on his bare ass check.

He landed a solid slap on her leather-covered ass. "Omara."

"That one," she shouted amidst her laughter.

Zain didn't care that he was acting like a Neanderthal. Maybe he had officially lost his mind. He was desperate to get a taste of her cream and sink his cock inside her pussy.

She'd said he had to be gone by morning before her kid arrived home. That gave him plenty of time to do what he had planned for Omara.

He stalked toward the door and nudged it open. Her bedroom was tastefully decorated in light colors that contrasted with her dark furniture. He dropped her on to the bed and tried to get control of himself.

The glint in her eyes and her sexy grin told him he wouldn't need to.

6

Omara licked her lips. The taste of Zain still lingered. She had always had a healthy sexual appetite. She was always a woman who knew what she wanted. Her demeanor had Zain fooled. Just because a woman was shy didn't mean she didn't like to get dirty.

Zain was a big man, and she wanted every part of him. That magnificent cock of his was to die for. She licked her lips, loving the salty taste of his release. Something had changed in Zain, it was as if he'd snapped. She wasn't worried if he would hurt her.

No.

It was something else. He had been holding back

as if she were a porcelain doll, afraid she would break. She wasn't sure of the women he had been with in the past, but she wasn't one to want cute and easy lovemaking.

But tonight wasn't for lovemaking. As he'd told her, tonight was for fucking, and that's what she was craving.

Hard, fast, hair-grabbing, skin-slapping, shouting-to-the-Lord-above type fucking. Sex that would have her on her knees at night taking a cock, and again in the morning, begging for forgiveness for what she had done.

That's what Omara wanted.

The feral look in Zain's eyes warned her she was in for a treat.

"Clothes off," Zain rasped.

Omara's smile faded. Her gaze locked on Zain's cock that was jutting out, once again erect.

That was one thing her ex had lacked—stamina.

Derrick would climax once and be out for the count. He'd never cared about her needs. He couldn't care less if she reached an orgasm. All that mattered was that she pleased him.

Omara blinked and shut down that train of thought. She refused to think of him now.

Not when she had Zain staring at her like she was a tasty snack he was about to devour.

He who she shall not be thought about had never looked at her like this. A chill swept through her at the intensity in Zain's eyes.

It had only taken her twenty-nine years to get it.

Omara peeled her nipple pasties off then reached for her leggings and slid them off. She was not going to think of her child's father right now. She scooted to the edge of the bed and stood. Zain discarded his shirt, tossing it over his shoulder.

Omara's mouth went dry at the hard lines of his chest and the perfectly chiseled abs. The grooves of his muscles were deep, and she had the sudden urge to trace them with her tongue but she would save that for later.

Zane watched her as she took off each item. His heated gaze had her pussy dripping wet. Her panties were thoroughly soaked from her sucking him off. Once the last of the offending articles were removed from her body, Zain pulled her close to him and kissed her. This kiss was different than the ones before.

She clung to him, her knees going weak. He caught her and lifted her and placed her on the bed.

He covered her body with us and leaned down, nuzzling her neck with his face.

"Please tell me you want me to fuck you hard." His lips brushed against her skin.

She tilted her head away from him, giving him more access to her.

"I've been thinking of nothing but fucking you since I saw you at the bar," he said. "I need to fuck you, Omara."

"God, yes," she hissed.

He nipped her sensitive flesh with his teeth, then soothed it with his tongue. He blazed a hot trail of kisses along her skin, traveling down to her breast. Omara groaned when his lips enclosed around her nipple. Her sensitive bud was bathed by his tongue. He sucked it deep inside his mouth. Omara's skin heated from his assault. His free hand palmed her other mound completely, rolling her tight bud between his thumb and forefinger.

Zain took his time drawing out her pleasure. He visited her second breast with his mouth, his tongue licking and suckling her mound. Omara writhed underneath him. She loved the feeling of his hard, toned body against hers.

She dove her fingers into his thick dark locks. His hair was soft and at the moment gave her something to hold on to. Zain continued his exploration and journey south. A whimper escaped Omara once he arrived at her pelvis. He pushed her legs apart and just stared at her.

"So fucking beautiful," he murmured.

Omara's breath stuttered when he zeroed in on her clit. His tongue trailed through her soaked slit.

A guttural groan escaped him. "Sweet as fucking honey."

Zain took his precious time swirling his tongue along her clit and dragging it though her slit. Omara was panting by the time he pushed one finger into her channel. She tightened her grip on his hair, needing to hold on to something.

She couldn't stop the moans spilling from her lips. He introduced a second finger into her, stretching her while he suckled her sensitive bundle of nerves. Tears blurred her vision as her body trembled. His fingers thrust in and out of her at a fast pace. Her hips rose to meet his hand with his pace quickening.

Her head thrashed around on the bed while the sensations became almost overwhelming.

"Zain," she moaned. She needed that euphoric release. It was close but just out of her reach.

"Let go, Omara," Zain demanded of her. He

withdrew his fingers from her and covered her clit with his mouth.

The sucking sensations intensified and sent her skyrocketing into the stratosphere. Tremors racked her body, and her scream filled the air. His hands rested on her thighs, keeping them from closing while he continued tormenting her sensitive bud with his tongue.

Incomprehensible words poured from her mouth while waves a pleasure washed over her. She couldn't feel if she was pleading or praising him. When the waves of her orgasm finally passed, she flopped back down on the bed, her muscles weak.

Zain lifted and, his heated gaze meeting hers, he crawled over her until he was braced above her. His length brushed her core. She widened her legs to accommodate him. Anticipation was building to feel him inside her.

He swooped down and captured her lips in a searing-hot kiss. She tasted a hint of herself on his tongue. Omara wrapped her arms around his neck and returned the kiss with the same fever. His tongue swept into her mouth and stroked hers. She held him tighter, her breasts crushed between them. She lifted her legs and braced them around his waist.

Zane growled, the sound going straight to her

core. He reached between them and pressed the blunt tip of his cock to her opening. He held her gaze while he sank fully inside her. Omara gasped at the invasion. His cock was thick and long. Her inner muscles screamed with the sharp, quick pain.

He waited for her to accommodate his girth.

"Breathe, Omara."

The strain was evident on his face that he needed to thrust. She exhaled and breathed in, only catching the scent of Zain and the aroma of sex.

"Move," Omara pleaded.

He withdrew slightly before thrusting deep. Her eyes rolled into the back of her head when he did it again.

The feeling of fullness was overwhelming. Her pussy was so full of Zain, and she wasn't going to complain. He set a brutal pace, pounding unto her. Omara's hips rose, meeting him. They synced together in a beautiful rhythm.

Where he was hard, she was soft.

She was the calm, while he was the storm.

They fit together perfectly.

His hands bore into her thighs, holding them in place. She was sure there would be bruising but she didn't care.

He changed angle, and she cried out. With each

thrust, his dick brushed against her clit, inciting a wave of pleasure to rush through her. Another orgasm was speeding toward her. Omara was unable to fathom having two orgasms back to back with any man, but it was happening tonight. She clenched around his cock, unable to get enough of him.

"You're so damn tight," Zain growled. His skin was covered in sweat. He paused, his chest rising and falling quickly. His eyes were closed, and the man looked as if he was barely holding on to his control.

Omara wanted him to lose it.

"You won't break me," she whispered. She slid her hands along his slick chest. The man should never wear a shirt. It should be illegal to be this sexy and hide it.

Zain's eyes flew open. He rested his hands on the mattress on either side of her head, and the intensity of his gaze shook Omara to her core. He leaned down and kissed her lips, hard.

She pulsated around him. She never wanted him to withdraw from the cocoon of her pussy. Everything felt so right. It was as if they were made for each other.

"You really think you can handle more?" His

voice lowered, filled with the promise of immense pleasure.

Omara nodded, unable to speak. He rotated his hips, his cock flexing inside her. Omara whimpered, needing more.

"You take my cock so good."

He shuddered then blinked. A dangerous glint appeared in his eyes. Omara clenched her muscles around his length.

"Please," she whispered, jutting her hips forward to meet his.

A shudder went through him. His cock swelled even more inside her.

"This pussy of yours was made to be fucked," he rasped. He pulled back and thrust forward.

Hard and deep.

Just like she needed. Zain came at her like a sudden summer storm. Omara held on to him, her cries piercing the air. Zain's fingers dug into her hips, and he pounded into her. She couldn't resist opening her legs wider so she could take more of him.

He withdrew from her with growl and flipped her over. Omara tried to lift herself on all fours, but he pushed her facedown and sank back into her. He wasn't showing her any mercy, not that she would need to ask for it. He was giving her everything she had craved. The rhythm of his hips grew faster.

"Oh God," she groaned. This new position allowed him to go deeper, eliciting her cries and moans.

"I wish you could see what I see," Zain ground out.

Omaha stretched out and gripped the sheets. She couldn't respond, her breaths were coming in pants. She rocked her hips, meeting Zain's. She picked up the sound of her wetness as her pussy took him.

"Your pussy is greedy and taking my entire cock."

His hand shot out and gripped her hair.

God, she loved having her hair pulled. There was something so dominating and sexy about a man holding her in place while he fucked her. His grip allowed him to anchor himself to her.

His pace increased, and the sound of skin slapping grew louder.

Everything became overwhelming.

The slight pain of her scalp.

The only thought on her mind was Zain.

Her body trembled. A slap landed on her ass cheek, and Zain palmed it, and that was all it took.

Omara crested, falling over the cliff into her orgasm. Her muscles tightened while she screamed into the mattress. Zain's bellow followed hers.

He lodged himself deep, filling her with his release.

———

ZAIN STARED at Omara lying on her stomach. The blanket barely covered her ample ass. He bit back a groan at the sight. His cock stiffened, and he had to fight the urge to wake her up. If he did, he was sure to find her wet and ready for him.

The ringing of a cell phone off in the distance broke through the silence.

Zain recognized the ringtone.

Duty called.

He cursed, remembering his jeans were still in the hallway and his phone had been in the pocket. He crept from the bed and padded out into the hallway. He snagged his pants and took his phone out.

"Roman," he answered, keeping his voice down. He didn't want to wake Omara. Not after the night they'd had. He had been completely surprised by the little sex kitten—no, tigress—she had become.

The first orgasm he'd had, amazing. The

second one was mind-blowing, and after the fourth, he'd begun to get scared. A woman like Omara could captivate him and make him do things he said he would never do again, such as start a relationship.

He shuddered.

No relationships.

They had an agreement.

Sex only.

"There's a situation," Declan's voice came through the line.

Zain rubbed his jawline. Of course there was. He glanced back into Omara's room. She had said he needed to be gone early, and it looked as if she would get her wish.

"Be right in." Zain disconnected the call, no need to ask any questions.

SWAT was needed to kick some bad guy's ass. He moved to stand in her doorway and stared at her. She had turned over onto her back. Light snores came from her. Not wanting to wake her, he grabbed the rest of his clothing from the room and took one last look at her.

She was absolutely gorgeous. Those full breasts were beautiful. They had filled his hands and mouth perfectly. His lips parted at the sight of her beaded nipples. If only he had time for one more round, but he didn't.

He was married to his job. That was the only relationship he would claim. He was never let down by fighting bad guys and protecting the city of Columbia.

Zain spun on his heel and stalked from the room. He quickly got dressed in the living room. He left the house and made sure to lock the door on his way out. The morning air was crisp and a little chilled. Jogging down the stairs, he made his way to his truck. The neighborhood was quiet and peaceful.

Zain hopped into his vehicle and tried not to look at Omara's house. He hadn't had any issues leaving a woman's house previously. He usually didn't think twice about it. Starting the engine, he threw it in reverse and backed out of the driveway. Once on the road he drove away, keeping his eyes forward.

"Don't look in the rearview mirror," he muttered. He gripped the steering wheel tight.

He wasn't going to look. He had rules and he had never broken them before. She was a beautiful woman and fucking great in bed.

That's all that was.

Fucking.

Straightening in his seat, he began to feel like himself.

His gazed flicked to the mirror and landed on her house that was growing smaller in the distance.

Fuck.

7

*Z*ain was in one foul mood when he arrived at the precinct. He slammed the door to his truck and grabbed his duffle bag from the back. The sun was beginning to rise, and the parking lot was still bare. First shift would be arriving soon. Thankfully, there wouldn't he many people inside.

Usually, this was the type of morning he would enjoy, but at the moment he couldn't take any happiness in it. Going out on a call was just what he needed to take his mind off her.

Maybe sleeping with Omara had been a mistake.

Who was he kidding?

Everything between them had been perfect. They'd both got what they wanted.

But why did this situation leave a bad taste in his mouth?

He shook his head. He would have to figure out a way to get her out of his mind. This was no different than any other one-night stand.

One thing that made him feel better was hunting bad guys

Zain stalked inside the building and immediately went to the locker room so he could meet up with his team. He ignored the people he passed and pushed open the door.

"You're late," Mac snapped. His hard gaze swung to Zain.

"Got here as soon as I could," Zain muttered.

What was Mac going to do?

Not let him go?

He brushed past his sergeant and headed to his locker. He opened the door then set his bag down on the bench. Iker stood silently with his boot propped up on the bench tying his laces. Iker took one look at them then shook his head. Zain scowled. He already knew he was going to catch hell for actually taking Omara home.

Now that his friend was finally settling down with Jessica, he wanted Zain to try love again. They'd already had one conversation about a month ago. Iker and Jessica had wanted to hook him up with one of Jessica's friends.

Zain Roman didn't need to be hooked up on a blind date. It had worked for Declan and Aspen, but Zain wasn't into settling down. He liked his life the way it was.

"I didn't quite catch that, Roman," Mac said, appearing at the end of the row.

Zain didn't turn his way. Tension grew in the air; not one person uttered a word. It was rare that they didn't speak before going out together. His team was close-knit and like a family.

Zain blew out a deep breath. Mac wasn't going to let this go.

"No problem, Sergeant." Zain pulled his shirt over his head and tossed it into his bag before drawing out a long-sleeved black t-shirt.

Mac paused where he stood. The room was quiet as a tomb. No one ever spoke back to Mac.

Zain clenched his jaw and glanced in his direction. "I'm good."

"Make sure you are." Mac glared at him for a moment more then walked off.

"What the hell is your problem?" Iker moved close to him. His eyes narrowed on Zain. "Things didn't work out with her?'

Iker glanced around at the other guys in the locker room. Jordan always got prepared in the women's locker. Ash looked barely awake. Myles was unusually quiet, and Declan and Brodie was nowhere to be seen.

Zain knew what Iker was hoping.

"I don't kiss and tell." Zain finished throwing on his gear. He was usually one of the first to arrive when they went out. Zain drove the BEAR. That was his baby, and no one else was allowed to drive their utility vehicle. Everyone knew that.

"You have very big balls," Iker muttered.

Zain slid his gun in his thigh holster and slapped his black skullcap on his head. He was officially ready. He turned to Iker and grinned. "My balls are of none of your concern."

"Roman!" Mac roared from the door. "Let's go!"

"You're going to get your ass kicked by Jordan and Mac. This I can't wait to see." Iker chuckled and walked away.

Zain headed to the door and found Mac waiting for him with his infamous scowl on his face. Zain looked around and saw the room had cleared out. Apparently, his teammates had left him to face Mac alone.

The pussies.

"I'm going to ask you one time," Mac began.

Zain held up his hand. "I promise it's nothing hunting bad guys won't solve."

Mac appeared to believe him. The sergeant was like a bulldog, stubborn and protective. He watched out for all of them. He was the big brother to everyone. There was never a time he wasn't available to the team. In trouble, call Mac. Need to go beat someone's ass, call Mac.

"That's what I want to hear. Let's go get briefed." Mac slapped him on the back and guided him from the room.

They met everyone outside. Zain took notice the BEAR was out of the garage. He scowled and strode forward.

"Who the hell is driving my baby this time?" he growled. No one was to drive her but him. He walked over and placed a hand on the hood. "Daddy's here. Did someone hurt you?"

He ignored the groans from his teammates. They just didn't understand.

"It was me." Declan rolled his eyes.

Zain narrowed his on his other sergeant.

"Had you not been running late, you could have done it yourself," Declan said.

Zain spun around and leaned against the truck

and ignored the comment. Had anyone else been late he would have been riding their ass and cracking jokes. Jordan caught his eye and smirked.

If only she knew where he had just come from. She probably assumed he'd met up with some random chick as he usually did, but she would never guess he had just left her sister's house.

"All right. Listen up," Mac began.

All eyes turned to hear what they were about to embark on. Their job was dangerous. When SWAT was called in, things were serious.

"There was a carjacking at a local gas station. A woman went in to pay for her gas since the pump wouldn't take her credit card. The robbers took her car at gunpoint."

"Why are we being called in for a car robbery?" Ash asked.

Zain shifted his stance, also curious why they would be called in for something the uniforms could handle.

"When they took her car, her three-year-old son was in the back seat asleep."

The silence was deafening. Zain didn't have kids, but he couldn't even begin to imagine the horror the mother was going through. He looked around at his team, and each of them had a deadly glint in their eyes. It was one thing dealing with adult hostage victims, but a child, that was crossing the line.

"Continue," Brodie snapped. The youngest member of the team had just welcomed his first child with his fiancée, Ronnie, not too long ago. Mac's wife, Sarena, and Ronnie were best friends and had gotten pregnant around the same time. They were all shocked when it was announced that Brodie and Ronnie had hooked up. It was then that Zain realized how big Brodie's balls were.

The man had slept with his sergeant's wife's best friend.

When Ronnie had been taken by the Demon Lords, his friend had almost gone crazy.

Zane remembered the look in Brodie's eyes. He had been ready to kill for the woman he loved.

Another reason why Zain was choosing to stay single.

Love made one do stupid shit.

"What kind of piece of shit steals a car with a baby in it?" Jordan snarled.

"Two who are going to meet the barrels of our guns," Mac rumbled. It was easy to see the former Navy SEAL was taking this personal. This could happen to anyone.

Zain didn't even want to imagine the guilt the woman may feel for leaving her child in the car while going inside the station. He was sure she thought it would be safe, but one could never be too careful.

"Using the car's tracking system, it was found. The uniforms tried reasoning with the robbers to return the child but were unsuccessful. This is now considered a kidnapping and hostage situation. Our primary objective is to safely retrieve the child."

Nods went around.

This was going to be a delicate situation.

"If there's no other questions, let's roll," Mac announced.

Everyone dispersed, heading to the back of the truck. Mac met Zain at the driver's door and gave him the address. He recognized the area.

He flicked his gaze back to Mac from the piece of paper. Mac saw the look.

"I'll update everyone in the back where we are headed. Stay sharp," Mac replied gruffly. He slapped Zain on the back and followed the rest of the team.

Of course it would be deep in Demon Lords' territory.

The gang had been a pain in their side for years. There had been plenty of fall outs between the notorious gang. SWAT had lost them millions of dollars in drug busts. It was because of SWAT that the head gangster, Victor Huff, was sitting behind bars. The leader before him had caught a bullet between the eyes when he was on a rampage to take out Mac.

In recent years, the gang had been in disarray. Too many people trying to prove themselves, creating division in the organization. This was allowing every federal agency the opportunity to pick them apart. Pretty soon, the Demon Lords would crumble. It was only a matter of time.

Zain hopped in the truck and started the engine. He slid the small window open that separated him and the team. He placed his headset on and threw the truck in gear. He drove the vehicle toward the main road. Luckily, the drive wouldn't take too long.

Mac updated the team while Zain drove. Mac was getting updates by the sergeant who was in charge of the scene. It helped that they knew exactly what was going on when they arrived.

So the robbers still had the child hostage. A federal negotiator had tried reasoning with them but had been unsuccessful.

The truck remained silent. Zain was sure his team was getting mentally prepared. There were times when hostage situations didn't go well and the medical examiner's office would need to be called in to process the bodies.

Zain sent up a prayer that no harm came to the child. God help the men if they put their hands on the kid. If SWAT didn't get to them, then the other prisoners in jail would hear of it. Nothing was ever a secret in the prisons. Word on why someone was arrested always spread through like wildfire. The men behind bars didn't take too kindly to child molesters or child murderers.

Zain turned onto the road the apartment building sat on and was greeted by organized chaos. Blue and white lights lit up the sky. Patrol and unmarked cars littered the street. As always, the press had staked their claim on one side of the road behind the yellow tape.

Zain scowled. The media could make or break a sting.

A uniform cop flagged him down and directed him to a spot to park. Zain gave an appreciative nod.

"We're here, ladies," he announced.

They exited the vehicle and congregated on the side while Mac and Declan met with the sergeant in change of the scene.

"They just need to leave these motherfuckers in a locked room with me for one hour," Ash murmured. He folded his arms and leaned back onto the truck. His son was the light of his life. It was obvious the man would do anything for his child and wife.

"I wouldn't even need an hour." Myles growled. He slid his sculley down over his bald head. Myles was the doting uncle of all the SWAT children and the godfather of Ash's son.

"Whoever finds them gets first dibs," Iker stated.

Nods went around.

"Don't worry, fellas, I'll leave enough for y'all." Jordan snorted, a cold, chilling expression encapsulating her features.

The woman could be downright scary, and with the look on her face, Zain was glad she was on his side. Her gaze met his, and it was then he saw slight similarities in her and Omara.

Jesus.

Zain swallowed hard.

Jordan as going to kick his ass.

He blinked.

What was he worried about? Omara wouldn't tell, and Iker sure as shit better not.

He sighed and faced Mac and Declan, returning their grim expressions.

"Listen up," Mac said.

The team gathered around him in a semicircle. The tension in the air thickened. Whatever he was about to say wasn't going to be good.

"The negotiator lost contact with the kidnappers about fifteen minutes ago."

Zain stiffened. No, this definitely wasn't good news. This could mean anything.

"We are going in hot," Declan chimed in.

His eyes hardened. The former Navy SEAL was one dangerous son of a bitch. Declan and Mac had served together, and Zain had heard some of their old war stories. It wasn't often that they shared tales. A lot of their time as SEALs was classified.

They led their team with confidence, and every member respected them fully and trusted their decisions.

"You need to be alert and sharp. This building is quite old and was originally condemned a few years ago. Be careful, we're basically blind going in." Mac paused.

Zain stiffened.

This was deftly upping the danger. Normally they would have a blueprint of the buildings or a general layout. Zain eyed the building and took in the crumbling brick, busted-out windows, and grimaced. There didn't look to be any electricity on that he could see.

Why would they come to this building?

"There are two main entry points. The front entrance and the back. We are going to split up into two teams of four," Declan instructed.

Zain blinked and brought his attention back to the sergeants. This information was vital for their mission. They went over what little they did know of the building. How many floors and how they would sweep through them. It was a shabby plan, but at least it was something.

"Is there anyone else living in this building?" Ash asked.

"From what we were told, there were some homeless in there, and they were evacuated," Mac answered. He rested his hands on his waist. "But we have to stay alert. There may be more inside scared to come out. Secure anyone you find, let the uniforms sort out them out."

"Any description or information on the kidnappers?" Myles asked.

"I was just about to get to that." Declan held up a few papers and passed them to Ash who stood next to him. "Rick Denvers and Melvin O'Connell. Both have a rap sheet about a mile long with plenty of burglaries and gun charges. Denvers has quite a few domestic violence charges against women, but it would appear they have both upgraded to grand theft and kidnapping."

Iker handed Zain the papers. He took in the men, Rick, a Caucasian male with short hair, and Melvin was an African American male with his hair in cornrows. Zain memorized their features before passing the papers to Jordan.

"Consider both of them armed and dangerous. Stay sharp," Mac said.

Grunts of agreement and acknowledgment went around.

"Zain, Iker, and Jordan, you're with me. The rest of you are with Declan."

"Sync up your communicators. These are the new ones," Brodie announced. He was always getting their team new technology to try out, thanks to a good buddy of his who happened to be a weapons expert who worked with the military. "Not only is the range longer, but these are trackable. Once it's snuggly in your ear, double tap it to activate it."

Brodie walked around and handed everyone a little contraption. Zain reached up and placed his in his ear. It was tiny and fit completely with no signs of the device showing.

Genius.

He did as Brodie had instructed, and a small beep sounded.

"Testing. Testing," Mac murmured.

Nods went around to confirm they'd heard him. They were now officially ready to go. In situations like this, their safety was of the utmost concern aside from the hostage.

"My team, we'll take the front," Declan ordered.

"Of course you will. That way the reporters will get your good side going in?" Iker snickered. The joke broke some of the tension.

"Thank God this week was glutes week." Myles chuckled.

"I'm still paying for it." Ash shook his head.

"We can talk about workouts on Monday," Mac said.

Zain had a strong feeling they would be in for team training next week.

The sergeant's scowl deepened. "All right, SWAT. Let's hunt."

A coldness slithered through Zain. Mac's infamous words always brought a clear sense of focus for the mission. It was a calling that brought out the warrior in each SWAT member ready to go to war.

Zain pulled his mask over his face and unsheathed his weapon. He glanced over at the run-down structure. There was a path that led to the back that they would use to access the rear entrance. Three floors was a lot of ground to cover, and not having the layout of the building made this extremely dangerous.

Mac moved out, and they immediately got into formation. They worked as a close-knit unit, following the path that headed toward the back, while Declan and the others stalked toward the front door. Jordan was immediately behind Mac with Iker tailing her. Zain brought up the rear.

They had practiced entries hundreds of times, and the sense of confidence in his team settled upon him. The sounds of the crowd slowly disappeared. The air was thick, and the light slowly faded as they got farther away from the street.

Mac paused at the edge of the building and held up a fist. Zain tightened his grip on his Glock, slowing his breaths down. A sense of calmness overcame him. This was his calling. Taking down bad guys and saving the innocent.

Mac signaled the area was clear. They moved

forward fluidly, soon arriving at the door. The building was eerily silent. Mac lowered his rifle and turned to them, giving them a slight nod. Jordan reached for the door and swung it open, entering first, with Iker and Zain right behind her. Mac pulled up the rear once they were inside the building.

Stale air met them along with the scent of human excrement and other unknown foul smells. It was dark with a few lightbulbs shining, giving them little light. They each flipped on their flashlights that hung on their bodies. Zain's was on his helmet. It gave him a better view of the stairs as they silently ascended them. Their team would take the second floor first and sweep it while the others ensured the first floor was cleared.

They arrived at the second level and stayed in close formation. They stopped at the first apartment that didn't have a door. Jordan slid in first, aiming her weapon true in what would have been the living room. The open plan gave them view of the kitchen also.

"Clear," she murmured, going over to the corner of the room.

Iker went forward with Zain right behind him. They canvased the entire small apartment, not finding anything but trash and random pieces of abandoned furniture.

Zain willed his heart to slow down. It was racing, and his gut was screaming something was wrong.

"Let's move," Mac murmured through the comm.

Zain swiftly went back to the main area and followed them out. They headed to the next three apartments and found only the same thing.

By this time, Declan and the others were finishing up the first floor, having not found anything but a young teenager hiding in a closet.

"Heading to three," Declan's voice came in on the communicator.

Zain led this time toward the stairs. They silently made their way to the next level. He bit back a curse feeling his forehead break out into a slight sweat. He tightened his grip on his weapon and held it true. He paused at the edge of the hall at the entrance and held up his fist.

A noise captured his attention.

The sound of a baby crying.

He glanced back and met the eyes of his squad. They each gave a nod, confirming they heard it, too. Hearing the baby cry could go either way. They needed to hurry.

"We can hear the baby," Mac spoke softly, alerting the other team.

Zain frowned, straining to hear. They strode forward. He stood outside the first two apartments they reached, and the cry wasn't coming from either of them. It was down the hall.

"It's from the north end of the building," Mac announced.

"Copy that. We're on our way up now," Declan replied. "Wait for us."

It didn't take them long to arrive. They moved toward each other. Declan signaled which apartment they would take. Zain nodded, confirming. He turned and motioned to the door. Mac strode forward and kicked it in. The weakened wood gave way immediately, slamming open. They swept into the apartment with a vengeance. The sounds of the crying grew louder.

The small apartment was like all the others. Abandoned, but this one held a couple of air mattresses on the floor, random boxes stacked around the room. Someone had been living here.

Mac drew to a halt and lowered his weapon.

They stood next to him to see what he was looking at.

Zain froze.

Two men were sprawled on the floor, blood pooling underneath both of them.

"What the fuck?" Zain whispered. He kept his gun trained on them. He went over the white male lying prone with his eyes still open. He kicked away the knife that was still lightly held in his hand.

"Dec, we have the two suspects," Mac informed the other team.

"The baby," Jordan muttered.

She and Zain continued on through the apartment while Mac disarmed the other body.

"Found him. He's safe," Jordan's voice came through the comm.

Zain bent down and pressed two fingers on the guy's neck, checking for a pulse, but he already knew what he would find.

Nothing.

"What the hell happened here?" Zain stood and looked around the apartment.

The others joined them with their guns brandished. Curses went around.

Well, no wonder the negotiator had lost communication with them.

Something had gone down between these two and they'd killed each other?

This didn't make sense at all.

Jordan and Zain came from out of the back rooms. She held the little one in her arms. He was bawling but appeared to be in good shape.

"Search the rest of the apartment," Mac ordered. He pulled his phone from his pants and made a call, no doubt updating the sergeant of the findings.

Myles, Ash, and Brodie moved through the living room and headed toward the other rooms.

Zain eyed the room and shook his head. There had been a struggle. What little items they housed in the apartment were strewn all over the place. This sure as shit didn't make sense. Steal a car together, don't give back the baby, but then fight each other to the death?

Over what?

8

"Mom, are you okay?" Jason's voice broke through Omara's thoughts.

She blinked and stared at her son who sat next to her at the table. It was afternoon, and they were eating lunch together. He had come home from his friend's house famished.

Her son was eating her out of house and home. He'd had a growth spurt and was already close to her height.

"Of course. Why would you ask?" She reached for her lemonade and took a sip. She glanced at her phone, checking the time. She was expecting Jordan any moment. She'd have to go to the shop soon. Today, she had blocked her morning off from her clients and was working the afternoon and evening. She usually liked starting early on Saturday mornings, but this was the one day that month she'd given herself time to sleep in and do some errands before going to work. Owning a salon could be taxing, but it was her business, and she could set her own hours. She had a good group of stylists and employees who she trusted.

"You look mad. Have you talked to Dad?" Her son was far too observant for his age.

She sighed and shook her head. One thing her son was correct to note was most times she spoke to his father, she would be angry afterwards. Derrick liked to try to control her even though they weren't together anymore. He pushed all of her buttons to get under her skin.

Unfortunately, she was going to have to deal with him for the rest of her life. He was the father of her child, and the courts had ordered him to pay her child support and had granted him visitation rights. It would be nice to think that once Jason turned eighteen she would never have to see Derrick anymore, but that wouldn't be reality. They would see each other at their son's college graduation, marriage, birth of grandchildren and so on. She was stuck dealing with the lunatic forever.

"No, I haven't spoken to your dad lately." She took a bite of her sandwich.

Jason loved peanut butter and jelly sandwiches, so she'd made them both one. She loved spending time with him like this, eating their favorite meals.

Come to think of it, Derrick should have been calling her. Next weekend was his time with Jason. He normally picked Jason up every other Friday.

Maybe she would send him a text so she wouldn't have to hear his voice. The man could be so condescending when speaking to her. She still couldn't believe she'd thought he had loved her. Their relationship had been filled with violence, hate, and abuse.

Omara had been embarrassed to face her family due to everything he had put her through. There were times she hadn't even gone around her family because of the bruising he had left on her. It hadn't been often he'd hit her in the face, but when he had, she'd have the proof.

She grew sick thinking of all the times she'd tried to protect him, claiming she was clumsy and falling to cover up the abuse. There were only so many times she could fall, and makeup could only hide so much.

Jordan hadn't let her excuses keep her from

coming around. She had figured it out. Quick. She'd moved from Atlanta to help Omara get away from Derrick.

Derrick was no match for her older sister. Jordan was one hell of a woman. Omara wished she was half the woman Jordan was. Derrick had thought he could pull the same crap he had on her with Jordan.

Boy, had her sister taught him a lesson. Omara would never forget his face when Jordan had laid him on his ass. The gun in his face sealed the deal that he'd better never come around Omara with his hand raised again.

No matter what they did, they couldn't get the courts to strip Derrick of his rights to his child. The judge had basically ignored the evidence of Derrick's abusive nature. Just because he had never laid a finger on their child apparently gave him the rights to still act as a father figure.

The system was definitely broken.

"Then why do you look mad?" Jason's dimples appeared with his smile.

Her son was just too handsome for his own good. She could see a little of herself in him, but hints of Derrick were becoming more noticeable. Jason was the only good that had come from their relationship.

"Oh, nothing. I just have a lot on my mind for

things for the shop," she lied. She did have things to do for her shop, but that wasn't why she was really pissed off.

She still couldn't believe Zain would leave her house without at least saying goodbye. She didn't know what the protocol was for one-night stands but she would think it would be a common curtesy to at least say goodbye or thanks for the fuck.

Something.

She blew out a deep breath.

Her body still tingled from the memory of everything that had transpired in her hallway and bedroom. Her skin felt flushed from her remembering the feeling of Zain pulsing inside her.

"Can I come help?" Jason asked.

She glanced back down at her phone, checking the time again. If Jordan didn't show up soon, she would have no choice but to take him with her. He wouldn't be in the way and liked helping her out at the shop. Some of the stylists would pay him to sweep up hair, and he earned some extra money. He had a small jar where he kept his earnings, saving it.

"Let me call your auntie first and see if she's still coming."

Jordan had promised to keep Jason with her so

Omara could go to work. There hadn't been word from her sister since she had left the bar last night. Omara hoped she wouldn't be catching her at a bad time.

She loved her and all, but there were some things they just didn't share with each other.

She picked up her phone and dialed Jordan's number. Winking at Jason, she stood from the table and walked back into the kitchen. The phone rang a few times before Jordan answered.

"Omara, hey," Jordan's voice sounded strained.

"Are you okay?" Omara immediately asked. Worry filled her at the thought that she hadn't called Jordan before now.

"Of course I am. Why wouldn't I be?" Jordan chuckled.

Omara blew out a deep breath. Jordan was right. Why wouldn't she be fine? Her sister could take care of herself.

"You sounded funny when you answered. You were supposed to be here an hour ago, and I was getting worried."

"I'm sorry, sis. SWAT got called out last night, and I'm just now leaving the scene." Jordan's voice changed again.

Omara could easily hear the stress in her sister's

voice. Wherever she had disappeared to last night must have been interrupted.

Then that was why Zain had left before she'd woken up.

He had to go because of work.

She should be used to that, being the sister of a SWAT officer. There were plenty of times Jordan had disappeared without a word because of getting called out on a mission. He could have still had the decency to wake her up. There didn't have to be any false promises made or anything.

She scowled, thinking she would give him a little piece of her mind. A gentleman would at least thank her for a wild night. She bit back a snort.

"Don't worry about it. I'll take Jason with me," Omara said.

She popped her head back into the dining room and motioned for him to get his shoes. He grabbed his empty plate and cup and rushed into the kitchen. She watched him toss his paper plate in the trash, rinse out his cup, and put in in the dishwasher.

She was impressed.

"Go ahead and do that. It will give me time to shower, then I can pick him up from you. Would that work?"

"That would be perfect." Omara chuckled

watching Jason disappear from the kitchen at a full sprint. It would be the best of both worlds. Earn a little money and then hang out with his cool auntie. She leaned back against the counter, her smile faltering. "No one got hurt last night, did they?"

She tried to keep her voice neutral. She didn't want to let on that she was asking about a certain tall, dark-haired officer who had rocked her world last night and into the wee hours of the morning.

"Yeah, everyone's good. A child was involved but thankfully wasn't injured."

"Oh my goodness." Omara's heart all but jumped into her throat. She closed her eyes, unable to fathom what her sister went through on the daily at her job. She knew there were some crazy things that cops got to see and deal with. Anything with a child would certainly tear Jordan apart. She loved Jason as if he were her own, and anytime she had a tragedy that involved children she would come over and just hug on Jason.

Omara didn't even want to imagine something happening to her son. She would lose her mind if someone hurt him.

"Who took you home last night?" Jordan asked, breaking through her thoughts.

"Um, Zain did," Omara stuttered. She cursed

internally, hoping Jordan didn't pick up on her nervousness. She twirled the end of her hair between her fingers, glad Jordan wasn't in front of her. Guilt was probably written all over her face. "He said that he didn't live that far away from me so he volunteered."

"He does. He better have been a perfect gentleman." Jordan snorted.

Omara blinked.

Oh, he had been.

He'd asked her if she was sure she wanted him in her home.

He'd confirmed if he could come in her mouth.

He'd been every bit of a gentleman when he'd fucked her just as she needed.

"He was," she replied. Omara had to shake her head to get the images from coming forward. Her heart was already racing with the memories springing to mind. There was no way in hell she would share with her sister the things she'd done to her coworker.

"Good. He does live close to you. I'll buy him a coffee or something," Jordan muttered.

Omara had to hold back a snarky comment that she didn't have to pay her coworker. Omara had taken care of that herself.

"So, you want to let me know where you disappeared to?" Omara asked. She couldn't help the grin that spread across her face. Jordan thought she was going to get away with not fessing up to what—or who— had her dipping out on her at the bar. If Omara didn't ask now, Jordan would just act like nothing had happened.

"How about I bring over a bottle of wine tonight. I'm off, and what I have to tell you will require wine."

"Oh, okay." Omara was officially intrigued. This was new for her sister. "I'll hold you to it."

"Mom, I'm ready!" Jason dashed back into the kitchen. He had his shoes and backpack on. He grinned and danced in place.

"Here, let me go. I have a client in less than an hour," she said, taking in the time on her watch.

"See you soon, sis," Jordan said. "Love you."

"Love you, too, big sis." She disconnected the phone and turned to Jason. "Let me get my keys, boo." She blew him a kiss and jogged into her bedroom. She paused in the doorway and inhaled. She could still smell the scent of Zain. She ran a shaky hand through her hair. There was no way she would be able to sleep in here with his cologne lingering on her sheets. Glancing at her watch again, she saw she could take a few minutes to throw them into the wash. They could dry when she got home.

Hurrying around her bed, she stripped the sheets from it. Snagging her keys from her dresser, she headed toward the garage where her washer and dryer were located. She quickly threw them in the washer and started it.

She'd had her one night with the sexy cop. Now it was time for her to move on.

Hopefully, the start would be to erase proof that he'd ever been inside her home.

Too bad she couldn't erase the memories like she could his scent.

But honestly, the memories of what they did would hold her over for a long while. The next man she chose to sleep with was going to have big shoes to fill.

Zain had certainly left his mark on her.

Walking back to the door that led to her kitchen, she snorted.

Oh, he'd certainly left his mark all right.

The soreness between her legs was proof enough.

"MISS ELAINE, lift your dryer and check to see if you're dry." Omara smiled at her older client. Miss Elaine had been coming to her for years. The elder woman came for the same thing each week. A wash and a roller set. "I'm almost done with her, then I'll comb you out."

"Okay, dear." Miss Elaine proceeded to do what Omara had asked.

"Scoot down in the chair a little, Marsha," Omara asked, turning her attention to the woman sitting in front of her. She would finish flat-ironing this client's hair and then would complete Miss Elaine.

Omara loved what she did. She had completed cosmetology school while in high school. When she'd graduated and received her license, she'd begun working at a high-end salon in Atlanta. She had met and fallen in love with Derrick then moved with him to Columbia after they'd found out they were expecting. Everything had appeared to be perfect. Her dream had always been to open her own salon, and when she'd moved to Columbia, she'd put that plan in place.

She had devoted too much time away from Derrick and focused on her business, and it was then that he'd begun to change. She wished she would have noticed the signs at first. Their constant bickering and arguing. She had attributed it to stress of a new baby, the move, her starting her business, his job.

But never had she put the blame on him.

She remembered the first time he'd pushed her.

They had been arguing over something as stupid as what would be for dinner.

Laughter brought her away from the dark memory. She took in everyone giggling about something she'd totally missed. Omara took in her small salon, and pride filled her. Everything she had been through to make her dream a reality was well worth it.

Fly Styles was her second child. The shop represented everything she wanted her clients to leave feeling. The decor was soft and feminine.

She bit back a smile remembering Zain sitting in her styling chair. He'd looked so out of place.

We are not going to think of him.

Thoughts of Zain would lead her to becoming aroused and aching again.

How was it she now had two men she wanted to shove out of her mind? One who'd brought her nothing but pain, and the other nothing but pleasure.

As promised, Jordan had come and scooped Jason up. Now that he was gone, the other stylists were back to their normal shenanigans. When Jason was in the shop, they had to be on their best behavior with their conversations and language.

"Who would you choose, Omara?" Sadie asked. Her smile was as wide as everyone else's.

Omara hated that she'd tuned them out while she was finishing her client.

"What?" she asked.

"Goodness, what could you be thinking about so hard." Sadie laughed. She reached for her hot comb and brought it back to her client's head and touched up her edges. "We are playing who would you rather marry. Choices are Jason Momoa or Dwayne 'The Rock' Johnson."

Everyone turned toward her, waiting for her response.

"You guys are brutal. How can I choose between them?" Her voice ended on a squeak. That was a hard choice to make. She pulled the flat iron through the last bit of Marsha's hair coiling the ends. Her hair was a cascade of curls and beautiful. "Do you want me to comb through it?"

"No, I like when they fall into place." Marsha smiled.

Omara placed her flat irons on the counter and handed Marsha a handheld mirror so she could see the back.

Marsha swiveled around in the chair, checking herself out. "Thank you so much for squeezing me in today."

"No problem."

"Same price?" Marsha handed her back the mirror and stood, taking her black smock off.

"Yes, ma'am."

Marsha passed her folded bills. Omara didn't have to check for she trusted her longtime client. Knowing Marsha, there was a hefty tip in there.

"Thank you. Stop at the reception desk to secure your next appointment. I'm getting booked out."

"Will do." Marsha nodded to the waiting stylists who were all staring at her. "I think you better answer them. Good luck with that answer."

Omara fell into a fit of giggles watching her client walk away and waving to everyone.

"We're waiting, boss lady," Alicia called out from her station.

Omara rolled her eyes and leaned back against her station.

"Okay!" She held her hands up and tried to think.

The choice was just too hard, but she knew her pick. "Well, I've had a crush on him since I was younger and was hooked on wrestling, so I'd have to say The Rock."

Laughter burst through the air. Nods went all around in agreement. Omara loved the atmosphere of her salon. It was always laid-back and fun. The five stylists who rented chairs from her were the best in the city. She was lucky to have them all under one roof. It kept the place busy, and her shop was getting a name for itself.

Omara's back pocket buzzed. She reached around and pulled it out.

"Asshole—Think Before Answering" was calling. She sighed, staring at the nickname she'd given Derrick. This was an expected call, but she never knew how it would go with him so she decided to take it back in her office.

"Miss Elaine, you can come have a seat in my chair," Omara called out. She scanned the shop and saw their intern, Kelsey, putting someone under the dryer. "Hey, Kelsey, can you take her rollers out. I have to answer this call."

"Yes, ma'am." Kelsey nodded. She was a twenty-year-old who was at the end of her beauty school and would be graduating soon.

Omara took in a few interns each year to help give them salon experience.

"Thanks." Omara spun around and headed toward the short hall where her office was located. She swiped the screen and answered. "Hello?"

"Took you long enough to answer," Derricks' smooth voice came on the phone. It was laced with the same malice that was always there when he spoke to her.

He had never taken too kindly that she'd left him. Which she'd never understood since he'd cheated on her multiple times.

"I'm at work, Derrick," she replied coolly. She shut the door, glad she'd made the decision to seek privacy for the call. She walked across the room and took a seat in her chair. There wasn't much to it, but this was her domain. It was decorated in soft colors, and a large white faux fur rug was placed beneath her glass desk. She had splurged a little on the desk, but she wanted her office to be professional and chic. She glanced at the small bay window behind her and leaned forward to open the blinds slightly to allow light to stream in. "What time are you picking Jason up on Friday?"

"I'm not."

"What?" She settled back in her chair and

pinched the bridge of her nose. This wasn't the first time he'd cancelled on their son. Omara just wished that Derrick was a better father. He could be a jerk to her all he wanted, but their son needed a strong, dependable man in his life. "Why not?"

"That's none of your business," he replied.

"Then what am I telling Jason?" she asked sarcastically.

"That I have some business to attend to and I promise to get him on my next weekend."

Omara rolled her eyes. Derrick worked for a construction company, but he always had little hustle projects on the side. There was no telling what this "business" entailed.

"You know what? Fine." She didn't want to argue with him. Her son was better off without him. She tried to not speak ill of Derrick in front of Jason. She was a firm believer that her son would see his father's true nature when he got older and know that Derrick was a deadbeat. She wasn't sure how much her son remembered of their relationship.

She'd tried to hide the arguments, fights, and beatings, but he'd been a witness to some of them. Omara hadn't been able to shield that side of his parents completely. Thankfully, Derrick never raised a hand to their son. He could hit her all he wanted as long as he left their child alone.

"Do you want me to have him call you?" she asked. Maybe he could just tell Jason himself.

"Sure. Where is he?"

"With Jordan." She was met with silence.

"I've told you countless times that I don't want him with your crazy fucking sister," he snapped.

"Don't talk about my sister." Her voice hardened. He wasn't going to sit there and talk about Jordan just because she was able to best him. He may be bigger than both of them, but her sister was still able to defend Omara and herself against him. "Do you want me to have him call you?"

"Not with her around. He can call me later this week. I'll talk with *my* son."

She didn't miss the emphasis on the word "my." During the court proceedings he'd tried to paint her as a woman who slept around and he wasn't sure he was the father. There had been a paternity test that proved he was the father of Jason.

"I saw the raise in your child support coming out of my check. You just make sure you are using that money for my son."

"Goodbye, Derrick."

9

*Z*ain guided his patrol car through the light traffic. It had been a week since he'd left the warm comforts of Omara's bed. It had taken everything he had to not ask Jordan about her. If he had, she would have been curious as to why he was asking about her sister. The sexy siren had been on his mind constantly. No matter how much he tried to block her, she showed up.

The sounds she'd made when she'd sucked his cock.

Her groans when he'd gone deep.

The memory of her pussy taking his entire length was burned forever in his mind.

"Fuck," he muttered. He had it bad. The one

rule he tried to stick with, and he was already contemplating breaking it.

He pulled to a stop at a light and recognized the area. He was near Omara's shop. Zain scrubbed a hand along his jawline. Maybe he could go see her. There had been a lot of burglaries reported in this area recently. He could drop by and warn her and the other stylists to be on the lookout when leaving at night.

Yeah, that's what he would do.

He was on the clock, and visiting shops was a great look for the Columbia Police Department. It would be good for community relations.

Yup, that was his excuse, and he was sticking to it.

He found a spot to park on the street near her building. He killed the engine and sat back.

His heart fluttered at the thought of seeing her again. Would she be receptive of his presence in her shop?

He pushed the door open and got out.

Zain Roman never got nervous around women. He'd closed that part of himself off after the ex-wife. He didn't care what women or anyone thought. He would have fun in life and live it to the fullest.

He shut the door and glanced around. A few

pedestrians ambled along the sidewalks, and traffic on the street wasn't bad at all. It was a calm, warm afternoon for a fall day. He started toward her shop. Zain gave a nod to two elderly women walking down the street. They smiled and carried on past him.

He arrived at Fly Styles and paused. From where he stood, he could see the waiting area was packed. It was a Friday afternoon, and he was sure there were lots of women wanting to get ready for their weekend plans.

Zain pulled the door open and walked in. He rested his hand on his utility belt and walked over to the reception desk. Conversation paused as the few women chatting all turned to stare at him. He bit back a grin at their expressions. He was in full uniform and hated it. What he wouldn't give to go out on missions every day, but unfortunately, that wasn't how it worked. When not decked out as if going to war, he patrolled.

The last time he'd been here, the shop had been closing, and the only person who had been there was Omara. He'd guess the owner of the shop would have late nights ensuring her business ran smoothly.

"Good afternoon, ladies." He gave them his kilo-watt smile.

They murmured a greeting, not taking their eyes off him.

He stopped at the desk and leaned against it. "Is Omara here?"

"Um, yeah. She is." The woman's eyes were wide as she stared at him. She was about fifty with her hair pulled up into a bun.

"Can I go back and speak with her?" he asked, raising an eyebrow.

"Oh, um. Yeah, you can go back. Do you need me to—?"

"No. I've been here before." He slapped the counter softly and pushed back away from it. He tossed her a wink and headed toward the back. He arrived, and the conversation amongst the stylists and clients ceased.

He bit back a chuckle. He was sure they weren't used to a male being in their sanctuary. Excitement was in the air. Women sat under the hood dryers in the styling chairs. The salon was filled with energy. He was sure they'd all had hard days at work and this was their treat to themselves at the end of the week. This was something his mother did. Nora Roman never missed her hair appointments. Now he could see why.

"Hello, ladies." He scanned the salon, and his

gaze came to rest on Omara who was organizing her station.

She swung around, her eyes going wide, and her mouth dropped open in shock.

"I'm Officer Roman with CPD."

"Hello, Officer," a sassy voice said.

He turned to the speaker and saw a woman with bright-pink hair staring at him. She didn't hide the way she sized him up like he was a fresh piece of meat. Zain knew what he looked like in uniform. He wasn't cocky by any means, but he took pride in his appearance. He looked damn good in his uniform.

"Who hired the stripper?" another one asked. Giggles went around. "Because my birthday is coming up, and I will gladly take a dance."

"I just went to the ATM," another one said.

Zain's cheeks warmed at the joke.

At least he hoped they were joking.

He faced the short woman with her hair in a high ponytail, tight jeans, and a red, low-cut top. She offered up a grin and rested her hands on her waist.

"I can assure you, I'm not a stripper, ma'am."

Groans went around. He shook his head at the women. He turned back and faced Omara.

"What are you doing here?" she asked. She folded her arms and leveled him with her gaze.

Shit, she was pissed at him. He could tell by the look in her eye and her body language.

Besides, she was related to Jordan, and their expressions were eerily similar.

What the hell had he done to her?

"Well, I was in the neighborhood and came to talk about the recent robberies that have occurred in this area," he announced.

The salon fell quiet. He saw all smiles were gone and they were paying attention to him.

"Really?" Omara asked.

"Yeah. There have been reports of some business owners and employees being robbed last night when they went out to their cars. When leaving at night, make sure you have a buddy, stay aware of your surroundings, and if you see anything suspect, don't hesitate to call the police."

Concern lined their faces, and he wanted to reassure them.

"If you aren't comfortable leaving, call and ask for a patrol car to come. We'll gladly keep an eye on your lot when you go to your cars."

"Can we call and ask for you?" Pink Hair asked.

Snickers met her question.

"Does all your unit look like you, because I think

I'm living on the wrong side of town," one of the clients sitting in a chair said.

"I'm on the wrong side of the law!" One sitting under the dryer hood snickered. "Let me go commit a crime."

He barked a laugh and walked backward toward Omara. He could take whatever these women threw at him. He was enjoying himself with their teasing.

"If I'm in the area, I wouldn't mind stopping by." Zain grinned and turned back to Omara.

"What are you really doing here?" she asked, tilting her head back to look up at him.

Damn, she was even more beautiful than he remembered. He could feel the eyes of every woman in the salon on his back.

"Can I talk with you in private, ma'am?" he asked.

Her gaze narrowed on him. His cock twitched at the expression. He was beginning to think he liked when she was pissed.

"Sure. We can go back into my office." She motioned for him to follow. She spun around and walked away.

His gaze dropped down to her ass covered in her bright-colored leggings. She had a t-shirt on that stopped right above the swell of her ass. He remembered the sight of her nakedness and had to reach down and adjust himself.

They stepped into a small room that was tastefully decorated. It reminded him of her. Soft, feminine, and all about business.

"What do you want, Zain?" she asked, shutting the door behind him. She leaned back against it and folded her arms. The move pushed her breasts up.

He stopped in front of her and trapped her with his hands on either side of her head.

"I can't come by and see you? Didn't you hear my speech out there?" He watched her chest rise and fall. The pulse of her heart rate throbbed at the base of her neck. Her heart was racing away.

He was affecting her just as much as she was him. His cock pressed harder against his pants. It was begging to be released. His gaze dropped down to her plump lips that were coated in a shiny lip gloss. He needed to taste them.

"I heard it. If that was all you had to say, you could have left afterwards, or the police department could have just sent a notice to the business."

"Me stopping by was making it personal," he murmured. He reached up, unable to resist touching her. He ran a finger along her cheek, trailing it over her soft brown skin to her lips. "Why are you upset at me?"

Fire blazed brightly in her eyes.

Oh, she was pissed at him all right.

"What makes you think that?"

"I am very good at reading people, and right now, the look in your eyes definitely gives off angry vibes." His finger reached her bottom lip. He traced it, remembering her mouth wrapped around his cock. "Tell me, Omara."

Her lip quivered. An unladylike curse escaped her.

"You left without saying goodbye." Her big, brown-eyed gaze landed on him.

The look in them took his breath away.

"You were sleeping so good, I didn't want to wake you," he admitted. The night they'd had together had been mind-blowing. He was shocked he'd had enough energy to go to work. He stepped closer and dropped a kiss on her forehead. "It was just a night of fucking, Omara. Or did you forget that."

She tried to push him away, but he was too big for her. He chuckled at the snarl that came from her as she tried until she finally gave up. She fell back against the door and glared at him.

"I know, but a common courtsey would be to say goodbye. You could have at least texted me."

"I don't have your number."

She paused and stared up at him. His lips tilted up in the corner. She glanced away, and it was obvious she was trying to hold back her smile.

"All it was the other night was fucking." She sniffed.

"Isn't that what we agreed upon?" he asked.

"It was."

"How about if I said I wanted another night with you?" he asked. He tipped her chin back to force her to meet his eyes.

"Another night?" Her eyebrows rose sharply. Interest was evident in her eyes by the way her pupils dilated.

He leaned down and kissed her lips.

"I keep thinking about you," he whispered.

"I've been thinking of you, too."

Another kiss.

"You lips and pussy felt so damn good around my cock."

Another kiss.

Her hands came to rest on his chest. He cursed having the ballistics vest on. He wanted to feel her hands on his bare skin.

"Your cock felt good inside me," she whispered. She gripped his shirt and rose on her toes. Her hands skated up and dove into his hair at the nape of his neck. "I want it again."

He swooped down, taking her lips in a hard kiss. His tongue swept inside her mouth, getting another taste of her. She met his kiss with the ferocity he felt inside for her. He angled his head and deepened the kiss. Desire for her rippled through him at the feeling of her back in his arms.

He slid his hands down her torso to her hips. He tore his lips from hers and blazed a hot trail of kisses along her jawline. He nuzzled his face into the crook of her neck. She tilted her head away to give him more access. He ran his tongue down the smooth column of her neck. He sank his teeth into her flesh just slightly. She moaned, her back arching away from the door. He slipped his hand underneath the elastic of her pants. Her legs separated, allowing him to reach for her center. He parted her slit and met the evidence of her arousal for him.

He cursed, dipping his finger inside her wet heat.

"When?" he demanded.

He toyed with her clit, watching her eyes flutter

shut. Her hips rocked against his hand. Her breaths were coming in little pants.

"Tonight," she exhaled. Her eyes opened, and her gaze landed on him.

He withdrew his finger, gathered more of her cream, and took his hand out of her pants. He glanced down and smiled at the slickness on his finger.

He lifted it to his mouth and sucked it clean. The taste of her exploded on his tongue. A growl rippled through him. He took her chin in his hand and kissed her mouth.

"I get off at eleven."

"Jason will be in the bed by then," she murmured. Her lips were swollen from his kiss. She patted his chest. "You will have—"

"To be gone before he wakes up." He nodded, fully understanding. "Got it."

His radio roared to life. He reached up on his shoulder to turn the volume down and cursed. He had forgotten that quick that he was still on the clock.

He dropped another kiss on her lips.

"You still didn't ask me for my number," she said, playing with a button on his vest.

"May I have your number?" He grinned and took his phone out of his pocket.

She rattled it off then took her phone out. She inputted his into hers.

"Now that problem is solved."

"It is." She pulled him down for another kiss.

Zain could lose himself in her lips. They were so soft and tantalizing. He could spend all day kissing her.

The radio sounded again.

"I got to go." His lips brushed against hers.

"Don't keep me waiting," she said.

He took a step back and swallowed hard, staring at her. She reached up and tucked a strand of her dark hair behind her ears. The move was simple, yet she made it sexy.

"The party might start without you."

She pushed off the door and opened it, escaping before he could say anything.

Running a hand along his jaw, he shook his head and prayed he didn't get any SWAT calls tonight. This might be one he would have to skip.

Damn the consequences.

ZAIN PULLED his squad car into the driveway of the house he'd been called out to. It was located in a quiet neighborhood, and the police were requested for a domestic disturbance. Yelling came from inside. Another police car arrived behind his. Zain radioed in that he was on the scene.

Leaving the engine running, he stepped from his car and gave a nod to the officer.

"Hey, Roman. How's it going?" Jones met him at his cruiser with his hand extended.

They shared a firm handshake. Jones was a veteran officer. He held the respect of many on the force, including SWAT. Jones had taken a bullet to the chest the night Brodie's woman had been kidnapped from the hospital. He had been pulling some overtime and had arrested a thug who had been stabbed and needed medical attention for his wound. The thugs who were after him turned up at the hospital, shot Jones, and took Ronnie hostage.

"Can't complain. How's the chest?" Zain asked.

"Good as new. Thanks to my vest, I just had some deep bruising." The older man looked around the neighborhood.

They faced the house and walked toward it.

"I'm getting to be too old for this. If they are just arguing then they get a warning."

"Agreed." Zain understood couples argued. He and Freya had been notorious for their rows. The woman had always gone against his word. If he said the sky was blue, she'd say it was green.

A scream and a crash came from inside. Zain and Jones raced up the stairs. Zain banged on the front door. He flipped the button on his thigh gun holster. Hopefully he wouldn't need to pull it out.

"CPD!" Zain hollered. Another cry had him reaching for the handle. It was unlocked. He glanced at Jones who gave him a nod.

Zain pushed the door open and called out again.

"Hello?" he said. He took a step in, his hand hovering over his weapon. "CPD. We were called about a disturbance."

Jones came in behind him. The living room had clothing strewn all over the place along with old takeout food containers. Voices sounded from the hall off the living room.

"Hold on. Here I come." A woman appeared, walking down the hall toward him.

Zain stiffened. She came into view, and he instantly zoomed in on the red area to her face. Her lip was split with a little blood oozing from it.

Someone had hit her.

"Are you all right, ma'am?" Jones moved to stand beside Zain. He'd seen what Zain had picked up.

"Of course she's all right," a booming voice came from the hall. A tall, dark-skinned man strode toward them.

"We weren't talking with you," Zain said.

He sized up the man and concluded this had to be the one who'd put his hands on her. He suspiciously held a cloth to his hand, covering it.

"Ma'am, would you mind stepping out onto the porch with me for a moment?" Jones escorted the woman outside.

"How the hell did y'all get inside my house?" The man scowled.

"Front door was open. What is your name?" Zain asked, cutting to the chase.

The man glared at him instead of answering.

"We're here because someone called us. Now just answer the question."

"Derrick. Derrick Allen," he finally replied.

"What was going on here?" Zain asked.

"Nothing. We just had an argument. Nothing worth the police's time," Derrick muttered. He stalked over to the window that looked out onto the front porch. "Why did he take Jenny outside?"

"We just need to speak with both of you," Zain

replied. His muscles remained tense. He didn't trust this man. There was something about him that didn't sit right with him. Zain hoped the woman wanted to press charges against the fucker. "Do you live here?"

"Roman. Can I talk with you for a moment?" Jones asked from the door.

Zain gave Derrick another glare.

"Don't go anywhere. I'll be right back."

"I'm not going anywhere," Derrick snapped. He went over and sat in the recliner.

Zain eyed him for another second before going back out onto the porch where Jones stood with the woman named Jenny.

"What's going on?" he asked.

"I want him out of my house," Jenny announced. She wrapped her arms around her waist. Her bottom lip trembled. She sniffed and wiped her nose with the back of her hand.

"He hit her, but she doesn't want to press charges," Jones said.

"Ma'am, with all due respect—" Zain was cut off by the raising of her hands.

"Your partner here already gave me the talk. Look, I don't want any trouble. I just want him gone. This is my house, he doesn't pay my mortgage or the bills here. He just needs to go." Her voice ended on a hiccup. She brushed her bangs from her face and leaned against the pillar.

Zain met Jones' hard gaze and gave a nod.

"Yes, ma'am," Zain said.

He and Jones went back inside the home. Derrick remained in the chair, his foot tapping the floor.

"What did she say?" he asked, eyeing Zain and Jones.

"She wants you out, sir. Please go gather your things—"

"She can't just throw me out!" Derrick snarled. He jumped up from his seat.

Zain's hand instantly went to his weapon. He calmly gripped the handle but left it in the sheath.

"Are you the homeowner?" Jones asked.

"This is her place—"

"Then she has the right to ask for you to leave," Jones said calmly.

Zain didn't take his eyes off Derrick as he paced.

"We're going to stay here until you leave," Zain said.

Derrick's cold gaze cut to him. His attention dropped down to Zain's hand.

"You want to shoot me, Officer?" he sneered.

"No, sir," Zain snapped. He didn't take his hand

off the handle. He met the angry man's glare with one of his own. Zain wasn't trying to be here for long. The sooner this asshole left, the sooner he and Jones could wrap this up. "Go get your things. Now."

Derrick sized him up, throwing his hands up in the air.

"Fine. I ain't got time for her shit, no way." Derrick disappeared down the hall and went into a room.

Zain waited for him in the living room. He kept his hand on his weapon. He never like being in people's homes. There was no telling what weapons they could pull out. A simple call could go wrong at the drop of a hat.

Jones went back out onto the porch to update Jenny. Zain was sure the man was trying to give her all the options she would have.

A few moments later, Derrick came flying out of the room with a duffle bag in his hand. Zain followed him outside and stopped on the porch next to Jones.

Derrick jogged down the stairs and went over to the SUV parked in front of the garage.

"Don't call me for shit, bitch," Derrick hollered. He opened the driver's door and tossed his bag inside.

"Don't worry, I won't. You sorry piece of shit," Jenny screamed. Tears spilled down her face.

"Ma'am, don't rile him. Let him go." Jones rested a hand on her shoulder.

She nodded and wiped her face with the back of her hand.

"What did you say?" Derrick took a step back toward them.

Zain walked down the stairs and pointed to his truck.

"Go ahead and leave, sir," he warned.

Derrick stopped and eyed him.

"Whatever." He turned his glare to Jenny before stalking back to his truck. "You were a lousy lay anyway."

Zain shook his head watching Derrick get into his truck. The engine roared to life. He backed out of the driveway and flipped the poor woman off then drove away.

Zain went back to the porch, stopping at the bottom stair. He didn't like the look in Derrick's eyes.

"Do you have someone you can go stay with for a night or two, ma'am? Or someone who can stay with you?" Zain asked.

"Yeah. I'll call my brother." She nodded. She

offered a small smile to both of them. "I really appreciate you coming so quickly. He can be a bit much. He used to be so nice and kind."

"Don't make excuses for him. I highly suggest you file a restraining order against him," Jones said.

She jerked her head in a nod. "I will."

Zain peered down the street in the direction Derrick had traveled. Something didn't sit right with him about that guy. He just prayed the man stayed away from Jenny. Zain didn't agree with her not wanting to press charges.

Men like that didn't deserve to see the light of day.

10

Omara walked into her bedroom with her towel wrapped around her. Fresh from her shower, she had to look and smell good for her late-night appointment. Tonight had been the fastest she'd had Jason get ready for bed. She had even allowed him to stay up late to make sure he was good and tired. He'd taken his shower and promptly fallen asleep.

Which was perfect.

She didn't want him to be awake when Zain arrived.

Omara had always been protective of her son. She refused to parade any man in front of him who wasn't going to be a long-term relationship.

What she had with Zain wasn't a relationship. It was two people who needed sexual release and who were good together.

She glanced at her phone and saw it was almost midnight. She had warned Zain that if he was late, she was going to get the party started without him. She sat on the bed and reached for her moisturizer. She quickly slathered it over her body, loving the scent. This was a new brand she had found, and it was amazing. Her skin was silky and smooth.

She put on the nightie she had placed on her bed. It was black and lacy and didn't really hide much. It had been a splurge purchase six months ago. She didn't know what occasion she had purchased it for. She had figured it would be something she could put on to walk around her house and feel sexy.

Now she had a good reason.

A six-foot-three-inch-tall SWAT officer.

Omara took her towel and hung it up on her closet. She turned back to her room, trying to think of what else she could do to set the mood. Not that one had to be set. The moment the two of them entered her bedroom, the sparks flew.

"Candles," she murmured. She walked over to

her dresser and picked up the small box of matches and went around her room, lighting the candles she had scattered around. She scurried over to the mirror above her dresser to look at herself one last time.

Her hair was down. There was no point in putting it up. It was going to get messed up tonight. She grinned and reached for her lip gloss. Once she was done, she smiled at herself. It had been a long time since she had been this excited about a man.

Or maybe that she was getting another dick appointment.

It had been a while since she'd had mind-blowing sex, and now, two weekends in a row was setting a record for her.

Too bad she couldn't call her sister and share the news.

Jordan would have a conniption if she knew she was sleeping with Zain.

Omara paused.

She and Jordan still hadn't had the chat she'd been promised. Her sister had been busy with work lately, and she had been perfecting her disappearing act.

Again, Omara decided she would wait on her sister to be ready to share whatever it was she was hiding.

Omara sauntered back over to her bed and sat on the edge. She reached for her phone, feeling bold. She settled back against the pillows and took a sexy selfie. She bit her lip and stared at it.

"What the hell," she mumbled. She sent it to Zain via text. Omara giggled. She couldn't even remember the last time she'd sent a pic to any guy.

Waiting on you.

She sighed and paused to see if he was going to reply. She double- and triple-checked to make sure she had sent it to him and not anyone else. She would be mortified if she'd sent it to one of her parents.

You better wait for me.

Omara bit her lip. She had warned him. She slipped one of her shoulder straps down and took another seductive photo. She paused then threw caution to the wind and sent it.

What's your ETA?

She squeezed her thighs together at the thought of Zain. Everything about him was perfect, from the dark curly hair to his thick cock. Even his laugh made her smile. If she was looking for a relationship, someone like Zain would be who she'd want.

But you have Zain, a small voice spoke up in the back of her mind.

Omara sighed.

She didn't need a relationship. There was too much on her plate right now, and having a man could complicate everything.

What she had with Zain was perfect. They each got what they wanted.

Hot, sweaty sex.

She would be content with that.

Her phone buzzed with a reply from Zain.

I'm almost there. Be there in less than five minutes.

She could almost hear him growling.

Omara stood and retrieved her black silk robe and put it on. She didn't want the doorbell to wake Jason, so she decided to wait for Zain in the living room where she would be able to see when he arrived.

She padded out into the room and didn't have long to wait. Knowing Zain, he probably ran all of the red lights. She wouldn't be surprised if he had his police lights on so he could get here quicker.

She paused, remembering him in her shop earlier with his dark uniform on. That man dripped sex appeal. Everyone in the shop had recognized it. The vest, his exposed forearms, the badge, the gun holster on his thigh, and those damn handcuffs. The look he'd given her basically melted her panties.

She had grown quite jealous of the looks and comments being thrown his way, but Zain being who he was just rolled with it. No matter how much she'd wanted to tell everyone to back off because he was hers, she'd kept her mouth shut. But he hadn't glanced at any of them. They weren't exclusive, and he could have, but it was her he'd taken in her office and mind-fucked her. Hell, she would have fucked him in her office and not cared who would have heard them.

The man had her strung.

Dickmatized.

What was a girl to do?

Omara took a deep breath at the sight of head-lights appearing in front of her home. Just as she was wondering if he should park in her drive, Zain backed out and stopped a few houses down on the street.

"Great minds think alike," she muttered.

Omara watched his tall figure stalk up her drive-way. She would recognize Zain's figure anywhere. She pushed off the windowsill and headed over to the door. She peeked around the curtain just as he arrived at the bottom step. She opened the door and smiled.

Zain's attention went to her face first before sliding down toward her curvy frame.

"Hey," she said.

Omara was slightly tongue-tied staring into his heated gaze. She might as well have come to the door naked. His nostrils flared as he got down to her bare feet then came back up to her face.

He liked what he saw. A twinge of excitement filled her. She could be self-conscious of all her curves at times, but the way he always looked at her had her proud of her thick figure. He'd changed his clothes, putting on a dark CPD long-sleeved t-shirt with the sleeves pushed up, gray sweatpants that had her holding back a whimper, and tennis shoes.

And tonight, for a few hours, he was all hers.

"Are you going to invite me in?" His lips curved up into a grin.

"Of course. Where are my manners?" she sputtered. She opened the door and stepped back, allowing him to enter.

He brushed past her, and she caught a whiff of his cologne.

It damn near did her in right there.

A handsome man with a good musky scent was a downright temptation no woman could resist.

Omara shut and locked the door. She felt his warmth at her back. Her hand was braced on the door. A familiar bulge pressed to her bottom. Her core clenched at the sensation of his hard cock on her.

"Miss me?" he murmured. He nuzzled her neck and pulled her back flush against him with an arm wrapped around her waist.

"More than you know," she whispered.

Omara had been in a state of arousal all day thinking about this man. Now that he was physically there and touching her, slickness coated her thighs. She tilted her neck to the side to give him more access. His tongue burned a trail along her skin while his other hand skated up her tummy and cupped her aching breast.

Omara panted, leaning back into his embrace.

"I've been thinking about you all damn day," he groaned. He squeezed her mound, then rolled her nipple through the material with his fingers.

"Bedroom," she gasped. She spun around in his arms and took in the feral look in his eyes. Her body was completely on fire, and if she wasn't careful, she'd let him take her out here. She couldn't risk Jason coming out of his room and seeing Zain.

Zain appeared in a haze. He lowered his head to her and pushed his face into the crook of her neck, nipping and licking at her skin. Omara whimpered, leaning into him, while wrapping her arms around his neck. She pressed her thighs together, a moan escaping her at the prodding of his cock against her stomach. Zain made his way to her chin before he claimed her lips in one scorching kiss.

All conscious thought just about left Omara. She fell into the hot, open-mouthed kiss. Zain was dominating, his tongue stroking hers, while his hands were full of her ass. He gripped her hard, holding her to him while he claimed her mouth.

"My room. Now," she demanded, breaking the kiss.

Zain bent down and lifted her. She squealed, wrapping her legs around his waist. He carried her through the house as if she weighed no more than a pillow. They arrived in her bedroom with him pushing the door shut with his foot.

"Lock it," she whispered.

He grinned and did as she'd asked. She didn't want to take any chances her son may walk in. He had a bad habit of not knocking when he was in a rush.

He put her down, her body sliding along every inch of him. She groaned, loving the feeling of his fit physique and his member vying for attention. He undid her robe and pushed it off her shoulders, allowing it to fall to the floor. His quick intake of breath had her smiling.

"Like what you see?" She took a step back and rested her hands on her waist.

His hungry gaze took her in. He gave a short nod.

"Very much so. Your body should never be covered," he rasped. He reached for the hem of his shirt and pulled it over his head. He tossed it on the floor and stalked toward her, backing her up against the bed.

The sight of him shirtless took her breath away. The candlelight showcased every edge of his muscles. The ones on his abdomen begged to be traced by her tongue.

"Yours shouldn't either, but I'm not sure what people would say if I walked down the street with no shirt on. I mean, men may appreciate it—"

"I don't want to think of another man seeing

your perfection," he growled, his eyes narrowed on her.

His hand shot out and gripped the back of her neck. They were so close, nothing could fit between them. Her breasts scraped his chest as she inhaled.

Hmmm...was someone jealous?

She bit back a smile, knowing the feeling was mutual. They weren't exclusive, she had no rights to tell him what to do.

"My perfection?"

The fire in his gaze flared. His hand slid down to her throat. A shiver rippled through her at his touch.

"You're a beautiful woman, Omara. I shouldn't have to tell you that," he whispered. His gaze held hers, and his hands traveled down her body. "Your soft lips, these full breasts, hips, ass, and pussy were made to be worshipped."

His hands somehow made their way back to her shoulders, where he pushed her straps off. The silky nightie slid silently to the floor.

"And as much I love seeing you in this thing, I prefer you naked," he said before crushing his mouth to hers.

She wasn't sure when they made it onto the bed. She lay underneath him, basking in the feel of him on her. She spread her legs to allow him to settle into the valley of her thighs.

Zain explored her body, taking his time kissing and nipping her breasts. His hot mouth suckled her breast as if he were a starving babe. Her hands dove into his soft hair. She loved running her fingers through it. She writhed on the bed, the sensations coursing through her sending waves of desire to her core.

Zain nipped her bud with his teeth, eliciting a moan from her. He continued on, kissing every inch of her skin. He stopped at her soft belly, not put off by her slight pudge. He slid down farther, pushing her legs apart. He stared at her core for a moment. She squirmed, needing him to put her out of her misery.

"What is it?" she asked.

He leaned in and inhaled her scent. Her cheeks warmed, and a nervous laugh escaped her. She was so glad she had been keeping up her lawn mainte-nance. She wasn't completely bare down there but kept it neatly trimmed.

"Zain. What are you doing?"

"Admiring you." His gaze flicked to hers, a smile hovering on his lips. "Taking the time to appreciate a masterpiece."

She stared at him. God, if this man didn't be careful, she would lock him in her bedroom forever and never let him go.

He lowered his head and captured her clit with his lips. Omara's head dropped back onto the bed. The man needed no instructions. He certainly knew what he was doing. She bit back a cry, knowing her son was in the next room sleeping.

Zain's tongue was magical. He slid it through her slit, lapping up all of her juices. He teased her with it, feasted on her. Her hips lifted, meeting him as she rode his tongue.

She shot her hand out and entwined her fingers in his hair. She thrust her hips forward, fucking his face. She loosened her hold, not wanting to tear his hair out.

"Grip it tighter, baby," Zain ordered.

She blinked and looked down at him.

"What?" she gasped. She could barely comprehend the English language at the moment. The man had her on the brink of orgasming that quick. Her heart was racing while she panted, trying to draw breath into her body.

"My hair. I won't break, baby. Pull it if you need to." He gave her that sexy wink of his before returning to what he was doing.

Omara gave a silent cry when he pushed a finger into her drenched opening. Her muscles clenched around it. Her hips rocked against him, wanting it all. She bit her lips, soft cries escaping her. He thrust his finger in and out of her slowly while he suckled her clit.

"Please," she begged. Her legs shook from the anticipation of what was to come. Zain was a very astute student. He had learned her body and was pushing her to the brink of her climax.

Another finger joined the first one. He was stretching her out, rotating them inside her. She was impatient and wanted his cock in her. She tugged on his hair harder with the pace of her hips quickening. She wanted—no, needed—that euphoric feeling of her release.

Sweat coated her skin, her breaths coming in heavy pants. Zain thrust his fingers inside, hard and fast.

The pressure on her clit increased, her muscles tensed, and she finally crested.

Her silent scream escaped her, and tremors racked her. Omara was no longer in control of her body. Her climax wiped away all conscious thought while she rode the waves. Her back arched off the bed as she turned herself over to all the pleasure coursing through her. Zain continued his sweet torture of her until she flopped back down.

"Oh God. Zain," she cried out softly. She tried to pull him up by his strands, but the bullheaded man wouldn't let up on her. Her feeble attempt to close her legs was thwarted by his strong forearms pushing her legs open wider. His fingers remained buried inside her while he continued his gentle sucking on her clitoris. "Zain."

"What?" He raised his head and met her gaze.

She whimpered at the sight of her release on the hairs of his beard on his chin. He gave her a little feminine satisfaction to see it. He withdrew his fingers from her and lifted them to his mouth. She watched with bated breath—he licked them clean.

She completely forgot what she was going to say.

He lifted and stood by the bed and shucked off his pants. His cock sprang free, standing to attention.

"Um, sir." She cleared her throat.

Her attention locked on that magnificent thick cock. She raised her eyes to his once he moved back to the bed. He crawled over her and braced himself with his hands on each side of her head. The weight of his cock rested on her belly. It was soft, hot, and hard all at the same time. She needed it inside her ASAP.

"You do know walking around with gray sweat-pants on with no underwear is the equivalent of a woman walking around naked with a trench coat on, right?" she said.

He grinned and shook his head.

"No, I had no idea," he smirked. "I'll keep that in mind."

He lowered his head and captured her lips with his.

11

Zain leaned back on his knees and watched Omara spread her legs wide for him. He gripped the base of his cock and stroked it. A shiver rippled down his spine at the sight of her. There were so many positions and things he wanted to do to her, but for now, missionary it was. He was wound too tight at the moment and didn't want to blow his load prematurely like an unseasoned teen.

The cute, sexy little pictures she had sent him had him breaking every traffic law to get to her. Just the thought of her touching herself without him had him careening out of control. Then when he had arrived and she was in her sexy lingerie, he'd almost come in his pants then.

What is it about her?

He was craving the feel, touch, and taste of her.

"Had I been late, what would you have done?" he asked.

A grin spread across her face. Her hands went to her breasts and molded them in her grasp. His breaths came faster as he continued to run his hand along his length. Curiosity was getting the best of him. He just had to know.

"Well," she began. Her hands slid along her mounds, then one dipped down, skating along her soft belly.

He didn't give a shit about her rolls or the stretch marks. The woman had given birth to a child. His mind instantly pictured her pregnant with his.

He paused his hand on his dick, almost spilling his seed right then and there. He had given up on the thought of having children.

Omara was a great mother. It was evident by her silent cries and orgasm, her not wanting to alert her child that she was having an adult sleepover with a member of the opposite sex.

From the little Jordan had shared, Omara's ex was an ass. Zain growled at the thought of this mystery man. Had he been there during her pregnancy? Was he a good father to her child? All these questions filled his head, but he had no right to ask them.

"I have a drawer filled with some things that would have occupied my time," Omara said. Her words were soft and breathless.

He blinked and found her finger massaging her clit.

"Where?" he demanded. He wanted to see what she used on herself.

"Bottom drawer," she murmured, pointing at her nightstand.

He leaned over and pulled it open, finding quite a few toys in there. His gaze caught sight of the tube of lube, and he brought it out.

"We're going to need this." He held it up for her to see. He jerked his eyebrows up and tossed it onto the bed.

"We are?" She arched one of her perfectly sculpted eyebrows. She gave a small moan, her finger still playing with her clit.

His cock thickened, growing impossibly harder. She rolled over, exposing her round ample ass for him to see. Many women paid money to get an ass like hers, and here she was, blessed with a natural one. He gripped his cock again, squeezing it at the base. A drop of his seed appeared on the tip. He was close to blowing and he hadn't even sunk inside her yet.

She gave him a sexy look over her shoulder, eyeing his hand stroking his cock. "And please tell me why you deserve this?"

She leaned down on her elbows, giving him a full view of her dark rim. The air flew out of his chest. He struggled to get air in. He moved fast, pressing his cock against her. He shot his hand out and gripped her hair. He yanked her head up so she could fully hear him. His hold on her dark strands were tight, more than he planned, but her little dig at him needed to be repaid.

"Why I deserve it? How hard did you just come on my tongue? How many orgasms have I given you? You know very damn well how wet you get thinking of me. Your pussy was drenched when I got here," he growled.

He was no longer in control of his actions. He rubbed his cock between her ass cheeks. Their simultaneous groans filled the air. He dipped his cock down and ran it through her slick folds. Her body was so damn responsive to him.

She wiggled her ass against him.

He was going to explode, but not before he pushed inside her.

His cock was coated in her juices. He rubbed it again against her dark hole, eliciting another moan from her. Tremors racked her body. He grinned and released her hair. She was just playing hard to get.

"Do you want me here?" he asked.

With his free hand, he cupped the roundness of her ass cheek. He pressed harder, running the underside of his shaft against her, guiding it between her cheeks. Her head jerked in a nod.

"I need to hear you say it, Omara."

She cursed, her head falling forward.

"Do it, Zain. Please." Her lust-filled voice was husky and low. She spread her legs wider and leaned down on her forearms, putting her in the perfect position.

He snatched the lube up and flipped the top open. He placed a substantial amount over her puckered rim. He tossed the tube on the nightstand. No use in putting it up. They may be using it again later.

He held his cock firmly. He ran it through her slit, once again getting her natural juices to coat him before moving back to the hole he had yet to explore.

He nudged the tip of his cock into the gel, coating her and himself. He carefully pushed forward. Her audible inhale could be heard when he breached her tiny opening. He bit back a curse at the feeling of her gripping the meaty head.

She was so tight.

He exhaled and pushed farther. With his length and girth, he couldn't go too fast at first. He didn't want to hurt her.

Sweat beaded on his forehead as he fed her another inch.

"Zain," she breathed.

He loved hearing his name on her tongue. Her hips rotated, her ass drawing more of him into her.

"That's it, baby. Take all of me." He ran a hand along her back, trying to calm himself down.

"It feels so good," she muttered. Her hips did their thing again, but this time she pushed back onto him. He sank fully into her. "So good, Zain. Please fuck me. Now."

Her words created an explosion inside him. He withdrew from her, leaving only the tip in before he thrust forward. She snagged a pillow and buried her head into it, muffling her cries.

Zain continued the motions, rocking his hips and taking what she offered. He watched his cock pull out and sink back in, and it was one hell of sight. Her hole stretched to accommodate him. He slid in and out effortlessly.

Her tight walls clenched around him. Her ass greedily accepted him. He held on to her waist while increasing his pace.

His orgasm was fast approaching. The sounds of their fucking had his balls rising close to him, a warmth flooding him, and he knew he was close, but he didn't want to come without her climaxing again.

"Play with your clit," he demanded. His strokes were long and deep.

She pushed up on one arm, sliding her hand between her legs.

She chanted his name repeatedly.

"Yes," he hissed.

He quickened his hips until he was furiously pounding into her. Her body shook, her climax taking hold of her. Her muscles spasmed, sending him spiraling into his release. He held back his roar while he emptied himself inside Omara. Ripples of his seed spewed from him. He pumped a few more times, filling her. He paused, leaving them connected. He tilted his head back and stared at the ceiling. Stars lined his vision. Her ass milked him for everything he had.

A smile came to his lips.

He was in Heaven.

Buried inside the most beautiful woman he had

ever known, he didn't ever want to leave. He glanced down at Omara, her face once again buried in the pillow. If he wasn't mistaken, snores were coming from her. He slowly withdrew from her. His cock was still semi-hard. The sight of his semen dripping from her hole had him feeling possessive like some chest-pounding alpha male who had claimed his woman. He lay down next to Omara and gathered her into his arms. He pulled the covers over them and tucked her in close to him. Kissing her forehead, he held her until he drifted off to sleep.

ZAIN WOKE UP, momentarily confused on where he was. Then all of the memories came flooding back. He reached out for Omara and didn't feel her in the bed next to him. He opened his eyes and didn't see her.

Her soft voice was muffled out in the hall. He sat up on the side of the bed and heard a smaller voice talking with her.

Her son.

Jason must have woken up.

Zain ran a hand through his hair, unable to believe he had slept through her getting up. He was usually a light sleeper. He snagged his pants from the floor and took his cell phone out. He cursed, remembering he'd left his gun in his truck. He'd been in such a rush to get to Omara he'd left it locked away in the glove box. He checked his phone and didn't see any missed calls. Dropping it on the nightstand, he pulled his sweats back on.

He silently walked over to the door and pressed his ear to it.

"Well, just wait and see if it comes or not," she said softly. "You probably just need a good poop."

"Mom," Jason groaned.

"When was the last time you had one?" she asked.

"I don't know," the kid responded.

Zain smiled at her being the overprotective mother. He could remember having conversations with his mother that were downright embarrassing for a kid.

He quietly opened the door. She stood inside the doorway to her bathroom. She leaned back and caught his eye.

"Take a minute and sit here. I'll be right back," she said to her son. She left the door partway open then walked toward him.

"Everything okay?" he asked, keeping his voice low.

"Yeah. He woke up with a stomachache." She tucked her thick hair behind her ear and slipped into the room with him.

He closed the door and pressed her against it. Her robe was back on, but her nipples were erect and obvious through the thin material.

"You're a great mother, Omara," he whispered. He kissed her on the forehead.

"I try to be." She sighed. She leaned back on the door. "Someone has to be a great parent for him."

"His father isn't around?" he asked softly. He didn't want to pry, but his curiosity was piqued.

"Sort of. This was supposed to be his weekend, but he cancelled on Jason." Her big brown eyes met his.

The strings of his heart were tugged by her expression. He felt sorry for the kid. Zain and his brother, Luca, had a great role model in their father, Benson. He was heavily involved in their lives, and there wasn't a day either him or his brother couldn't go to their father with any problems.

"I'm sorry," he said. He reached up and caressed the soft skin on her cheek.

"There's nothing for you to be sorry about. It's not your problem to deal with." She sniffed.

He wasn't sure why, but that hurt a little.

But she was right.

It wasn't for him to worry about. They weren't together, and this between them was physical only.

I want more, he realized. He almost took a step back from her.

He lowered his head and nuzzled her neck. He didn't know what shower gel or perfumed she used, but he loved it. He breathed in her scent and nipped her neck. Her body arched to his, pressing her full breasts against his.

"When you're done seeing to your son, I need you," he whispered.

A whimper escaped her. He lifted his head and kissed her soft lips. Her brown eyes were locked on him.

"Is that so?" She smirked.

He moved closer to her, showing her how much he needed her. His cock was thick and engorged, ready to be back in the depths of her heat.

"How can you be ready again?" she asked.

He barked a laugh and dropped another kiss on her lips.

"Well, when you get the attention of a very

beautiful woman, you take full advantage of it," he murmured.

"Mom!" Jason called out.

"Give me a second," she replied. Her hands came to rest on Zain's chest.

He placed his hands on hers and raised them to his lips. He kissed both of her palms. Her teeth snagged her bottom lip, and he bit back a groan.

"Go ahead, babe. Take care of your son. I'll be waiting for you." He stepped back to allow her to turn and escape out the door. He stood watching her go back to the bathroom.

She opened the door and peeked her head in.

"Anything yet?" she asked.

"No, but it doesn't hurt anymore," Jason said.

"Okay, well, at least you tried." She leaned against the doorjamb.

"Who were you talking to, Mom?" Jason asked.

Zain stiffened. Shit, the kid must have heard his voice even though he had tried to keep it low.

"Nobody, babe."

"You sure? I heard a man's voice. Is Dad here?"

The air whooshed out of Zain's chest. He felt as if he'd been hit in the solar plexus with a two by four. He coasted a hand along his face and closed his eyes. He opened them and closed the door the rest of the way. Of course the kid would assume his father was back in the home.

Didn't all kids want their parents to be together?

Was Omara hoping her child's father returned?

Was that why she'd agreed to their arrangement?

"No, Jason. You know your father wouldn't be here at this time of night. My television was still on. That's probably what you heard."

Zain walked away from the door to give Omara some privacy with her son. He sat on the edge of the bed, raking his hands through his hair. He'd never been involved with a single mother before. Did he even want to deal with a crazed ex or a kid who wasn't his?

The door opened slightly, and Omara returned into the room. Her lips were pressed in a firm line. She leaned back against the door and stared at him.

"I'm sorry," she said.

"For what?" He lifted an eyebrow. What did she have to apologize for?

"For hearing what Jason asked. About his father." She walked to him and stopped in front of him.

Zain sat straight up and reached for her hand. He pulled her to stand between his legs.

"It's all good. I'm assuming it's a question any kid would have," he admitted.

She reached up and pushed his hair back from his face.

"Well, I can guarantee that me and his father will never be back together," she said softly.

He jerked his head in a nod, unable to speak around the lump that had formed in his throat. He didn't want to admit that jealousy was rearing its ugly head. Hell, if they had wanted to try to get back together for the sake of Jason, he would step aside. There was no way he'd stop a man from trying to get his family back.

"You want me to go now?" he asked. He rested his hands on the back of her naked thighs. Her skin was so soft, he couldn't help but touch it. He skated his fingertips underneath the robe.

"Only if you want to." She tilted his chin up and kissed him softly. "He'll drift off to sleep soon. In the meanwhile, you would have to be extra quiet."

She untied her robe and pushed it off onto the floor.

He swallowed hard, taking in her naked form. His cock jerked to attention beneath his sweats. She dropped to her knees in front of him. She pointed to his pants.

"Um, what's this?" she asked.

"I wasn't sure if I was going to have to leave or if he'd see me. I was thinking I'd rather not meet your son with my dick out." He grinned.

She giggled and sat back, watching him stand and push down his pants. He kicked them off to the side. He engorged member stood to attention against his belly. He sat back down on the bed and widened his legs. She scooted forward.

"Thank you for such consideration," she murmured. Her brown eyes deepened as she gazed upon his cock. She wrapped her hand around him and stroked the length of him.

Zain blew out a shaky breath, loving the feeling of her soft grip on him.

"No problem, at all," he breathed.

Omara leaned forward and kissed the tip of his cock. A little bead of fluid appeared on it. She licked it off, moaning.

His eyes closed when her lips wrapped around the head. He reached out and threaded his fingers into her hair while she took more of him. Omara's hand slid along the length of him while she sucked him off.

His body shook from her sweet torture. Her hot mouth was so inviting to his cock. He pulled her head down, pushing him farther into her throat. She swallowed, taking every inch he fed her.

He tightened his hands into fists while her head bobbed up and down. Her warm saliva coated him, allowing her hands to slide along his shaft. Zain tried to think of anything else but the sensation of her sucking.

His balls drew up quickly.

He wasn't going to last long. It was amazing how the second her lips wrapped around him, he was ready to blow.

"Fuck, Omara," he breathed.

The sounds of her sucking enhanced along with the pressure. He trembled and tugged her hair so he could withdraw. He blew out a shaky breath; he was not coming inside her mouth this time. He needed to be inside her.

"What did I do?" she asked. Her hand skated along his length.

He couldn't take his eyes off her. Her plump lips glistened, and her breasts rose and fell fast.

"Nothing. Come here." He helped her stand and pulled her down on his lap. He gripped the base of his cock and held it in place. "Hop on, little lady."

She rose and allowed him to nudge the blunt tip

of his cock at her entrance. Her juices coated him as she slowly impaled herself onto him.

Their simultaneous groans filled the air.

Her breasts were in his face. He wrapped an arm around her to hold her in place. She rotated her hips, taking him deeper.

"God, you're so deep," she moaned.

Her arms settled around his neck, bringing his face to rest between her breasts. He breathed in her scent before looking up at her. He watched the emotions play on her face while she rode him.

Her muscles clenched around him, and his eyes rolled. She slipped her hand between them and strummed her little bundle of nerves. Her mouth fell open, no sound escaping, and she continued to lift then fall onto his cock.

"Yes," she hissed.

Her breasts bounced around in his face. He captured one with his lips, sucking the nipple into his mouth. Her soft cries increased his desire for her. He moved his hands to her bottom, helping her bounce on him.

"Zain. I...oh."

Omara threw her head back, her walls constricting around him while she crested. He released her breast, his hold on her tightening, his climax engulfing him. He pulled her down, holding her in place, his release filling her.

She remained seated on him while they held each other, trying to catch their breaths. Omara leaned her forehead against his. He wrapped his arms around her, never wanting to let her go.

12

Omara stood in the doorway and watched Zain drive off down the road. She closed the door and inhaled sharply. She had thrown on a cami and shorts when he'd got dressed. As promised, he'd left before Jason woke up.

She padded into the kitchen with the plan to cook her and Jason breakfast. That growing boy of hers loved pancakes. She adored cooking and gathered all of her supplies she would need to make the pancakes from scratch.

A yawn overtook her. She would need coffee, too. Her single coffee machine sat waiting for her on the counter. She moved over to it and turned it on so she could make her a good cup of joe.

Her phone sat on the counter. She contemplated calling Jordan and having her come over for breakfast.

The doorbell rang.

"Who the hell could that be?" she murmured. The only person she could think of stopping by without calling would be Jordan.

But she had a key.

"If that girl didn't bring her key again," she muttered. Omara left the kitchen and went to the front door. She opened it without looking out of the peephole. "Did you forget your—"

She froze.

Derrick stood on the porch.

Her smile faded away. Why was he here? It was Sunday morning, and he said he couldn't pick Jason up this weekend.

"Well, hello there." He sick smile spread across his face while he took her in.

Omara's skin crawled at the expression. Eons ago, she might have thought it was sexy, but now all she felt was sickened by the look.

"What are you doing here?" She folded her arms. Now she wished she'd thrown on a thick sweatshirt or something to hide herself away.

"I'm here to see my son," he snapped, his smile disappearing.

She tightened her grip on the door. She glanced out into the neighborhood and didn't see anyone in their yard. It would be embarrassing if he caused a scene where everyone could see. Her neighbors were all kind and good people. She'd hate for them to see her dirty laundry.

"Derrick, Jason is still asleep. He was up in the middle of the night with a stomach bug and—"

"Go wake him up." He narrowed his gaze on her.

Omara's stomach lurched at the sound of his voice. She knew what was coming next. He'd yell and scream, and in the good ol' days, knock her around.

She was strong. He didn't hold any power over her. She repeated this to herself.

"Derrick, it's early—"

"I said wake him up," he snarled, pushing his way into her house.

She staggered back from the force of his shove.

"Wait a minute," she gasped. He didn't belong in her home. This was a place she had built without him, and she didn't want the calmness broken because of his rage. "Are you even listening to me? Your son was sick last night."

"I don't give a shit." He grabbed her by her arm and dragged her into the hallway.

She fought to break free of his hold, but his grip tightened on her. He worked construction and was naturally built. When they had first started dating, she'd been captivated by his strength until he'd turned it on her. He pushed her against the wall, his hot breath blowing into her face. She smelled alcohol on his breath.

"You trying to keep me from my son?"

"No, Derrick," she whimpered. She hated the sound of her weakness. His hand was digging into her flesh, and she knew a bruise would appear. "You're hurting me."

"Mom?" Jason's door opened, and he stood in the doorway. His big, brown-eyed gaze landed on her and Derrick. "Dad?"

"There's my boy." Derrick released her and shoved her aside.

She stumbled before righting herself.

He grinned at Jason as if nothing had just happened between her and him. "Your mom said you were sick last night."

"I was, but I'm all better now."

Derrick pulled Jason into a hug. Concern filled Jason's eyes as he looked at her. She offered him a small smile of reassurance. Tears blurred her vision, and she blinked them back, trying to not let them fall. He guided Jason toward the living room.

"I thought you couldn't come get me," Jason said.

Omara followed them into the living room. She moved to go into the kitchen to give Jason some time with his father and to give her time to get herself together. She didn't want to Jason to see her like this.

"I have some things I need to take care of, but I wanted to see you," Derrick said.

Omara rolled her eyes. According to Jason, most times he was with his dad, Derrick dropped him off over at his mother's house. Jason loved spending time with his grandmother, but Omara found it funny it was to be his time with his dad, but he wouldn't be around.

Not that she had any problem with Mrs. Allen. The woman was a saint, and Omara didn't know how a man like Derrick had come from the sweet older woman. Also spending time with his grand-mother gave Jason a chance to play with his cousins.

Omara opened her cabinet and pulled a mug out so she could make her coffee. Jason was currently updating his father on the happenings at his school and his science project that he was working on.

She breathed a sigh and placed her cup in the

machine and hit the button to start brewing. Her gaze landed on her phone sitting on the counter. She wondered if she should text Jordan to tell her Derrick was here.

If she did, Jordan would stop whatever she was doing and show up.

Jordan and Derrick in the same room would not be good.

She'd wait and see how much longer he would be here first.

Once her coffee was done, she doctored it up the way she normally took it. Some flavored cream and a couple of Splenda. She was a simple girl when it came to coffee.

Cooking breakfast would have to wait. There was no way she was going to give Derrick a reason to stay any longer than necessary. She took her mug and stood in the doorway.

Derrick turned his attention to her, a false smile on his lips. "You not going to make me a cup of coffee?"

"You're not staying long," she replied dryly.

The muscle in his jaw jumped while his gaze narrowed on her.

He didn't like her response, and frankly, she didn't care.

"Is aunt Jordan coming by today?" Jason asked innocently.

"She is. She should be here soon," Omara lied. She was normally against her son telling untruths, but this was one she didn't mind telling. She'd text her sister, and Jordan would stop by.

"Well, your mother is right. I can't stay long. I'm in the middle of moving," he said.

"Oh?" Omara couldn't help it. This was the second time he'd moved in the past year. The current girlfriend must have kicked him out.

"Yeah. I need something bigger. Maybe I'll find something where you can get your own room when you come to visit." He ran a hand over Jason's head playfully.

"That would be cool. Can I get a gaming system there, too?" Jason asked.

"Sure. I don't see why not." Derrick stood from the couch and motioned for her to follow him. He dropped a kiss on Jason's forehead. "You make sure you behave yourself for you mother."

"Dad, of course I will." Jason laughed.

Omara rolled her eyes again. This was his "I'm a good father" act. She wasn't sure who he was trying to convince of this, him or her, but Omara wasn't fooled by it. She pushed off the doorjamb and trailed Derrick to the front door. He opened it and stepped out onto the porch. She followed him, leaving the door slightly ajar.

"Yes?" she asked.

"I don't like your fucking attitude," he snarled.

"You can't just drop by here," she snapped. She gripped her mug tight, trying to prevent herself from throwing the contents in his face.

"Why? You got a man now?"

"That's none of your business."

He snatched her arm and pulled her to him. She grimaced at the pain that zipped through her muscle. It was the same one he'd manhandled in the hallway. He grinned. The son of a bitch always liked to see her in pain.

"Listen here, Omara. Don't have no other man coming around my son. You need dick, all you have to do is call me." His gaze raked her body again. "The extra weight you've put on looks damn good on you. I have no problem fucking you when you need it."

"What I need is for you to leave," she exclaimed. She stepped back, breaking his hold. Her skin was crawling, and she now felt dirty. She needed a shower—a scalding one.

"You sure you want me to leave? Your tits say otherwise." He eyed her breasts.

Her damn nipples were pushing against the cotton material. It wasn't from arousal but from cold. It was early and chilly outside.

"Goodbye, Derrick." She spun around and went back inside.

She felt completely violated by his look. His chuckle followed behind her. She slammed the door in his face and leaned against it. She tried to inhale and not sob at the same time.

Omara was impressed she hadn't thrown her coffee into his face, but then again, she'd hate to waste it on him.

"Are you okay, Mom?" Jason asked, walking toward her. His big brown eyes watched her curiously.

"Sure I am." She smiled, praying he didn't see the truth on her face. "Want some pancakes?"

"Yes!" He jumped up and down. He raced out of the room, disappearing into the hallway. "I'm going to go wash my face and brush my teeth now."

She laughed at his antics. Of course food would distract him. He was a growing boy and ate a ton. She went into the kitchen and picked up her phone.

She sent off a text to her sister, inviting her over for breakfast.

Jordan's reply was almost immediate: *On my way.*

Omara snickered. Jordan and Jason were just alike. Food always ruled them.

Now she felt a slightly better about her little white lie.

She dropped her cup and phone down on the counter. She winced at the pain in her arm. She looked at it and saw the beginning a very large bruise. She hurriedly showered to get the feel of Derrick off her. She found a long-sleeved shirt to put on.

She didn't want to have to explain to Jordan what happened. If she did, Jordan would hunt Derrick down.

"YOU HAVE to be the worse client ever." Omara chuckled.

"What I do?" Jordan snickered. She twirled the styling chair around and glanced at her. A wide smile was on her sister's lips.

It was the middle of the week, and Jordan had

stopped by to get her hair done. The shop was a little slow, but that was normal. It usually picked up in the evenings and was jam-packed on the weekends.

"Well, for one, you don't pay," Omara started. Not that she wanted her to pay. She did so much for Omara and Jason and never asked for anything in return.

"Okay?" Jordan rolled her eyes.

The move reminded Omara so much of her son. It was amazing how much Jason was like his auntie.

"What else?" Jordan asked.

"It's been a minute since you referred someone to me."

"One of the girls from work should be calling you," Jordan said, smiling. She sat up straight. "Speaking of girls from work. Shaunte's birthday is Friday, and we wanted to take her out for drinks. Why don't you come with us?"

"Is she one of the cops?" Omara asked. She spun the chair around so she could finish Jordan's hair. She had two more clients due to come in after her and didn't want to get behind. Omara was always conscious about her clients' time.

"She's one of the dispatchers. It would be fun and do you some good to get out the house."

"I don't know. Last time you invited me out with

your work people, you ditched me..." Omara ended her words in a singsong voice. Her sister had yet to come clean about why she'd left her and why she'd been acting so suspiciously lately.

"See, about that. I had to go handle something," Jordan murmured.

Omara parted her hair and snagged a piece and ran her flat iron through it. She moved on to the next section, quickly styling Jordan's hair.

"It didn't happen to be a dick, did it?" she whispered.

Jordan barked a laugh. Omara followed, tears streaming down her face. Everyone turned to look at them while they were in a fit of hysterics. She waved her hand, not willing to share the joke between them.

That was one thing about their sisterhood. There were some things they shared amongst themselves, and some things were private. Omara didn't know what to think if Jordan was keeping someone a secret.

They had shared plenty between themselves about their love and sex life. Jordan was two years older than her, and they'd pretty much run in the same crowds when they were younger. Both of them had their "ho period" in life.

"You know me so well, sis," Jordan said, wiping her face with the back of her hand.

"Of course I do," Omara murmured. She wasn't going to let on that she had a secret, too. If Jordan could keep her secret man hidden away, then Omara would keep hers to herself.

But Zain technically wasn't hers.

She pushed that thought aside and continued working on Jordan's hair. What would it be like to officially claim him? She had thought not having a man would be fine. She'd run her business, raise her son, and she'd be okay.

But having two nights of Zain staying over showed her how nice it was to have a man beside her at night. One who would hold her, make love to her to the point where she was exhausted afterwards.

Memories came of Zain watching her as she'd teased herself with him watching.

The way he'd lost control when she'd challenged him on whether or not he deserved her forbidden hole.

He had definitely proved his point. A shiver slid through her at the memory of him taking her there. She bit back a silly grin she was sure would appear.

Omara had fallen into a deep sleep once she'd climaxed. It had been so hard, it had zapped all of her energy. She didn't even remember him tucking them into bed. She hadn't woken up until Jason had knocked on her door.

What they had was fine. She'd leave it be.

She had to stay focused on her business and her son.

She sat her flat iron down on her counter and winced. Her damn arm was still sore. There was a huge dark bruise where Derrick had grabbed her.

"What's wrong with your arm?" Jordan asked quietly.

Omara glanced at her sister and shrugged. There wasn't much her sister missed.

"It's nothing," she said, turning away. She reached for her oils and sprayed a little in her hands before turning back to Jordan. She ran her fingers through her hair then she combed out the curls.

"Nothing, as in, a six-foot dipshit?" Jordan met her gaze in the mirror.

"Leave it alone, Jordan," Omara whispered. She didn't want anyone else in the shop to know. She'd kept that part of her life hidden from the other stylists. She didn't want to see pity in their eyes. She hated for anyone to think she was weak or less of a woman because her ex was hitting on her. She knew it wasn't her fault, but that's what some people thought.

She'd heard it all in the past.

"Jason told me he stopped by on Sunday before I came over." Jordan wasn't going to let it go. It wasn't in her nature. She was too damn stubborn—and protective. "Why didn't you call me the second the asshole walked into your house?"

"My phone was in the kitchen," she replied. She lowered the comb, her vision blurred. She blinked back the tears. She turned around and rested her hands on her station. She didn't want to cry. A sob lodged its way into her throat. She dropped the comb on the counter and spun away. She headed into her office.

Jordan's curse sounded behind her.

Omara arrived at her office and flew into it. She tried to close the door, but Jordan was right there with her.

"I'm sorry, sis." Jordan shut the door and wrapped her arms around Omara.

The floodgates broke.

She tried to be strong, but it was so damn hard. Derrick had lodged his claws in her so deep that had it not been for Jordan, she would never have gotten away. He had stripped everything from her. Her confidence, her spirit, her bright outlook on life. She had become a shell of herself around him. The only thing she had to live for was her son.

Jason was her focus.

She didn't care what Derrick did to her as long as he left their baby alone.

"I hate him," she sobbed.

"I know. I do, too." Jordan ran a hand along her back, soothing her.

Omara held on to Jordan who had been her rock. She had always been able to count on her sister. Jordan didn't like hiding what Derrick had done to her from their parents. It would have broken her parents' hearts if they had known what Omara had gone through.

She had felt like a failure. How had she not seen the warning signs when they'd first got together? She had thought she would spend her life with that man.

Omara's sobs finally quieted. She blew out a deep breath and pushed away from Jordan. She moved over to her desk and snagged her box of tissues, taking a few out and wiping her face.

"What happened on Sunday?"

"Nothing. Jason was there, so he put on his act." Omara paused and blew her nose. She tossed the tissues in the trash and reached for more. "He grabbed my arm. That is all."

"He has no right to put his hands on you in any way," Jordan growled. She paced the room. "I should take the guys and remind him—"

"No!" Omara gasped. She didn't want anyone to know of her past with Derrick.

Especially Zain.

She loved the way he looked at her. She wouldn't be able to stand it if the pity was in his eyes, too.

"No?" Jordan came to stand in front of her. "I told him if he ever put his hands on you again, I'd break his fucking arm."

Omara remembered, and Jordan would do it, too. Omara had never seen her sister in action before until that day. Jordan was definitely a force to be reckoned with. It was the day Jordan had come to her rescue and helped her move away from Derrick. They'd packed up her small sedan with their meager belongings and left.

It was the day she'd started over in life.

"Just leave it be. Please," Omara begged.

Jordan stared at her for a moment before jerking her head in a nod.

"That was his last time. He does it again, and I

promise you, he will regret it, and I won't be asking or telling you anything."

Omara swallowed hard at her sister's threat. This was a side of Jordan she had never seen before. That was why she was a badass cop. She didn't take shit from anyone.

"I love you, big sis," Omara breathed.

Jordan's features softened, a small smile playing on her lips.

"I love you, too." She reached out and hugged Omara again. "And you're coming out with us this Friday."

13

*Z*ain stepped out of the showers in the locker room. He and the team had just returned from a call. This one had been a midday call for a drug bust. The DEA needed the assistance of Columbia's finest. Occasionally, they were called in to help the Feds out when it came to infiltrating drug houses and disband the illegal operations. It had been an easy, clear-cut mission.

Of course, it was the Demon Lords that were involved.

This house had been a small operation.

He and his SWAT team had dealt with the notorious gang for years. There was a war out there, and the Demon Lords were at the center of it. Ever since their leaders keep changing, their organization had been centered in chaos. Word around town was that there was a new boss ascending the throne. Recently, the gang unit had been keeping their ears to the streets and calling SWAT in more frequently.

Zain arrived at his locker and opened it. He glanced at the sweats he had folded and chuckled, remembering Omara's claim about men and their sweatpants.

His phone sat on top of them. It had been burning a hole in his pants all week. He was trying to get up the nerve to ask Omara out.

What the hell?

He snagged his phone and sent off a text to her.

Thinking about you.

He grimaced. Was that too much? It had been a while since he had asked a woman out on a date.

Hopefully all good thoughts.

He grinned, sensing her sassiness through the phone.

"Why the hell are you grinning at like that?" Iker came by and stood in front of his locker. He eyed Zain warily while he opened his door and sorted through his clothes.

"None of your business." Zain glanced down at his phone, trying to figure out what to say next.

Hope you are having a good day.

There. Something simple.

"Who are you texting?" His friend slid his jeans on and buttoned them up. He raised an eyebrow at Zain, then as if coming to a conclusion, his gaze narrowed on Zain. He moved closer to him and lowered his voice. "Seriously? You're still involved with *her*?"

Zain wasn't even going to act like he didn't know who *her* was.

"Yeah." He shrugged. He brushed a hand through his wet hair, pushing it away from his face.

"Does *she* know?" He didn't need to ask who the *she* was.

Iker was looking at him as if he had lost all of his marbles.

"Nope, and you're not going to say anything either. Just give us time."

"So there's an us now?" Iker moved and took his shirt out of his locker and threw it on.

"Maybe. I'm working on it."

"Well, I'll be damned." Iker grinned. He slapped Zain on the back. His smile was genuine.

Iker had been there when he had gone through his divorce from Freya. He had been Zain's biggest support aside from his family. Only his family didn't know the dark path Zain had traveled afterwards.

That's why they were best friends. They had stood beside each other at their worst and still loved each other as brothers.

"Happy about what?" Myles asked, stopping at the end of their row.

"That his STD test came back clean," Iker replied, not even missing a beat.

Zain scoffed at his friend. It had always been a running joke between the two of them with all the women they had each slept with. Even the other team members were in on the joke.

"Congratulations." Myles snorted before moving on.

Laughter sounded around the locker room.

Zain chuckled and snagged his underwear and slid them on before his sweats. He wasn't sure what Omara was talking about. Men walked around with just sweats on all the time. What was wrong with that?

Do you have plans Friday night? I want to take you out.

There, he'd put everything on the table. He wanted to move to the next level with Omara. She wasn't a woman to hide away. He wanted her seen on his arm.

He sat his phone back down and finished getting

dressed. His phone buzzed, and he snatched it back up.

As in a date?

Yes, he replied. Then waited. He watched the bubbles on his screen signaling she was typing.

This Friday I can't. I'm going out with my sister and her friends.

He nodded. He'd heard something around the precinct about one of the girl's birthday celebration.

Saturday night?

He slid his boots on and waited for her response. He was going to head home and get some much-needed sleep. He'd been on the clock now for a full twenty-four hours between his shift and getting called out for SWAT. He was dead-ass tired. He couldn't wait to jump in his bed. Tossing his dirty clothes in his bag, he zipped it shut and hefted it up on his shoulder.

"I'm out. I'll see y'all later," Zain announced. He slapped Iker on the shoulder in passing.

"Later," Myles and Ash called out from their row.

Zain exited the locker room and ambled through the station, leaving out the back door. He got into his truck and hit the start button to turn it on. His phone sounded with a text. His heart sank at Omara's reply.

Saturday isn't good either. There's a hair show going on, and I'm a judge this year. It starts at seven, and I'm not sure what time I'll be home.

I'll call you, and we'll figure something out.

He pulled out of the parking spot and began the drive home. He was surprised she hadn't questioned him on the request of a date. They'd both had said they didn't want commitment.

He gripped the steering wheel tight, hoping she had changed her mind, too. He grinned, still in disbelief that he was willing to settle with one woman.

But being with Omara wasn't settling.

She was a prize he was lucky to have.

There weren't many women like her. She was the type to hold on to. He wanted to get to know her and her son. Zain realized this could be his second chance at happiness.

He pulled into his driveway and gave a wave to his neighbors, Chuck and Carol. They were an older retired couple who love putzing around in their yard. Their carefully manicured lawn put everyone else's on the street to shame. Carol had even made her way to his, buying and planting flowers in his yard. She never let him pay her for any of it, stating it gave her something to do.

Zain grabbed his duffle bag and got out of the vehicle, walking to his front door.

"Evening," Zain called out.

"How are you, Zain?" Carol smiled.

It wasn't her usual bright one, and Zain felt that something was wrong. Chuck stood back at the hole he had just finished digging and turned back to him. He tossed off his gloves and headed toward Zain.

"Can we have a moment of your time?" Chuck asked.

"Sure." Zain walked over to meet them halfway.

He held out his hand and took Chuck's in a firm shake. Carol gave him a hug before stepping back to her husband's side. Something was worrying them. They were good people, and Zain wouldn't mind helping with something if he could.

"What's going on?"

"Well, it's our granddaughter, Ivy. She just moved in with us the other day. She's been having some hard times, and we were wondering if you could talk with her."

Zain was taken aback. He didn't think he'd be the best choice to talk with a young girl—

"She was in the police academy and got in trouble," Carol said, obviously seeing Zain's expression. "She's waiting to hear if she'll be kicked out."

"Okay," Zain said cautiously. He still wasn't sure if he was the right person.

"If not you, maybe you have a lady cop friend who could talk with her?" Carol said.

"She's been through so much. Her boyfriend and her broke up, and her parents sort of disowned her." Chuck's shoulders slumped. He shook his head and rummaged a hand through his balding hair. "I never thought I'd see the day my son would do something like this. We're going to have a talk with him and that wife of his. This is no way to deal with—"

"Chuck, honey. Zain doesn't want to hear about our family problems, dear." Carol's calming voice instantly defused the riled-up man. He faced his wife, his features softening as he took her in. He reached for her hand and brought it to his lips.

"You're right, my dear." He turned back to Zain and sighed. "Would you be able to help? Being a cop is something she's wanted to be since she was seven years old. I'd hate for her to lose her dream because of something stupid."

"Yeah, I know the perfect person for her to speak with," Zain said. He'd talk with Jordan and see if she be up to it. If not her, he could think of a few other female cops who would probably want to help. There weren't that many women on the force, and they always stuck behind each other. He was sure he could get one of them to talk with her. "Let me reach out to a few of the girls at the precinct and I'll get back with you."

"Thank you so much, Zain." Carol smiled. This time it was a genuine one, reaching her eyes. "Now you go get some sleep. You look like you're about to fall on your face."

"Yes, ma'am." He grinned. He took Chuck's hand again in a firm shake.

"Thanks, Zain," Chuck said.

Zain went inside his home. He should eat, but his bed was calling his name. He stopped in the laundry room and tossed his bag on the floor in front of the washer, promising he'd go through the bag later.

He went upstairs to his bedroom and shucked off his clothes and shoes. He climbed into bed naked and reached for his phone. Should he call Omara now? He glanced at the time, unsure of what she'd be doing now. Was she at the shop still? Was she at home with her son, winding down?

He had so many questions, realizing he didn't know her routine or anything she did throughout the week. Their relationship so far had been one of the physical. He wanted to get to know her. The real Omara.

He scrolled through his phone and saw a missed call from his brother earlier that day. Zain had been out on the raid and wouldn't have been able to answer it if he had heard the call. He hit Luca's name and settled back on his pillows.

"Yo," Luca answered on the first ring.

"What's up, little brother?" Zain grinned.

He and Luca were close. He hadn't seen him in a minute. Between his job and Luca teaching and coaching, this time of the year it was hard for them to get together.

"Football practice has been underway, and you haven't stopped by once."

"Been busy as shit," Zain admitted. He swiped his hand along his beard and shook his head. "Don't tell me you need your big brother to come whip your team into shape."

"Never that. But the kids love having you come help out. I figured I'd call and make sure my brother was still alive for one."

One thing that worried his family about him being on SWAT was the unknown. He never lied about the dangers of his job with them. They always worried about him. It didn't help when the media broadcast stories of their adventures that had gone wrong.

When Ash had got shot, and Brodie, Zain's phone had blown up from his family trying to make sure it hadn't been him. His mother worried consistently about him. He grimaced, realizing he hadn't checked in with his parents in a while.

"Mom told you to call me, didn't she?"

"Of course she did. That woman stays glued to the news when she doesn't hear from you." Luca's tone shifted.

"I'm sorry, man. I'll give her a call when I wake up. I just got home—"

"Go ahead get some sleep. You sound like shit." Luca chuckled.

Zain rubbed a hand along his face. He could feel his body shutting down. It had been the longest twenty-four hours ever.

"I'll talk with you later," Zain said.

They disconnected their call. Without a doubt, he'd head over to his parents' house so they could see him in the flesh.

He set an alarm on his phone then tossed it on the nightstand and rearranged his pillows to get comfortable. A yawn overtook him.

He closed his eyes, and the image of Omara came to mind. He slowly drifted off to sleep, hoping to see her in his dreams.

―――

"MOM, I promise me and Jason will come to visit." Omara laughed. She flew around the kitchen finishing their dinner. She'd had a hankering for some fried fish so she'd stopped at the market and picked up some catfish filets. Jason loved her fish and fries. Their fries were currently in the air fryer while she finished cooking the last pieces of fish.

"I need to see my grandbaby, Omara." Her mother's voice was stern with a slight hint of humor.

Irene Knight was the perfect grandmother. From the moment Omara had announced she was pregnant, Irene, and Cecil, Omara and Jordan's father, had gone crazy. Everything was about the baby. Omara and Jordan were almost forgotten.

"What about me? What am I, chopped liver?" Omara gasped.

"How are you, my dear?" her mother asked.

"I'm good. Business is doing phenomenal—"

"That's nice, dear. Now when will you bring

Jason to Atlanta? Does he have a long weekend coming up? Maybe we'll just come get him."

Omara barked a laugh at her mother. She leaned against the counter and shook her head.

"I'd have to check the school calendar. I think he does have a four-day weekend coming up, but I'd have to make sure it's not on Derrick's weekend." Omara's smile faded.

"Hmmm...has he been skipping his weekends again?" Irene asked, not biting her tongue. She hadn't really liked Derrick and if she knew what he'd put Omara through, Omara didn't think her mother and father would be able to handle it.

They would blame themselves, when in reality no one was to blame for his actions except Derrick. It had taken Omara a long time to realize that. She'd assumed his anger and rage was because she was lacking.

"Yeah, he did. Then showed up here wanting to talk with Jason." She blew out a deep breath. She reached over and eyed the fish in the cast-iron skillet. Another minute or two then she'd flip it over.

"Really? What was his excuse?"

"He had business to attend to and something about moving," she said, settling back against the counter.

"And you believed him?" Irene's sarcasm could be heard clear through the phone. Her mother didn't hold back when it came to Derrick. She respected Omara's wishes to not talk against him in front of Jason. But the moment Jason was out of earshot, her mother didn't hold any punches.

"Of course not, but I didn't care. I got to keep my son with me."

"Well, check my grandson's schedule and see when he can fit in his gram and pops."

"Yes, Mom." Omara gave a dramatic sigh.

"Is dinner done yet, Mom?" Jason walked into the kitchen.

She eyed the timer on the air fryer.

"In a few minutes. Go wash your hands, young man," Omara said.

"Is that my grandbaby? Let me talk to him," Irene demanded.

"Here, Jason. Gram's on the phone." Omara handed her cell phone to him.

He took it and walked out of the kitchen with it. Knowing them two, they'd be on the phone for a while. Omara felt guilty that she hadn't been home to visit. She hated the distance between her parents and her. If she could have, she would have gone back to Atlanta, but thanks to the courts, she couldn't live out of state with her son.

Even though she'd won primary custody and child support, she still felt like she had lost.

Fussing over the court ruling wasn't going to fix anything. She moved back to the stove and gently flipped the fish over. The air fryer signaled it was done. She gathered their plates and condiments they would need. Dinnertime with her son was important to her. This gave them a chance to eat as a family and talk about their day.

She finished off dinner and made their plates. She began setting things on the small table and called out for Jason. "Dinner is ready! Come eat."

Jason came running into the dining area with her phone in his hand. He set the phone down on the table and ran into the kitchen.

"What are you doing?" She strode in the kitchen behind him, getting cups from the cabinet.

"Getting the barbecue sauce for my fish," he said. He grinned at her rolling her eyes.

She never understood her child. He ate barbecue sauce on all of his meats. No matter what it was. He rushed back in the dining room and took his seat. She snagged juice from the fridge and followed him, taking her seat next to his. She poured them both some into their cups.

After she made Jason say the blessing, they dug into their food.

"Mom, when I was talking to Granny, somebody was calling you," Jason said.

"Oh?" She raised her eyebrows. She took a bite out of her fish, the taste exploding on her tongue. It was everything she'd been imaging and was curing her craving.

"Yeah, it was a weird name. Big D, Always Answer?"

Omara choked on her fish that had been sliding down her throat. She wheezed, trying to get air in. She reached out for her drink and took a long swig, clearing her throat from the food that had lodged itself there.

Oh God. Why had she given him a crazy name in her phone? She fell into a fit of laughter with her son eyeing her as if she'd lost her mind.

"That's just a friend of mine," she said, clearing her throat.

"I told Gram who was calling, and she said I should let that call go to voicemail."

Omara froze.

He'd told her mother? Omara closed her eyes

and couldn't even look Jason in the face or she'd laugh harder.

Omara could expect another call from her mother tonight.

No doubt Irene was going to want to know who this "Big D, Always Answer" was.

She was just thankful Jason hadn't asked her what Big D stood for.

14

"Happy birthday!" Another one of Jordan's coworkers arrived to celebrate Shaunte's birthday.

Omara was trying to learn everyone's names, but people were coming and going.

Shaunte stood and hugged the newcomer. She was all grins and alcohol. Everyone was buying her a shot, and Omara had lost track of what number she was on. Her boyfriend stood by quietly, smiling at her antics. The woman was three sheets to the wind.

"That's Michelle from accounting," Jordan said. She leaned over and updated Omara on who was who, but Omara was horrible at names. There were too many to remember.

"Well, look who graced us with her presence," Michelle teased, waving to Jordan. She ran around the table and gave Jordan a hug. "SWAT didn't have nothing going on tonight?"

"No, and please don't jinx me. I doubt Mac would want me showing up with a few drinks in my system." Jordan laughed and shook her head. She turned and waved for Omara to join them. "Michelle, this is my sister, Omara."

Omara stood next to her sister. She smiled and offered her hand, but Michelle waved her away and pulled her in for a tight hug.

"We aren't formal around here. It's good to finally meet you! Jordan talks about you all the time."

"She does?" She eyed her sister. There was no telling what Jordan had shared.

Jordan tried to look innocent, but Omara wasn't fooled.

"All good. I promise!" Michelle giggled. She faced the table filled with women from the department. "Who's turn is it to buy a round?"

"Yours!" everyone exclaimed.

Laughter went around. Omara chuckled at Michelle's face.

"Fine." Michelle dramatically sighed. "Even though I just got here."

"You shouldn't have been late," someone shouted.

Omara was thoroughly enjoying herself. They were at a bar she had never been to. It was a trendy spot with loud thumping music and a small dance floor with tables spread throughout the building. There were two bar areas where people could go up and order their drinks and sit and mingle.

Omara sat her empty glass down on the table beside theirs that was vacated. She stood to the side while Jordan spoke to one of the women who had been sitting at the table. She didn't mind letting her sister chat and have fun with the girls from the precinct. She was just happy to be out of the house. This was the most she'd gone out in months. Jason was spending the night over at Ricky's house. Ricky's mother, Samantha, didn't have a problem having Jason over. Ricky was the eldest child, his little sister was six months old, and having Jason over preoccupied him.

"Want to go get a drink from the bar?" Jordan asked.

"Sure." Omara followed behind her sister,

threading through the crowd. Tonight she had put on a dress she had purchased last year and never worn it because she hadn't anywhere to wear it. The moment she'd seen it, she had fallen in love with it.

The halter-top dress was a gold shimmery material that stopped mid-thigh. She'd paired it with black heels and a matching gold small purse. She hefted the strap of her purse up high on her shoulder.

She noted plenty of appreciative glances being thrown her way. None of the looks were from a certain person she wanted to see. Too bad he couldn't see her tonight.

She had been shocked when Zain had texted her, asking to take her out. That had been out of the ordinary. He had started them off stating what was between them was fucking only, since he wasn't looking for a relationship.

Which she'd been okay with.

But lately, she wanted more.

She hated that she couldn't accept his offer this weekend. There was no way she could cancel on her without Jordan being suspicious. The hair show, she couldn't back out of it. She was a judge, and canceling last minute wouldn't look good for her or her shop.

They arrived at the bar and stood together waiting to snag the barhop's attention.

"Having fun?" Jordan asked.

"I am," she admitted.

"Good. We need to get you out the house more often." Jordan smiled. Her gaze went over Omara's shoulder. "Oh, that guy who was eyeing you when we first got here is making his way over here."

Omara glanced in the direction Jordan was staring. When they had first arrived, a tall, handsome man had been staring at her. His dark-blond hair was brushed back away from his face. His tanned skinned was decorated by a few tattoos peeking out from underneath his sleeves that were pushed up. His button-up shirt fit his form well, highlighting a toned physique. He'd smiled at her, and Omara had turned away, shy. It had been a long time since she'd been hit on in a bar.

"Jordan," Omara squeaked. Her heart raced while panic set in "What do I do?"

"Just talk with him. Let him buy you a drink. Enjoy yourself." Jordan nudged her with her elbow. She winked at Omara. "You deserve it. Hell, play your cards right, go home with him."

"What?" Omara's voice went even higher.

"I'm just playing. You think I'd let you leave here with a stranger?" Jordan fell into a fit of laughter.

Omara shoved her sister, sensing a warm figure standing next to her.

She looked over and found Mr. Tall and Handsome standing beside her. She caught a whiff of his cologne that was pleasant and inviting.

"Hello," he said, offering her a warm smile.

"Hi." Omara returned his smile. She rotated his way, allowing her playful side to come out. Or maybe her drink was kicking in, giving her this newfound confidence. "You were staring at me earlier."

He barked a laugh and gave a nod.

"I was. I couldn't help it. I hope I didn't come off as a creep." He held out his hand. A dimple appeared in his cheek as his smile widened. "My name is Maverick."

"Omara." She slid her smaller hand into his. "It's nice to meet you."

"Well, since you caught me watching you, allow me to buy you a drink."

Omara glanced at Jordan, and a guy had sidled up to her. She focused her attention back to Maverick, her sister's words coming to mind.

Just talk with him. Let him buy you a drink. Enjoy yourself.

"That would be nice," she said.

He stood to his full height and waved down the bartender who stopped in front of them. They placed their order then turned to each other once the bartender disappeared.

"Are you here alone?" Maverick asked.

"Oh, no. I'm here with my sister and some women from her job." She motioned to Jordan who spun around.

"Hi, I'm Jordan," her sister yelled, giving a small wave.

"Maverick," he said.

"What brings you out?" Omara leaned against the bar.

"My brother, Gunnar, is in town to visit. We figured we hit the town for a little fun while he was here." He nodded to the guy Jordan was speaking with.

Omara eyed the guy and saw the resemblance between the two of them.

"That's nice."

The bartender brought their drinks. Maverick slipped him a bill and then lifted his glass to her.

"New friends." Maverick clinked his glass to hers.

She smiled and took a sip of her drink.

"New friends, huh?" She grinned.

"What'd you'd say?" He bent down. The music changed and appeared to get even louder. He rested his hand on the small of her back while she stood on her tiptoes.

"I said new friends?" She raised her eyebrows at him.

"A guy could always wish," he said into her ear.

She stepped back slightly but didn't have much room. The bar was pretty packed, making them have to stand close together. Jordan's back was touching hers.

"There's a ton of people here tonight. I'd love to have your number. I'd love to take you out for dinner," he said.

"Oh my god!" Jordan exclaimed.

Her sister nudged Omara hard, sending her flying into Maverick's arms. He was rock-hard. His casual business clothes were definitely deceiving. This man must do some type of hard labor for work.

"Oops! I'm sorry." Omara laughed.

Maverick grinned and helped her stand up

straight. She tilted her head back. He was as tall as Zain. As much as Maverick seemed to be a nice guy, she just couldn't lead him on. If Zain hadn't been on her mind so much, maybe she could see herself at least going out once with Maverick.

"Omara." Jordan grabbed her forearm and spun her around, laughing.

"What is it?" Omara asked.

"Guess who is across the bar with some skank who barely looks legal."

Omara followed her sister's finger and froze.

A small woman with dark hair and heavy mascara sat at the bar with a tall muscular man with a mop of dark curly hair speaking into her ear.

Zain.

He glanced up at that moment and met her gaze. He paused, not even blinking as they stared at each other. He flicked his gaze to Jordan who was making faces at him. Her sister didn't pick up on the tension that flew across the bar.

"Oh, wait until I get to work tomorrow." Jordan wiped her face with the back of her hands.

"Do you know that guy?" Maverick leaned down and asked in Omara's ear.

Zain glanced back at her, then his gaze landed

on Maverick and darkened. The small muscle in his jaw tightened.

Omara blew out a deep breath.

Well, she guessed she'd got her real answer about what Zain wanted.

"Yeah," she admitted. She faced Maverick and tried to drum up a smile. "He works with my sister. They both are cops."

"Really?" His eyebrows rose as he eyed Jordan before turning back to her. "Are you a cop, too?"

"What? God, no." She burst out laughing. She reached up and tucked her hair behind her ear. "I'm a hair stylist. I own my own salon. What about you?"

"My brother and I own a few car dealerships here in the state of South Carolina, Georgia, and Florida." He leveled her with his gaze.

"Impressive," she teased.

He laughed at her, running a hand through his hair.

"It pays the bills." He shrugged.

Omara glanced back over and saw Zain talking to the female. His face was cold and unreadable. They almost appeared to be arguing. The woman finally stood and leaned into Zain. He wrapped his arm around her and guided her away from the bar.

He looked back in Omara's direction and held her gaze for a moment more.

She didn't know what to think.

Again, she had to remind herself for the millionth time, they weren't exclusive. He could date and do what he wanted with whoever he wanted.

That left a bad taste in her mouth.

Was this jealousy?

She gave herself a mental shake.

"I can't believe him. He just goes for anything now." Jordan snorted. "He's such a man whore. I guess he'll put his dick in anyone no matter the age."

Omara's eyes widened. She'd heard some of the stories her sister had talked about the guys. She guessed she was part of his list of anyone.

She turned back to Maverick with a small smile.

"I'm sorry. What were we talking about before?" she asked.

"I would love to take you out for dinner." Maverick smiled at her. He leaned against the bar, his eyes locked on her. "How about it?"

Omara scanned the bar around them and didn't see any sign of Zain anymore. Maybe this was for the best. What were the odds they would land at the same bar? She faced Maverick and took in his warm, friendly smile. Maybe Zain wasn't the guy for her.

"I'd like that," she replied.

ZAIN CURSED, carrying Ivy out of the bar. Chuck and Carol had called him with the information that she was currently getting wasted at some bar in town and if he could go get her.

He loved his neighbors and had promised he'd helped them.

So off he'd gone to track down their granddaughter. He'd known Ivy as a kid and a teen when she'd come to visit her grandparents. She'd argued with him the moment she'd seen him standing next to her.

"I'm fine." Ivy groaned. She stumbled for the hundredth time.

Zain cursed and bent down and lifted her into his arms. He stalked across the parking lot toward his truck.

"I'm not a kid anymore."

"Well, you're certainly acting like it," he snapped. Zain arrived at his truck and opened the passenger door. He sat her down in the seat and placed her safety belt on. "I shouldn't have to track you down and take you home."

"No one told you to come and get me." She sat

up straight and focused her glazed-over eyes on him. Her hair was a mess, her makeup smeared underneath her eyes, making her resemble a raccoon. She smelled of booze and cigarettes.

"Your grandparents did. They care about you and want to help you." He slammed the door in her face and stalked around to the driver's side.

He paused at the door and glanced back at the bar.

Zain blew out a shaky breath. Omara had been in there. Jordan, too. He couldn't care less what Jordan was thinking when she'd sighted him with Ivy.

It was Omara he was worried about.

Her unreadable stare had unnerved him.

She looked so damn beautiful in the gold dress. He wished he could have seen the entire thing. There had been too many people around her for him to see it when he'd left.

But then again, the fuckwad standing next to her, touching her and whispering in her ear, was the real reason Zain had almost forgotten his promise to Chuck and Carol. He had wanted to walk around that bar and plant his fist in that fucker's face and drag Omara away. He had been standing entirely too close to Omara. He bet the dress was sexy and short, showcasing her beautiful legs.

Legs that wrapped around his waist perfectly.

Legs that spread open for him, revealing her delicious core.

He bit back a growl thinking of the piece of shit standing next to her trying to get her attention. What had the fucker whispered in her ear? There was one other thing Zain had noticed.

She hadn't moved away from him.

Zain cursed and pulled open the door and got in the truck.

Ivy's head was resting on the headrest, her eyes were closed, and her mouth was wide open.

He started the engine and guided the truck out of the parking lot and onto the road. He didn't live that far away from here. He'd drop Ivy off and go back to the bar. He'd find Omara and take her away from there. He didn't care that Jordan was there.

It was time to stop hiding.

He tightened his grip on the steering wheel and tried to keep his truck close to the speed limit. They drove in silence with Zain glancing over at Ivy occasionally to make sure she was still breathing.

"Do you know anyone who got kicked out of the

academy?" Ivy asked quietly. She leaned her head against the glass and sighed.

"Um, yeah. People get kicked out all the time," he said.

She appeared dejected and lost. He felt sorry for the kid. Hopefully, Chuck and Carol would be able to help her.

"And then what?" she asked. A hiccup escaped her, then a belch.

"You better not throw up in my truck," he warned. He rolled her window down some to allow some air to come in. "You feel queasy, say the word, and I'll pull over."

She gave a nod and closed her eyes.

"Listen, I heard you were suspended. If you want to be a cop then I would suggest you go and beg whoever you need to in order to stay. Apologize for whatever. Maybe they will give you a second chance." He glanced back over at her and found her sleep.

He turned down his street and pulled into his driveway. He killed the engine and looked at Ivy who was slouched. The light on his neighbors' porch turned on with two figures stepping out onto it.

Zain sighed and exited his truck. He walked over to the passenger side and opened the door. He gently picked Ivy up and carried her across the lawn to Chuck.

"Is she all right?" the older gentleman asked.

"Yeah. She fell asleep on the ride here," he said.

Chuck led him to the house.

"She didn't put up much of a fight, did she?" Chuck asked. It was apparent the man was worried about his grandchild. The hair he did have left on his head was in disarray. He held the door open for Zain.

Carol stood in the living room with a blanket in her arms.

"Put her here, Zain." Carol motioned to the couch.

He walked over and gently lowered the slumbering girl. Carol immediately threw the cover over her. Tears streamed down her face. She gazed up at Zain, a small smile playing on her lips.

"Thank you so much. You just don't know how much this means to us."

"It's not a problem, Carol. I'll call you on Monday and let you know who I could get to come and talk with her." He backed away and spun on his heel in an attempt to make a quick exit.

Chuck was behind him, his eyes reddened and

wet. "I know you have better things to do with your time—"

"Don't. Anything I can do for you two, I will," Zain cut him off. This family was going through so much, and they needed him. The couple reminded him of his parents. Zain held his hand out to Chuck. He brought the older man in for a hug. "Whenever you need something, just call me."

"Thank you, Zain. You're a good man." Chuck stepped back and scrubbed a hand across his face. His gaze landed on Ivy and softened. "I guess she'll need to sleep this off. I remember what it was like to be this age."

"She'll have one hell of a hangover in the morning." Zain slapped Chuck on the back and headed to the front door. "Have a good night."

"Night," they echoed behind him.

He shut the door and stood on their porch, staring out at the neighborhood.

He breathed in the night air, needing to clear his head. He jogged down the stairs and strolled to his house.

Should he go back to bar and drag Omara out? Or should he wait for her at her place?

He took his keys from his pocket as he arrived at his front door.

His cell phone sounded.

"You have got to be fucking kidding me." He pulled the damn thing out of his pocket, and sure enough, it was work. He swiped his finger across the screen and brought the phone to his ear. "Roman."

"We're being called in. Let's roll," Mac's voice came in on the line.

Zain closed his eyes and sighed.

"On my way."

15

"**G**irl, I don't know if it was fair for you to be a judge tonight. With the way you're looking, you were putting everyone to shame," Apollo said. He navigated his luxury truck through the streets. He was one of the other judges and owner of Divine Designs on the other side of town. He and Omara had opened their shops around the same time.

He had offered to pick her up for the show. The Hair Show was an annual event that was put on in the city to allow up-and-coming stylists a way to showcase their talents. Omara had been thrilled to be invited to judge.

It had been so hard to pick amongst all of the contestants and their models. Everyone had worked so hard to try to win the grand prize of the claim of "Hottest Stylist in Columbia" and a five thousand dollar check.

It had been so much fun. Stylists and people in the hair industry came from all over to attend it. The atmosphere had been electric.

"Well, you know I can't come to judge and not be fly myself," Omara teased. She was finally getting to dip into the back of her closet where she had stashed outfits she'd only hoped to wear one day. Tonight's dress was a little black number that hugged her curves and stopped mid-thigh. Red knee-high boots completed her outfit. She had gotten so many compliments throughout the night. Her hair and makeup had been done by her, of course.

Not only was she working as a judge, but it was a night to network and talk about her shop. She'd passed out business cards and spoke with so many potential clients to try to drum up business for her and her stylists.

Omara and Apollo had become friends years ago. They had been contestants in the same show. She'd taken second place while he'd taken third. After that, they had stayed in contact with each other.

"You aren't looking so bad yourself," she said.

Omara would kill for his high cheekbones and flawless skin.

"You think so?" He batted his eyelashes at her and rested a hand on his oversized pearls on his neck. He kept his hair faded short with waves and was a mix of different styles. Apollo was unique. There was no one like him. His clothing was one of a kind, designed by him. She'd been telling him for years to start selling what he made, but he refused.

Didn't want anyone copying him.

"I wouldn't say it if I didn't mean it." She laughed.

Apollo was a drama queen and always fishing for compliments.

Omara was glad she'd had fun at the show. It had helped keep her mind off a certain someone. She didn't even want to think where he'd gone after last night when he'd left with that young girl. She was almost sickened to think that he would be messing around with someone like that. Zain was thirty-five years old, and that girl was way too young for him.

But that was none of her business.

"So what else you getting into this weekend?" Apollo asked.

"Boy, my weekend is over. I'm going to go home, take a hot shower, and binge watch a show.

Tomorrow will be my time with my son." Tonight she'd hired a babysitter to stay with Jason. One of the neighborhood teens was always looking for extra money. Glancing at her watch, she saw it was late. Jason should be in bed asleep. On the weekends she allowed him to stay up an hour later.

"Ugh, you and being Mom of the Year. How dare you be such a good mother?" he scoffed, rolling his eyes. He grinned. "How is little Jason?"

"Getting big. That boy is keeping me busy. He's been begging me to let him sign up for football."

"Girl, let him. I played peewee football, and it was so fun. I'm still friends with several of the guys, and some of them went on to play in college and professional ball."

Her gazed whipped to him. Apollo playing football? With his size, she could see it. He was tall and stocky.

"But he's my baby." She sighed. Omara was deathly afraid of Jason getting hurt. She always heard horror stories of kids with brain injuries.

"You never know. Football can pay for college. You're a single mom, you'll need that help. Plus, it will give him discipline and the chance to be around other kids his age."

Omara sat back and watched the scenery fly by.

The permission slip for Jason sat on the counter in the kitchen.

"When did you get to be so smart about kids?" she joked.

"I'm the eldest of eight, honey. My parents ain't raised them kids by themselves." Apollo laughed. He patted her on the leg. "It will be fine. Now when are you going to take me out to lunch?"

She burst out laughing at his dramatics. She had been promising to take him out to lunch so they could talk business. They'd had a few ideas that they wanted to talk about, but she just hadn't had the time.

"Soon," she promised.

He snickered at her response.

"As long as I owe you lunch, you'll never go hungry," she said.

He gave her the side-eye that made her laugh even harder.

"Whatever." They rolled down her street and pulled into her driveway.

Tara's, the babysitter, sedan was parked in her drive. The light in the living room was on. Her house was still standing, so Jason must not have terrorized her too much.

"Thanks for driving." She turned toward her

friend. She wished their night didn't have to end, but she had to be super mom come morning and would need her beauty rest before Jason woke up starving.

"Anytime." He leaned over and kissed her cheek. "Don't be a stranger. Call me next week."

"I will." She exited the vehicle, shutting the door. She jogged up the few stairs and pulled her keys from her purse. Once the door was unlocked, she spun around and waved.

Apollo tapped his horn, then backed out of the drive, heading down the street. She waited until he was out of sight before closing the door.

"Ms. Knight, you're home earlier than I thought," Tara said. She lifted her head from the couch. She was snuggled under one of the throw blankets watching a movie.

"I'm getting old. Late-night partying isn't for me." Omara dropped her purse on the edge of the couch, digging in it for her phone. "He behave himself?"

"Of course. He's a sweetie pie." Tara stood and stretched. She folded the blanket and disappeared down the hall.

"Apple Pay okay?" Omara asked.

"That's fine." Tara reappeared. She was a senior in high school and very responsible for her age.

Omara was actual shocked Tara wasn't studying. The girl always had her nose in her school books.

Omara sent the payment then walked Tara to the door.

"Thanks again," Omara said.

"No problem. I'm available most weekends. Goodnight." The young girl jogged down the stairs and made her way to her car.

Once she'd driven away, Omara shut the door. She breathed a sigh of relief, ready to get these four-inch heeled boots off. She'd had them on for hours, and her feet were complaining.

Now that she was home, she could relax. A cami, house pants, a blanket, and her show were calling her name. She may even open the bottle of wine she had been saving for a special occasion.

She pushed off the door and went into the kitchen.

Wine made itself to the top of her list.

She grabbed the bottle out of the fridge and searched her cabinet for a glass. She twisted off the cap, not ashamed of her cheap wine. Four-dollar bottles tended to get her tipsy quick and were so tasty. She poured herself a hefty glass and took a gulp.

"You sip wine, my dear," she said, mimicking her mother's voice.

Irene hated when Omara and Jordan downed wine like it was Kool-Aid. Her mother was a classy woman. Too bad both her daughters got their class from their father.

Omara giggled and stored the bottle back in the fridge to keep it chilled. "I'll be back for you."

After a ladylike sip, she went and checked on Jason. She stood in his doorway and took in her wild sleeping child. He was lying at the foot of his bed with his pillow cuddled in his arms. There was no need to move him. He'd just end up right where he'd started.

She quietly closed his door and went back into the living room to shut off the television.

A knock sounded at the door.

"Did she forget something?" Omara murmured, glancing around the living room. Not seeing anything that would belong to Tara, Omara walked over to the door. She flicked the switch on the wall to turn the porch light on and peeked out the window.

She froze.

The floor of her stomach gave way. She tightened her grip on her glass to keep from dropping it.

Zain.

He returned her stare. The muscle in his jaw tightened as she stood there and downed the rest of her wine. He appeared exhausted. His hair was a skewed, his beard fuller. She hadn't seen Jordan since she'd dropped her off when she'd got called in for work. Apparently, Michelle had jinxed her sister and the SWAT team.

"What are you doing here?" she asked, opening the door.

He pushed his way in and shut the door.

"I wanted to see you," he said.

She snorted then spun around on her heels and went back in the kitchen. He followed behind her.

"Come to see me or come to fuck me?" she snapped.

She opened the fridge, but he slammed it shut and pushed her up against it. He removed her glass from her hand and sat it on the counter.

"Keep your voice down. I'm sure your son is sleep," he murmured. He closed the gap between them.

She cursed at how well they fit together. Even with her heels, he still towered over her. She tilted her head back to meet his gaze.

"Don't worry about my son." She poked him in the chest.

His eyes darkened, and his hand resting on her waist tightened.

"Answer my question," she said. "Are you here to fuck me?"

"Omara," he bit out through clenched teeth.

"I mean, yesterday you had a young chick who didn't look old enough to be in a bar. Was she not satisfying for you? Could she not handle you? Is that why you're here tonight? Am I better?" She didn't know what had gotten in to her, but the words just spilled from her lips. She hated how jealous she sounded, but seeing him with another woman after he'd asked her out stung.

A lot.

"You don't know what you're talking about," he rasped.

She tried to push him away, but the man was a solid wall. He didn't even budge an inch.

"Omara, listen to me."

"I find it funny that you finally asked me out, I can't go, so you replace me?"

His hand shot out to her neck and gripped tight. His mouth slammed onto hers in a brutal kiss, shutting her up. She tried to fight him off, but the feeble attempt failed.

Her body was a traitor.

She fell into the kiss. She channeled all of her anger into it. She slid her hands along his chest and landed at the nape of his neck. Her fingers threaded themselves into his thick hair. The pressure on her throat lightened. His hand moved to cup her jaw, tilting her head as he deepened the kiss.

"Then who was she?" she asked, tearing her mouth from his. She stared up at him, panting, trying to get control of her breathing.

"Who was *he*?" He glared at her. His hand slipped back down to the column of her neck.

She didn't fear Zain at all. He was nothing like her ex. He would never hurt her.

"No one," she whispered.

"He didn't look like no one. He was too close to you, touching you, whispering in your ear. The sexy dress you wore, those damn heels of yours. He wanted you." He leaned down, his lips brushing her earlobe.

A shiver drifted down her spine at the firm hold he had on her. If he squeezed hard enough, he could do damage, but she trusted him. Her traitorous body was awakening to Zain. She bit back a whimper that was threatening to escape. Heat engulfed her, the flames of her desire for this man growing.

"I don't share. Ever."

"Neither do I, but I'm not yours, Zain."

Apparently, that was the wrong thing to say.

A strangled growl rippled from him.

He swooped down and buried his face into the crook of her neck. Her back arched, pressing her breasts to his chest. He nipped her sensitive skin, soothing it with his tongue. A moan slipped out of her. His hands were everywhere.

"Did you bring him back here? Did you fuck him?" His warm breath skated along her neck. "Did you suck his cock as good as you do mine?"

"Zain," she panted, moaning his name.

His hand gripped her thigh, sliding under her dress. He dove beneath her thong, gliding a finger along her slit.

She was sopping wet.

It didn't make any sense how wet she got around him. Little did this man know, her body responded to him in a way that no other man could elicit.

He pried her thighs apart and pushed a finger inside her.

"Tell me, Omara. Did he make you come as hard as I can make you?" He fucked her with his finger.

Her hips thrust forward, seeking more. She gripped his shoulders, throwing her head back in ecstasy. Her pussy pulsed, clamping down on his finger. She rotated her hips, trying to get him farther inside her.

But that wasn't what her body was demanding he push inside her.

"No!" she panted.

He paused, leaving his finger inside her moist channel. He brought his face up and stared into her eyes.

"No, what?" The look in his eyes was feral.

All of his buttons had been pushed, and there was no going back. She felt just as crazed as he appeared. She didn't want to play any games. It was Zain who she wanted. She reached up and cupped his cheeks.

"I didn't fuck him," she whispered. "I gave him my number."

Something exchanged between them. She didn't know what it was, but it was like a bomb had gone off. Zain captured her mouth again in a hard kiss. He withdrew his finger from her. They scrambled to get him free from his jeans, pushing them down. He hefted her up against the fridge, pushed her panties to the side, and lined his cock up to her drenched opening. One thrust, and he sank fully into her.

Omara bit down on his shoulder to keep from screaming. He shuddered before he pumped his hips. His pace was hard and fast. Her internal muscles quivered from his invasion. Her walls screamed from being stretched so fast and wide. He hadn't given her time to adjust to his size before he'd started fucking her. Each stroke seemed to put him deeper inside her.

Zain was a massive storm rolling in, destroying everything in his path. Omara wrapped her arms and legs around him as she took whatever he gave her. She gripped his face, kissing him, chanting his name while rocking her hips to meet his.

It didn't take them long to reach their peak.

Omara's climax came crashing into her. His cock brushed her clit with each stroke. She trembled, riding the waves. His grip on her thighs was bruising, but she didn't care, she barely felt the pain.

She buried her face in his neck, whispering his name.

He stiffened, the muscles in his body going taut. A warmth fill her as he pumped her full of his release. The only sound he made was a low grunt when he came. After what seemed forever, they grew still. Omara wasn't sure how he was able to hold her up.

He dropped her legs and withdrew from her. She instantly missed the feeling of him. She felt almost empty without him inside her. He leaned his forehead to hers. They stood like that for what felt like eternity before his deep voice broke the silence.

"I didn't hurt you, did I?" he asked.

"No," she whispered. She rested her hand on his chest above his heart. It pounded away underneath her touch. The slight trail of his release coated her thighs, running down her inner thigh. Her lips curved up into a tiny smile.

"What's so funny?" His voice was gruff.

She opened her eyes and saw he was already growing hard again.

"Nothing." She shook her head, eyeing his dick. His huge member twitched against his stomach.

He tilted her chin up to meet his eyes.

"You are mine, Omara. I want you and I'm claiming you." He leaned down and kissed her swollen lips.

Her heart did a little pitter-patter of a dance. She had never been claimed before. His words brought out all kinds of feelings she couldn't name.

"Well, then I'm claiming you, Zain Roman. This is definitely mine." She slid her hand around his cock that was still slick with the evidence of their coupling. It pulsed in her hand.

He smiled and reached up, brushing her hair from her face.

"Just so you know. That young girl is my neighbor's granddaughter who'd been on a drinking binge, was in trouble, and they needed help with her. I picked her up and took her home to them."

Her mouth formed an "O," but no sound came out.

Well, that wasn't what she'd expected to hear. That explained why they'd looked as if they were arguing. What young girl wanted to be dragged out of the bar and taken home to her grandparents?

"And if you think I'm done with you now, think again." He yanked up his pants and led her to her bedroom.

Omara couldn't form a word if she tried. He closed the door and remembered the lock. He'd turned to her with a scorching intensity in his eyes that took her breath away. He reached for his shirt and tugged it over his head, tossing it to the floor.

He eyed her boots. "Clothes off. The boots stay."

She exhaled sharply. Her pussy clenched at his orders. More moisture slipped from her. She sensed the mess between her legs. She disrobed and felt Zain's hands on her. He tossed her on the bed and followed her down. He covered her body with his.

His knee prodded her thighs open, allowing him to settle between them.

The blunt tip of his cock breached her opening. Their simultaneous groans filled the air as he sank back inside her.

"Tell me you're mine," he growled in her ear.

She wrapped her arms around him, pulling him completely down on her. She wanted to feel his full weight on her.

"I'm yours."

16

*Z*ain awoke to Omara lying in his arms. He leaned down and pressed a kiss to her forehead. She snuggled in closer, putting her warm, naked body against him. His cock took notice of her and thickened.

He grinned in the darkness but wasn't going to wake her up. He could have and he knew she'd be down, but he didn't want to leave her sore. He shifted her off him for a moment and reached for his jeans that were still on the floor. He pulled his phone out and sat it down on the nightstand then reached for his gun and its sheath that was still attached to the back of his jeans. He opened her top drawer and slid it in there.

In the morning, they would have a long conversation. He hadn't been playing when he'd said she was his. He didn't give a shit what anyone would say, Omara was his woman.

He readjusted himself in the bed and brought Omara back next to him.

"Everything okay?" she mumbled.

"Yeah, go back to sleep, babe." He ran a hand along her back.

She sighed, nodding. He continued to rub her back with the tips of his fingers while staring at the ceiling. It was time for him to officially meet her son. If he was going to be in her life, he didn't want to be hidden away.

He hadn't had much experience with kids but he'd learn. A little boy couldn't be too hard to handle. He'd been one at one point in his life.

He wondered if the kid was into sports. Zain and Luca had always been in some type of sports growing up. They'd run their mother in circles with all of their after-school extracurricular activities.

Zain grinned, imagining the SWAT cookouts. They always had a friendly game of football at Mac's house. Maybe he was putting the cart before the horse, but he couldn't wait to have a little Zain of his own or a smaller version of Omara running around.

A woman like Omara wasn't one to let go. She was a good woman he could trust, unlike his ex-wife.

"What are you thinking about?" Omara whispered. She sat up slightly, eyeing him. "I can hear the gears in your head turning."

"You cannot," he mused. He guided her face to his, planting a kiss on her lips. "To be honest, I'm excited to meet Jason," he admitted.

"We should take that slow." She stiffened, leaning on her elbow. Her hand skated along his bare chest.

"Why?" He frowned. "I meant what I said about us."

"I know you did, but I don't just bring men around my son. I'm not sure how he will react to his mother being with someone. His father and I split a few years ago, and it's just been him and me. It will be an adjustment for him." Her warm breath caressed his mouth as she lowered her head to him. "Trust me, okay. I know what's best for my child."

Zain struggled with not arguing with her that they should just do it and get the meeting over with. But she knew her son and was a great mother. Who was he to demand anything when it came to her kid? He knew next to nothing about kids. He would have to follow her lead on this one.

She placed kisses along his jawline and down to his ear. He growled playfully when she nipped his ear. His cock thickened, growing aware of Omara's closeness.

"Don't start nothing, Omara. I don't want to make you sore." As much as he would love to sink inside her again, he didn't want to hurt her.

"How about you let me worry about that." Her hand closed around his shaft.

The woman was downright sneaky. He hadn't even realized her hand had disappeared underneath the cover.

"Don't say I didn't warn you." He rolled them until he was braced over her.

She cupped his jaw, bringing his head to her. His cock rested on her belly. If he checked her cunt, he knew what he would find.

"There are some things a girl is willing to sacrifice." She kissed his lips. "And walking is one of them."

"Good to know." He grinned, loving her silly nature. He lowered his head, then paused.

He picked up a sound coming from the house.

"What is it?" Omara whispered.

"I heard something," he murmured. He heard it again. It sounded as if it was coming from the kitchen. It was too far away to be Jason leaving his room. He rolled off Omara and snagged his boxer briefs. If he was going to surprise a burglar, he'd at least do it with his shorts on instead of completely naked. He stepped into them and stood.

"Wait a minute—"

"Stay here." He pushed her back onto the bed and reached for the nightstand. He slipped his gun out and softly walked to the door.

"Zain," she whispered fiercely.

"Stay here. I may need you to call the cops."

She nodded and tiptoed over to her closet while he headed out of the room. He didn't make a sound as he crept down the short hallway. Whoever was in the house wasn't even trying to remain quiet. What the hell would they be looking for in the kitchen? Was it a homeless person searching for food?

He flipped the safety off and aimed his weapon true. He turned the corner into the dark kitchen.

"Freeze! CPD," he barked. He flew into the kitchen and grabbed the assailant's arm.

A curse went up in the air while they tussled. The person was fast, slipping through his grasp. They slammed into the refrigerator.

"I said freeze, dammit," Zain growled.

A punch landed in his stomach, then a knee

came up hard. He turned to the side, narrowly missing it. He didn't want to shoot the person.

But if he had to, he would.

Zain was taller than the person and outweighed them. He kicked their legs out from under them. They went down and rolled away from him. The figure jumped up and darted toward the living room.

"Dammit," he roared and took off after them. He slammed into them from behind, falling to the floor.

"What is going on out here?" Omara cried out.

Zain had his hand around the person's slender neck.

She flicked the light on.

Zain froze.

Oh shit.

Jordan.

"You son of a bitch," Jordan screamed. She bucked him off her.

He jumped up, warily eyeing her as she pushed off the floor. She glanced between him and Omara. "You have got to be kidding me!"

"Jordan," Omara started, but her sister held up a hand while glaring at Zain.

"You're fucking my sister?" Her voice went up a notch.

"It's not what it looks like," Zain said but immediately regretted it. Things were just how they appeared. He slipped the safety back on the gun and stood to his full height.

Omara was dressed in a navy-blue cotton nightgown with thin spaghetti straps. She looked thoroughly fucked. Hair all over the place, lips swollen, and a darkening area on her neck from his nipping and sucking on it.

"You could have fucking fooled me. You're in your damn boxers," Jordan snarled.

"We we're going to tell you," Omara said. Her eyes were wide with unshed tears. She moved toward her sister, her eyes pleading with Jordan.

"Let's sit and talk—"

"Shut up, Zain," Jordan interjected. She took a step toward him with a hardening glare. She turned to her sister, pointing at him. "This is what you want? Someone who doesn't sleep with the same person, has a ho list a mile long? Hell, we just saw him last night with some young bimbo."

"I don't cheat," he growled.

"Don't cheat?" Jordan swung her gaze to him. Her glare would have struck down a weaker man. "Do you even know how to keep your dick in your pants?"

"I don't cheat," he roared again. "You know me,

Jordan. I know the guys told you what happened with my wife who slept with any man who could advance her career. How she lied to me. Manipulated me. Used me and when I had nothing else to give, left me." He stopped, running a trembling hand along his face. He hadn't meant to yell, but he couldn't help it. He would never put anyone through what his wife did to him.

Omara's eyes widened at his admission. Tears spilled down her cheeks.

Jordan watched him, not saying a word.

"I like Omara. More than I should. She knows who that young girl was, and it's not anyone I was sleeping with. I don't owe you an explanation, and the only person I did was your sister." He turned and walked over to the window, trying to will his racing heart to slow down.

"Mom, why is everyone yelling?" a small voice asked.

Zain spun around, his heart all but leaping into his throat at the sight of a little boy the same shade of brown as his mother and aunt. The resemblance between the three was uncanny. The shape of his eyes was Omara. He was almost as tall as she was, his hair a close fade. His nose was where they were different. He must have inherited it from his father.

"Jason, I'm sorry we woke you." Omara gathered him to her side. She dropped a kiss to his forehead.

The little guy looked around the room, his gaze stopping on Zain. It moved down to the gun in his hand before coming up to his face.

"We just got excited about what we were talking about," Omara said.

Zain cleared his throat. Standing in their living room in just his underwear was not how he first wanted to meet the little man.

"But Auntie was yelling bad words." Jason eyed Jordan who shrugged.

"Is that new?" Jordan asked. Her features softened as she moved over to him. She stood in front of Jason, blocking his view of Zain. She threw small punches at the kid who giggled and blocked her advances.

He peeked around Jordan.

"Who's he?" Jason pointed at him.

Zain glanced at Omara who shrugged. She wrapped her arms around Jason and maneuvered him around Jordan.

"This, baby, is Mommy's friend, Zain," she said. They stopped in front of Zain.

Jason tilted his head back, his eyes going wide.

"It's nice to finally meet you, Jason." Zain held out his hand.

Jason stood up taller, his chest puffed out slightly as he took Zain's hand.

"Nice to meet you," Jason said. His eyes skated to his mother. "Um, Mom. Why is he in his underwear?"

He stepped back and wrapped his arms around Omara.

"Ouch, baby," she grimaced.

"I'm sorry, Mom. I forgot about your arm."

Zain's eyes zeroed in on the black-and-blue bruise that was in the healing stage.

What the fuck?

That wasn't from him.

"What happened to your arm?" Zain stepped closer and lifted her arm. If he wasn't mistaken, the bruising looked to be in the shapes of fingers.

"It's nothing," Omara tried to brush him off.

"Yup, start off a relationship with covering shit up." Jordan snickered.

"Shut up, Jordan." Omara swung around to her.

"Why should I? You don't tell me about you and my teammate. Maybe I should finally tell him why I left Atlanta to move to Columbia."

"Stop it," Omara's voice grew louder. She placed

her hands on Jason's shoulders. "Go back to your room, baby. Mommy will come tuck you in."

She offered a smile, but Jason shook his head, fat tears rolling down his face.

"My daddy did that to you, didn't he? When he was here the other day."

The room went deathly silent.

Zain's hand tightened on the handle of the gun he still carried.

What did the kid just say?

Omara's head whipped toward him, and he saw the answer in her eyes before she turned away. She pulled Jason to her in a tight hug while the kid sobbed. She tried to console him with tears streaming down her face.

"It's okay, baby. You don't have to worry about anything, okay?" She eased back and wiped his face with her hands. "He can't hurt me anymore."

Zain's attention locked on Jordan. It all made sense. She'd transferred to CPD to be near her sister. To protect Omara. Rage like he had never known reared up inside his chest. Omara's ex was a dead man.

"I'll be back," Omara said, ushering Jason out of the living room.

Zain stalked to Jordan, his gaze narrowed on her.

She didn't back down away from him. The woman had nerves of steel.

"I want the name of the asshole who put his hands on her," he rasped. He would tear the man limb from limb. He'd destroy the man who'd brought tears to Omara's and Jason's eyes.

"Why should I tell you?"

"Don't fuck with me, Jordan. Look me in my eyes and tell me you don't believe I have feelings for Omara," he dared her.

She straightened, meeting his hard glare with one of her own. She studied him, and whatever she saw, she must have been satisfied with.

"You hurt my sister, and I promise you, there won't even be enough of your soul left to send to Hell."

Zain nodded in understanding, but he wasn't worried. He planned to be around as long as Omara would have him.

"He never put his hands on Jason," Jordan began. "She hid everything from me and our parents. I started doing surprise visits and would find bruising all over her. She'd lie and cover up for him, saying she was clumsy. But I knew my sister was covering up for that son of a bitch. I told him the last time that if he put a hand on her again, I'd break his arm."

Zain glanced down the hall before turning back to her.

"And?" He raised an eyebrow in question.

"She made me promise I wouldn't go after him this time."

"Yeah, well, I didn't promise shit," Zain growled.

OMARA LAY beside Jason with him cuddled in her arms. Warm tears slid down her cheeks while she held her child. He had been the only ray of sunshine in her life. It was this child who gave her the strength to get up each day.

She couldn't thank her sister enough for making her see that leaving Derrick was for the best, if not only for herself but for Jason. Omara had thought it would be ideal for Jason to be raised in a household with both of his parents like her and her sister.

But as Jordan had pointed out, their home had been a loving, nurturing environment. Living with Derrick was a step away from Hell.

Jason sniffed and snuggled closer to her. As

much as she had tried to hide things from him, her kid was smart.

"Mom?" Jason lifted his head.

She jumped slightly, having thought he was sleep.

"Yeah, baby?" She ran a finger down his back. As a baby, he was always comforted when she'd rubbed his back.

"Is Zain your boyfriend?" He studied her quietly.

Omara decided she wouldn't lie to her son.

"Yes, he is." She nodded, a small smile playing on her lips. "He's a good man. He's works with your auntie—"

"He's SWAT like Auntie?" His eyes widened.

"Yes."

"That's cool. Auntie says SWAT is badass."

"Jason, language." She tried to keep her voice stern but couldn't help the giggle that escaped. Of course her sister would teach her son swear words.

"But that's what she says. She said that she has to trust the guys to have her back because her job is super dangerous."

"That it is." Omara shivered. She always worried about her sister when she didn't hear from her. They talked every day if they didn't see each other.

Now there were two people she would fret over when they went out on dangerous calls.

"Why did he have his gun out?" Jason fiddled with his blanket.

She shifted him closer and exhaled. She stared at the ceiling, imaging the two of them in a little bubble. She was afraid of what she was going to step into once she left Jason's room. Omara didn't hear any other arguing out there. Her heart had seemed to jump in her throat when she'd heard fighting out in the house.

It was rare for Jordan to not text her that she was stopping by the house at night. Her sister had a key, but then again, it was late, and she probably hadn't wanted to wake Omara.

"He heard a noise in the kitchen. We didn't know it was Auntie."

"He was going to protect us?" Jason's hand paused. He turned his gaze to her.

"Yes."

"Yeah, he's a badass." He rested his head back on her arm.

Omara smirked, letting her son's cursing pass. She'd have to have another conversation with Jordan about her language when around her son.

"Will he be here in the morning?" Jason yawned, his eyes fluttering closed.

She ran her fingers along his spine. Sleep was coming for her son again. She softly kissed his forehead.

"Are you okay with that?" she asked.

"Yeah."

She nodded, listening to his breathing even out. She held him a little longer. She wasn't sure she was ready to go back out there.

It was cowardly, she knew, hiding in here with her son. But she didn't want to face Zain. It would tear her apart if he looked at her like everyone did when she shared she was a survivor of domestic abuse.

The door opened with Zain peeking his head in. His eyes softened when his gaze landed on her and Jason.

"Everything all right?" he asked.

She nodded.

He held out his hand to her. "Come on, babe. No hiding from me."

How did he know?

She slid out of the bed and turned around, tucking Jason in before heading to Zain. She took his hand and allowed him to guide her out into the hall-way. He closed the door quietly.

He seized her other hand and raised it to his lips. His kiss was gentle, bringing tears to her eyes.

"Don't look at me like that," he murmured.

"Like what?" She moved closer to him, needing to feel his warmth and strength.

He wrapped his other arm around her, closing the gap between them.

"Like you expect me to run away from you."

"You should." She chuckled. Her laugh died at the expression in his eye.

He leveled her with a serious gaze.

"Is that what you really want?" His voice dropped a few octaves.

"No." Her answer was immediate. She wanted him with her. There was no other man she wanted to belong to but him.

"I meant what I said, Omara. You're mine."

17

*Z*ain guided Omara back into the bedroom. He had waited long enough for her to come out of Jason's room. He could tell she was procrastinating after she'd been in there for thirty minutes.

Jordan had stormed out of the home. Things were not over between them. The woman was pissed, and all he could do was give her breathing room. He wasn't leaving Omara because of Jordan. His teammate was going to have to come to grips with the fact he was with her sister.

Zain had ensured the house was secure before going to get Omara from Jason's room. His heart had stuttered at the sight of her cuddled with her sleeping child. A yearning like he'd never known hit him.

He wanted that.

He wanted the right to bring her and their child into his arms and hold them.

Be their protector.

Lend her his strength.

Be as one.

Omara's hand tightened on his. He shut the bedroom door and flicked the lock. He escorted her to her side of the bed and helped her climb in before going to the other side and joining her. Once in the bed, he pulled her to him.

This just felt right.

Together, they lay in complete silence and darkness. Only the faint rays of the streetlights breached the room through the curtains. Omara's head rested in the crook of his arm. Her soft hair brushed his skin. He breathed in her scent, never wanting to forget it.

She shifted closer to him. Her warm breath fanned across his chest. His cock jerked at her closeness, but he ignored it.

"Tell me about her," Omara whispered.

Zain hesitated. Should he share how he had

failed at his marriage? That he hadn't been enough for Freya and that she had to run to the arms of many men in order to get what she needed? Men who were able to provide the lifestyle that she wanted. A man like him on a cop's salary sure couldn't do it.

He blew out a shaky breath and knew he couldn't hide anything from Omara.

"We met the summer after I graduated from the academy. Freya caught my eye. I was cocky and just signed on with CPD. We ran around in pretty much the same circle, had some common friends. I saw her out one night and asked her out." He paused, remembering how she had eyed him when he'd approached her. She'd slowly slid her gaze over him as if studying him. "She turned me down. Three times."

"So even though she wasn't interested, you asked her out two more times?"

"I was determined." He gave a slight chuckle.

"Sounds desperate to me," Omara muttered.

"Focused on obtaining what I wanted," he argued. He shook his head at the noise she made at the back of her throat. They wouldn't be able to agree on this one. He hadn't been desperate. No matter what she thought. "We went on our first date and got along great. One date turned into two, and before I knew it, we were married, moved in to together within a year."

They had a whirlwind relationship. Maybe if they had taken their time, he would have seen some of the red flags early.

"Sounds like love," she whispered.

Zain released a grunt. He sighed and brought her closer, not wanting to share the next part of the story.

"Everything was going fine. At least I thought it had been. I had been doing well as a patrol cop. I loved being able to get out in the community, keeping the streets safe. I felt as if I had found my calling. Freya got promotion after promotion at work. I really thought she was doing well, working hard. She pulled crazy hours at work. Some weeks working eighty hours, going on business trips for conferences and meetings. She was really advancing fast at her company." He paused, the horrors returning.

He had trusted her, and she had stepped on it and his heart as if it were an insect.

"You don't have to finish." Omara patted him on the chest.

He shook his head. "I do. You have to understand. She fucked me up something serious. Over the years, we started arguing over everything. She wanted me to sit for detective, lieutenant, any position that would take me up the ranks. She never understood how I liked where I was. When I made SWAT, she thought I should be going after Mac's position next. But that's not me.

"Hell, she wanted me to be the damn captain. Something she felt she could brag about because, quite frankly, me being a 'regular cop' was embarrassing for her." He stopped, his breaths coming faster as the arguments of the past came to mind. He could never understand where all of her hatred and scorn had come from because of his position. There was nothing wrong with being a cop. He had been proud to be a member of the Columbia Police Department.

Omara stilled beside him. He was so lost in his memories that he kept going.

"She had to attend her company's fundraiser function at a swanky hotel, and I went along with her. She had excused herself, saying she needed to go meet with her boss and that she would be right back. Imagine my fucking surprise when I went to the men's bathroom and found her blowing him there."

"Oh my God."

"It all came out later. I thought I was stunned then to see her on her knees for her boss. Come to find out each of her promotions were due to her sleeping around to climb to the top of her company. She'd fucked her way to the top. Those conferences and trips? She'd gone on vacations with rich executives she'd been sleeping with. They gave her anything she wanted."

"Zain stop." Omara leaned up on her elbow and stroked his cheek.

"Nothing I did was good enough for her. I couldn't provide the type of lifestyle she wanted."

"Zain, that's enough. I don't want to hear anymore." Omara's voice broke. She tried to turn his face towards her, but he couldn't look at her.

"And you know the worse part?" He released a shaky breath. "Before I found out about the cheating, we agreed to try for a baby. Even though we'd argued so much about my job, lack of high promotions, we agreed we both wanted children. Was it a smart idea, I don't know, but I wanted children. I thought it would fix what was between us. Ground us to each other. I just wanted what my parents had. I grew up seeing how well they worked together for my brother and me. She had told me she stopped taking the pill, and we tried. Month after month, no baby."

"Oh, Zain." Omara sniffed.

He felt the wetness on his face and knew Omara was crying, too.

"She got an IUD. So I never saw pills. That broke me, Omara. She knew how much I had wanted children. The divorce was messy and felt as if I were in a war zone. It was like we had never been in love. Hell, I still don't know to this day if she ever did love me."

Omara's fingers wiped the wetness from his skin. He shook his head, remembering the divorce proceedings. Freya had thought she would escape with everything. She'd tried to tear him down as a man, as a human. But the law had been on Zain's side. His flawless record on the force and in the community were in his favor. The looks of hatred on her face still puzzled him. He hadn't done anything but try to love her.

Who was that woman he had been married to?

The woman in the courtroom was not the same

one he had married and promised to love until death did they part.

She had tried to hide all of her bank accounts from him that her lovers had put money in. But seeing how she'd gained that money while married, it became communal property, and he was awarded half.

"Come here." Omara shifted in the bed and brought him to her. She slid her arm around him and pulled him into her embrace and held him.

He settled against her and breathed in her lovely scent. He felt comforted in her arms. Omara was completely different from Freya. She accepted him as is and hadn't made any demands but for him to please her. He wrapped an arm around her waist and held her tight.

This woman was who he needed.

"It would seem we know how to pick them, huh?" Omara whispered.

He grunted.

Freya may have mentally fucked with him, but this Derrick character was a different breed.

Using a woman smaller than him as a punching bag was uncalled for.

Zain was going to ensure that he never even looked at Omara again.

"WELL, Jason, since your mother cooked breakfast, it's only fair we clean up the kitchen," Zain said. He pushed back from the table.

Omara watched, stunned, as her son stood along with him without complaining. Jason gathered dishes from the table.

What in the world?

He usually grumbled when she asked him to clean the table or load the dishwasher. Not that she had him doing full chores like cleaning the kitchen yet, but she had started him on light things to help teach him responsibility.

So far, their morning with Zain had gone well. Jason thought Zain was cool because he was a cop like his auntie, carried a gun, and played football in high school.

She didn't think her son's eyes could get any wider.

Guilt filled her. Jason craved the attention of a male role model. His father was useless. He had a good relationship with her father, but he didn't see his pops all the time. Zain had been wonderful with Jason, answering all of his questions, engaging with him. In just that short time, they had already become buddies.

She had awoken to find the bed beside her empty. She had found Zain and Jason on the couch watching Jason's favorite, *Scooby Doo*. She had introduced the show to her son when he was younger, and he'd fallen in love with the cartoon dog. While they'd laughed and were engrossed in the television, she'd slipped into the kitchen and made breakfast.

"What position did you play?" Jason asked. His arms were full of plates, and he followed Zain into the kitchen.

"Safety, cornerback were just a couple positions I played," Zain replied.

She looked around the table and saw they had grabbed almost everything. She stood and snagged the napkins that had been left. She walked into the kitchen and stopped at the doorjamb. Jason was loading the dishwasher while Zain was starting the water in the sink.

"You fellas need any help?" Her eyes felt a little scratchy. This moment had her all up in her feelings. For this brief second, it felt like a real family. This was what Sundays should be like. She tried to rein her feelings in, but they were running wild.

Zain guided her son in what to do, and her core

clenched. She bit her lip and took in his strong form as he moved around the kitchen.

Omara exhaled. She would not take this man back into her bedroom and have her way with him.

At least not right now while Jason was seeking their attention. Maybe she could offer a distraction with his video game...

She pushed off the doorjamb and busied herself by throwing the trash away to try to curb her sinful thoughts. She leaned back against the counter and eyed them.

"I think we're good," Zain said. He glanced over his shoulder at her and tossed her a wink. Did he just dismiss her? He must have seen her shocked expression. He dried his hands on a towel and came to stand in front of her. There was that playful glint in his eye. He braced his hands on the counter, trapping her. "Are you feeling left out?"

She nodded, a silly smile coming to her lips. Jason was watching them with the curiosity of a child. This was new for him. The relationship between his father and her was always strained, and she couldn't even remember the last time they had shared a laugh together.

"Maybe." She folded her arms and tilted her head back to meet his gaze. She poked his stomach, feeling those hard ripped abdomen muscles under her fingertips. "What am I supposed to do?"

His fingers slipped to her sides and tickled her. She squealed, immediately trying to get away from his torturing. He held on to her, whipping her around in front of him. Tears slid down her cheeks. She'd always been extremely ticklish. Jason's giggle filled the air as he watched them. She swung away from Zain and ran behind Jason, pulling him in front of her. She wrapped her arms around him, laughing.

"Seriously? You're hiding behind your child?" Zain snorted.

"Yes. My son will defend me." She stuck her tongue out at Zain.

"You sure?"

Zain jerked his head to Jason who spun around and tried to tickle her, too. She screamed, breaking away from him and jogging from the room. Laughing, she turned to find Zain and Jason sharing a high five.

Did they just bond and band together against her?

"Guess I'll go take a shower." She sniffed.

"Okay," Jason said. He moved to Zain's side and began helping him.

She guessed she wasn't needed. Looked like the guys had the kitchen taken care of.

Omara couldn't erase the smile from her lips and didn't know if she wanted to.

She headed to the bathroom and planned to take a long, relaxing hot shower.

18

Monday morning rolled around before he knew it. Zain entered the conference room of the station where his team was meeting. His eyes briefly met Jordan's who sat off to the side. She narrowed her gaze on him but didn't say anything. She had left soon after their confrontation. He had the name of Omara's ex. It sounded familiar, but he couldn't put a finger on it. He'd give the name to Brodie after the meeting and have him look the son of a bitch up. One glance at her, and he knew she was still pissed at him.

He got it.

He'd crossed a line he probably shouldn't have, but he really did care for Omara. She was a great woman.

He nodded to her then headed to the back and took a seat next to Iker, where he could lean up against the wall. Everyone was present but Mac and Declan. They usually came in last. Low conversations were going around the room.

He'd spent all day with Omara and Jason. It had gone over better than they'd thought. Jason was very interested in learning about him. The kid had perked up when they'd started talking football. Jason had been trying to talk Omara into letting him play, but she had been hesitant. The way the boy had screamed and danced around when she'd told him she'd signed the permission slip had Zain grinning even now.

Omara's son was amazing. He was such a great kid and reminded Zain of himself when he was younger. They'd had a good day together lounging around. When it was time for him to head home, he hadn't wanted to leave them. Jason appeared sad when he'd grabbed his things.

"Do you really have to go? Jason asked.

The kid might as well have taken a knife and stabbed him in the heart.

"I do, but I'll be back. This isn't goodbye forever." *Zain's voice was gruff. He held out his hand for a fist pump.*

Jason's smaller one met his. That seemed to satisfy him.

"He doesn't live here, silly." Omara dropped a kiss on Jason's head then followed Zain to the front door. She stepped out on the porch and pulled the door halfway closed.

He brought her into his arms.

She wrapped hers around his waist, tilting her head back to meet his gaze. "He really likes you."

"He's an awesome kid, Omara. You've done good." He trailed a finger along her cheek while taking in her beauty. He had every mole, freckle, and blemish memorized on her body. He'd explored and tasted every bit of her. He leaned down and took her lips in a soft, deep kiss. He skated his fingers along to the nape of her neck and threaded them into her hair, holding her in place.

"Is it crazy that I don't want you to go either," Omara whispered.

"Don't tell me that, babe." He blew out a deep breath.

They remained close, their lips brushing each other. He was half tempted to stay another night, but he had to report to the station bright and early in the morning. He softly kissed her lips again and stepped back. Her big brown eyes were wide. Need and lust *burned in them, sending a ripple of fire through him. His cock jerked to attention.*

But he couldn't stay.

"Tomorrow after work?" he murmured. There was no way he could stay away from her now that Jordan knew.

She nodded.

"Text me when you get home," she said, dusting off a piece of invisible lint from his CPD t-shirt.

Another scorching kiss, then he had to drag himself away from her.

Zain blinked, coming back to the present. He made a mental note to call his brother back about him going to a practice. He wanted to take Jason to one. It would be a great way to introduce Omara and Jason to his brother while letting Jason see the high schoolers practice.

"You're awfully quiet today," Iker said. His friend eyed him, giving him a strange look. "You okay?"

"Yeah." Zain rubbed a hand along his face. He glanced over at Jordan then back at Iker. His friend's eyebrows rose sharply, catching on to what he was not verbalizing.

"She knows?"

Zain jerked his head in a nod.

"And you're still breathing?" Iker let out a low whistle and settled back in his chair.

"I'll tell you about it later," Zain muttered. He wasn't ready for everyone to know yet.

Declan and Mac stormed into the room. He sat up straighter so he could try to pay attention to what they were going to discuss. His time with Omara and Jason had been amazing. He already couldn't wait to go see them again.

"Morning." Mac stood behind the podium in the front of the room.

Declan took his seat on the front row where he normally sat.

"Mornin'," echoed around the room.

Zain eyed Jordan again. He had much respect for her. The woman had uprooted her life to come to her sister's rescue. He'd have to make her see she wasn't going to be doing this alone. He was now in Omara's life, hell, the entire SWAT team would back her up. She had never mentioned the issues with her sister's ex. Had she, their team would have been made a visit to this Derrick character. Omara was an extension of their SWAT family.

They protected their own.

As if feeling his eyes on her, she glanced over her shoulder at him and met his gaze. Her face was expressionless as she held the stare for a few moments before turning back to Mac.

"The sentencing for Officer Cruz has been rescheduled," Mac began.

The room grew eerily silent. It was a few months before they had all attended the court hearing. Thanks to a bombing at the courthouse, the sentencing had been put off. Thankfully, SWAT had been outside the courthouse when the bomb had gone off.

Just remembering had Zain itching to go hunt down whoever had tried to off not only Cruz, but anyone in the room that day. Namely the SWAT team. It was no secret that the Demon Lords had it out for the SWAT team. They had cost them millions of dollars in drugs and had been destroying their establishment.

That bomb had been targeted for Cruz who was turning on the gang. The disgraced officer was caught in bed with the gang, and now his life was on the line, he was turning over gang secrets to the Feds to get a lighter sentence.

"We're going?" Myles asked.

Considering everything that Cruz had done in the past, they all wanted to be there to look him in the face when it was read off how long he would be spending in jail. The mole had leaked vital information of the SWAT team and their missions to the gang.

"This time it will be a virtual hearing," Mac said. He took in the room with a hard gaze. "We can all attend together, or you can log in from wherever you want. If you want to do it together, I'm sure Brodie can set us up here."

"Yeah, I can do that. It's simple," Brodie said. "When is it?"

"Next Monday at nine in the morning," Mac answered.

"Did the bomb squad come up with who actually planted the bomb?" Ash asked.

"There are a few suspects they have on video going into the courtroom, but I don't think they've narrowed it down. The investigation is ongoing," Declan said, addressing the team.

Mac continued on, going over boring updates. Employee reviews were approaching, fixing errors on forms, new protocols for requesting vacations.

All of this could have been sent out in an email.

"Again, thanks to Jordan for representing SWAT at the mayor's task force initiative. I'm sure she will have a report at this week's meeting."

"That I will. It's actually not bad. At least for me

since I'm new and it's allowing me to get to know the other teams. I think this will help when the department needs to work together." She faced the room. "There's been a lot of brainstorming, and we're coming up with some good issues that all teams can address together that deals with internal police business and community."

"I can't wait to hear what is going to be proposed," Mac said. He cleared his throat, flipping over the papers in front of him.

He glanced around the room, and Zain knew that look.

They were about to be tortured.

"It's that time of the year where we need to come together for team building. The captain knows we are already a close-knit group—"

He was interrupted by Jordan's snort.

Zain tensed. He sat up straighter, watching her. She wouldn't dare. He glanced at Iker who had the same shocked expression.

"Is something funny about what I just said, Officer Knight?" Mac asked, zeroing in on her.

"Nope, Sergeant. Not funny at all," she said. She leaned back, folding her hands together in front of her. "It's just that you mentioned how close of a group we are."

Zain ran a hand along his face, blowing out a deep breath.

"Jordan," he said. "Let's talk about this later."

He could feel the eyes of everyone shifting between him and her. The other guys appeared confused. She swung around and hit him with her hard glare.

"So you don't want everyone else to know either?" she asked.

"Not like this," he said.

"What's going on?" Mac snapped. "Knight, spit it out."

"I sure will. I want to bring our close-knit team up to speed on some things I learned this weekend."

"And what is that?" Mac murmured. The sergeant was as tense as a rattlesnake prepared to strike.

"Oh, my teammate is sleeping with my sister." She shrugged calmly, but her voice was laced with malice.

Shit.

All eyes turned to him. Sharp intakes of breath were the only sound in the room.

"Jordan." Zain stood from his seat.

"Isn't that fucked up? Someone who is your

partner can't even tell you he's messing around with my sister." She ignored him.

"What do you want me to do?" Zain retorted.

"How about respect me enough to tell me that you're involved with my sister!" she growled. Her eyes threw daggers at him.

"That's why we didn't say anything because of the way you're reacting now," he shouted.

"Roman. Hallway. Now," Mac snarled. His cold gaze was on Zain.

"Knight, with me." Declan stood and motioned for her to go with him.

Zain shoved a hand through his hair. Ash, Brodie, Myles, and Iker didn't say a word as they both left the room trailing the two sergeants. Jordan followed Declan into the room next door while Zain and Mac went down the hall. They dipped into an empty office with Mac shutting the door.

"Please tell me she's—"

"It's true," Zain admitted. He walked over to the window and stared out of it. "We hadn't meant for her to find out like that."

"But you were going to tell her that you're involved with her sister?" Mac asked, his voice low.

It was calm, and Zain glanced over his shoulder. He'd known Mac a long time and had massive amounts of respect for him. He was a true leader and was trustworthy.

"Of course we were. Hell, we were trying to figure out what it was between us. It all happened so fast. I really like Omara. She's..." He was trying to find the right words. Until one hit him in the chest. "Everything. She's everything."

Mac knew what he'd been through when Zain had got divorced. His sergeant had been a great support and would step in if he thought Zain was spiraling dangerously out of control.

"I hate to ask, but how did Jordan find out?"

Zain exhaled and went into the story of him checking out the sound in the kitchen, fighting an intruder who'd turned out to be Jordan. Mac held a straight face while listening to the story.

"Well, I'm happy for you, Zain." Mac came to stand in front of Zain. He reached out and laid a hand on Zain's shoulder. "But you are going to have to work this out with Jordan. Sounds like it was a shock and she's hurt."

"I know. I will. I promise you this."

There was a knock at the door. Mac went over and opened it. Declan and Jordan stood in the doorway. She exhaled and walked inside with Dec motioning for Mac to join him in the hall.

Zain braced himself. Jordan was a firecracker, and he didn't doubt she'd come at him swinging.

"You sure this is smart?" Mac muttered.

"Come on. She promised to behave, and I checked her for weapons." Declan said, closing the door.

"Jordan—"

"No, let me go first. That was uncalled for back in the other room." She held up a hand. "I shouldn't have done that and I'm sorry to put you on blast in front of everyone."

"Jordan, you're the last person who should be apologizing."

"No, I need to." She blew out a deep breath. "I came clean to Declan on why I really transferred to Columbia. I told him about what my sister was going through and everything. She and I have always been close, and I'm her older sister and I've always protected her. It's ingrained in my brain to watch out for her. Not that she's weak, because she is the strongest person I know."

Jordan paused and glanced down at her hands.

"She's lucky to have you as a sister," Zain said.

"And she's lucky to have you," Jordan said. She looked back up at him, her eyes bright with unshed tears. "She's been through so much, and I know you are a good man. I had noticed she'd been acting different. She's smiling more, and now I know it's because of you. I was just taken aback to see you there the other night and reacted the only way I know how."

Zain moved to her and took her hands in his. He made sure he met her eyes so she could see the truth in his.

"I would never hurt her. She makes me feel things I didn't even know I possessed inside me. She and Jason belong to me."

There he was, putting his claim on them.

She squeezed his hands and gave a nod.

He pulled her in for a hug. She wrapped her arms around him tight. Relief filled him that Jordan had come to terms with his relationship with Omara. Work would have been very strained if they hadn't fixed the divide. He chuckled, resting his chin on the top of her head. She mumbled something into his chest.

"What?" he said.

"Just know I meant what I said before." She narrowed her eyes on him.

You hurt my sister, and I promise you, there won't even be enough of your soul left to send to Hell.

He chuckled again, seeing the Jordan he worked

with coming back. The badass had officially returned. Zain didn't know which one he was more afraid of—the feeling-sharing, apologizing Jordan, or the one who could kick his ass.

"I wouldn't expect anything less."

The door opened, and they turned, finding the team crammed out in the hallway looking in with concern.

"We didn't hear anything and was expecting a body on the floor," Iker said, leaning against the doorjamb.

"What?" Zain rested his arm around Jordan's shoulders. "Whose?"

"Yours, of course." Ash snorted.

"Well, the verdict is still out on that." Jordan elbowed him in the side.

The team shared a laugh and poured into the room.

Brodie came forward. "Who is the asshat we need to research? Sounds like we need to pay a visit to him."

Zain's smile vanished. His brothers in blue would always be counted on. Omara was officially one of them now. Declan must have shared that he and Jordan had made up.

"His name is Derrick Allen," Zain announced.

"I CAN ALREADY TELL you all that you need to know about Derrick." Jordan leaned back against the table next to Brodie's desk.

Everyone was crammed into his little hole-in-the-wall at the precinct. Zain had taken over a vacated office of one of the administrative assistants who had retired.

"Yeah, but it's always fun to search the database for the lowest of scum." Brodie snickered. His fingers flew across the keyboard.

"You shouldn't have waited this long to share with us that you were having an issue." Mac leveled her with his hard gaze.

The air in the room dropped a few degrees. Zain had to agree. If he had never met her sister and become involved, he would have had no issue helping Jordan straightening Derrick out.

The entire team would have volunteered.

"I had it handled," Jordan replied, shifting her gaze back to Brodie. Even she wasn't brave enough or crazy enough to go up against their hard-nosed sergeant. "I believe Jason said something about Derrick moving, so if that's true, I don't know where he lives now."

Zain's hands balled into tight fists. He just wanted to get the information he needed and go pay a visit to the deadbeat.

"How often is he supposed to get Jason?" Zain asked.

"Every other weekend, and they split major holidays. It's not unusual for him to cancel."

"Well, I can tell you why he cancelled this time." Brodie sat back, chuckling. He motioned to the printer that sat next to Ash. It roared to life and spit out papers. "Grab that for me, will ya?"

Once it was done, Ash gathered the papers and handed them to Brodie. He shuffled them and searched through them before putting them in whatever order he wanted.

"It would appear Mr. Allen doesn't know how to keep his hands to himself. He was arrested and jailed early last week." Brodie passed the papers to Zain.

"For what?" Myles asked.

"Domestic abuse," Brodie responded.

Zain took the papers and glanced down at the first page. In the top-left corner was a picture of Derrick Allen. He paused. He'd met this fucker before.

At the domestic disturbance he'd gone to with Jones.

"Son of a bitch," Zain swore.

"What is it?" Jordan came to stand by him.

"I've met him before." He looked over at her. His gaze swept the room, and he shook his head. There had been something about the guy that Zain couldn't put a finger on. He shared with them the call he and Jones had answered together.

"So you unknowingly get called to his house where he had been putting his hands on another woman?" Mac growled.

"Yeah. She didn't want to press charges and just wanted him out of her house," Zain said.

"Well, turn the page. There's more. He went back to her house." Brodie motioned to the papers.

Jordan tilted them down so she could read along with Zain. He shifted to the next page where it described a call from the same house. Dispatch sent two officers to the home. The altercation became physical. The officers had to call in backup and physically take him down. He was carted to jail and posted bond a few days later.

This monster was Omara's ex.

He'd put his hands on her.

Zain flipped the pages and scanned the rest of

what was in his hand. A murderous rage came over him at the pages that described the phone calls to a house where a young female had called for help. There were multiple calls with the same documentation.

There was even a few hospital records entangled with Derrick's rap sheet.

Emergency room visits for one Omara Knight.

"I see that look in your eye, Zain," Iker's voice broke through his thoughts.

He flicked his gaze to his friend.

"He's not worth what you're thinking."

"You don't know what I'm thinking," Zain snapped.

Mac snatched the papers from his hand and paged through them. He moved over to Declan where they reviewed them together. Their grim expressions matched what was festering in Zain's chest.

"You are having the same thoughts I've had for years," Jordan said softly. She rested a hand on his arm, shaking her head. "Believe me when I say Omara wouldn't want to come and visit you in prison. He's not worth it."

He may not be worth it, but it would sure as hell make Zain feel better.

19

"Are we there yet?" Jason asked for the eighth time in a matter of ten minutes.

Omara groaned and turned around in her seat to glance at him in the second row of Zain's SUV.

"Jason Allen. Have some patience," Omara said. She smiled at her son who rolled his eyes and fell back against his seat. The kid had no patience when it came to secrets.

Zain grinned and guided the truck to a stop at the red light. He peeked over at her and snagged her hand in his.

The butterflies in Omara's stomach were in overdrive. She knew where they were going, and Jason was going to have a kick out of watching the high school football team practice. This also meant that she was going to be meeting Zain's brother, Luca.

Meeting family members solidified their relationship status.

Omara smiled back at Zain. This outing of theirs had all of the feelings of a family. She didn't want to rush anything, but Zain had jumped in feet first when it came to Jason. He wasn't shy at all in getting to know her son or letting her son get to know him. In the back of her mind, she knew this was going too fast, but then so had everything else with her and Zain.

She and Jordan had their talk. It had been a few days since that night. Jordan had stopped by the shop, and they had gone for lunch. She had been shocked how Jordan had apologized. She had been ready for her sister to tell her all the reasons why she shouldn't be with Zain.

"He's honestly a good man and he's a great partner to have my back when we're out on calls." Jordan reached across the table and took Omara's hand in hers.

"This means a lot, sis." Omara squeezed her hand.

"But can I ask a favor?"

"Sure, anything." Omara sat back and took a sip of her drink.

They'd stopped in one of their favorite taco joints. Omara didn't even think of what she'd eaten. It was all going to her ass and hips, but it was well worth it. She loved authentic foods that were made up of fresh ingredients.

"Can you not share the, um, sexual stuff?" Jordan grimaced.

Omara burst out laughing. She and Jordan normally shared everything with each other. But she saw how it could be a little uncomfortable for her older sister since she worked with Zain.

"Well, I would say this," Omara started.

Jordan's eyes widened as she waited to hear what Omara was about to say.

"This one, I was going to be keeping to myself."

"Thank God," Jordan sighed. She sat back, relief evident on her face.

"Because the things that man does to me are downright illegal." She couldn't help but tease her sister.

"Ugh, gross!" Jordan balled up her napkin and tossed it at Omara.

"What are you smiling about?" Zain's voice broke through her thoughts.

She focused on him and shook her head.

"Oh, nothing. Was just thinking of my conversation with my sister when we went to lunch."

He eyed her before turning back to the road.

"Not sure I want to know," he muttered. His lips still tilted up in the corners. He guided the truck onto a road that led to the school. They drove past it and headed toward the back.

"Are we here now?" Jason asked.

"Yes, we are, bud." Zain glanced into the rearview mirror. "You'll see in just a moment where we are."

"It looks like a school." Jason sat forward, his face plastered to the window. "Is this the high school?" His voice went up an octave.

They arrived at the parking lot behind the school where there were cars spread around. The football team was already on the field. A few kids walked out of the building and were headed toward the field.

"Know where we are now?" she asked. She loved the play of expressions on his face.

Jason took in the kids on the field warming up.

"Is this their football practice?" Jason wiggled around in the seat, dancing. Zain had told him to wear shorts, a t-shirt, and tennis shoes. The kid hadn't had a clue where they were going. "Yes!"

Omara laughed at her son dancing in his seat. She loved seeing him this happy. Zain parked the truck, and Jason was out of his seat and the vehicle before Omara could even unhook her safety belt.

"Jason!" She laughed at his enthusiasm.

Zain hopped out and came around to open her door. Jason stood by the hood of the truck, waiting impatiently. Zain entwined their hands together.

Her heart did a little pitter-patter. He was dressed in a long-sleeved CPD t-shirt, basketball shorts, and tennis shoes. His sunglasses hid his eyes, but she felt them on her. Jason ran ahead of them over to the fence that separated the field from the parking lot.

There were quite a few coaches integrated with the kids. There were some spectators in the bleachers watching the practice. There seemed to be about a hundred kids out there. Some were running drills, others speaking with their coaches, while a few others were tossing the ball to each other.

"I see my brother." Zain pointed to a guy with a similar build as him.

As they walked around the fence and drew closer to him, Omara could immediately see the resemblance between Zain and his brother.

"Luca."

Luca turned around at the sound of his name. He was speaking with a few other men. He headed their way, a wide grin spreading across his face.

Oh, yeah. These two were definitely related. Zain had shared with her that his brother was two years younger than him, but they were as close as could be.

"You made it."

The brothers embraced each other with a strong hug and laughter. Luca took his shades off and pushed them to the top of his head. He even shared the same eye color as Zain.

He took both her and Jason in, his grin widening. "And who do we have here?"

Zain snagged her hand and brought her flush to his side, sliding his arm around her shoulders.

"Luca, this is my girlfriend, Omara, and her son, Jason," Zain said.

Luca's eyebrows rose high, but it didn't stop him from reaching a hand forward to her.

"It's so nice to meet you." He snagged her from Zain's embrace and hugged her.

She laughed, hearing Zain's playful growl behind her.

"Don't worry. I ain't trying to steal your girl."

"You couldn't even if you tried." Zain laughed.

He pulled her away from his brother and tucked her right back at his side.

"Jason, I hear you want to play football." Luca turned his attention to her son. He held out his hand to him.

Jason stood to his full height and took Luca's hand in a shake. Omara bit her lip to keep from smiling.

"My mom just signed me up for peewee football," Jason announced proudly.

"That is awesome. Both me and my brother played peewee." Luca grinned at Jason. He glanced over at the field before turning back to Jason. "Why don't you come out there with me. I'll introduce you to the team and coaches then show you around."

Jason spun to her with wide, pleading eyes.

"Go." She waved him on.

He dashed toward her and wrapped his arms around her.

"This is the best day ever," he exclaimed.

The hug was so fast, she didn't have time to return it. He was off walking away with Luca before she knew it.

"Oh my. He's going to be talking about this forever." She sighed.

She and Zain followed behind them. They

stopped at the edge of the field. She glanced around and took it all in. So far, this is what her son wanted. The grass was bright green, the numbers painted on it. She took in the open stadium. She wasn't a big football fan, but she knew the town loved their football.

The kids running around were huge. She didn't know what their mommas were feeding them. She eyed Jason standing next to Luca who was introducing him to some of the coaches and players. He was tall for his age. Derrick had height to him, as did other male members in his family.

"Come on. We can sit over here." Zain guided them to a row of chairs sitting on the field.

The sun was beaming high. Omara wished she had remembered to snag her glasses she'd left in her purse that was locked up in the truck. She had half a mind to run back to it to grab them.

"Do you usually come here for their practice?" she asked.

"Yeah. Once in a while to help out. The kids are amazing. They won the state championship last year. My brother has worked really hard with them. A few years ago, they didn't win many games. Now, they are known as a powerhouse." Zain spoke with such pride when it came to his brother.

They reminded her of Jordan and herself.

"Wow. That's great." She turned back to watch her son with Luca.

There were a long line of tires on the ground. She was completely confused on why the football team would need tires to practice. At the moment, some of the teams were running a few plays Luca put them through. Jason was soaking it all up.

"Yo, Zain." Luca motioned for him to come over.

"Be right back." Zain handed her his car keys and planted a kiss on her cheek. "Let me show these kids how it's done."

"Oh?"

What was he talking about? He was entirely too old to be out there running around with teenagers. Omara may not know much about football, but she knew the difference between a sixteen-year-old and a thirty-five-year-old's body. Just because he was in shape did not mean he could hang with these youngsters.

"I got to see this."

She glanced around and took notice of a group of women in the stands staring at Zain. They were giggling like schoolgirls and pointing in his direction. She scowled and turned back around. Not that she had anything to worry about, but she didn't want them ogling him. He was hers.

He spoke with his brother for a moment. She watched how he rested a hand on her son's shoulder, joked with him, and had him laughing. He rubbed the top of Jason's head, saying something before he jogged out on the field.

What was he doing?

She soon found out.

The man was crazy. He joined the kids out on the field. He was a graceful runner, going up and down the turf. He and his brother were giving tips. She watched as he took off, did a zigzag, and caught the ball the quarterback threw at him.

He laughed, in his element. A few of the boys surrounded him, listening to him as he pointed to a few areas on the field.

She swallowed hard, trying to keep from fanning herself. When did the temperature rise? She shifted on her seat and was suddenly dying for a cold drink of water. Her throat had grown parched watching him.

The kids laughed, egging him on about something. He reached down and took his shirt off, rubbing it along his forehead to wipe the sweat from his face. There was a collective sigh behind Omara.

She turned around and found the same group of women fanning themselves and laughing while drooling over her man. She had half a mind to walk over there and poke them all in their eyes.

He tucked the edge of the shirt in the back of his shorts and followed the kids. She had to remember to breathe. It wasn't like she hadn't seen him naked, but for some reason, the sweat coating him in this perfect sunlight was doing things to her.

"Breathe, girl."

A few whistles sounded behind her, and she bit her lip to keep from letting them have a piece of her mind. There were children around.

Zain stayed out there with the team, filling in where his brother needed him to. Omara pulled her phone out of her pocket and opened up one of her mindless games she kept on it. She wasn't sure how long they would be there. Jason and Zain were having too much fun with the high school kids.

She had lost track of time and glanced up, catching sight of her son walking along with Zain and some members of the team toward the row of tires. She watched, fascinated, as the players began doing a drill with jumping through the tires. Their knees went high as they made their way through them. She didn't know how they could go so fast. If she tried, she'd land right on her face.

Jason was right in the midst of them. She took her son in and did a double take. When had he taken his shirt off? His t-shirt was tucked into the back of his shorts. He stood watching until the kids motioned for him to try. He didn't even hesitate. He took off to the beginning, and even though he was much slower, he completed it. She cheered him on from her seat. The players high fived him. He ran over to Zain and jumped to hit his hand that was held up in the air. The two of them laughed, with Jason guiding Zain over to the tires.

"Okay, okay!" Zain shouted, smiling.

Omara's smile faded as she observed him take the tires. Watching him was like looking at a beautiful live-action painting. His arms, those abs of his, and the dark wavy hair that fell into his eyes. She bit her lip and sat forward.

The peanut gallery behind her was growing rowdier by the minute, and she was beginning to question what they had to drink in their water bottles.

Omara eyed her phone and saw the time. It was getting late, and she didn't feel like cooking. They had picked Jason up from school, changed, then came to the practice. She was sure her son wouldn't mind getting takeout.

She looked back out onto the field. Things appeared to be wrapping up. Zain and Jason we're headed her way. She smiled at the sight of the two of them. Zain reached over and gently elbowed Jason who laughed at something he said. He tried to push Zain back, but Zain didn't even falter in his steps.

"Hope you weren't too bored over here," Zain said.

"Not at all," she said. She stood and brushed off the back of the skirt of her maxi dress. It was one of her newer ones that had pockets.

"Mom, did you see me?" Jason exclaimed. Her son was sweaty and dirty, but the look on his face was priceless. He had loved every moment out there. He held a football in his hands, a gift from Luca.

"I did. You were amazing." She grinned.

"I had so much fun." He wrapped his arm around her and squeezed her tight.

She caught a whiff of his underarms. The moment he finished eating, he was getting into the shower.

"Can we come back another day?" he asked.

"I don't know. I'm sure we'd have to ask."

He nodded and stepped back from her, his attention once again drawn to the field.

"Did you see me?" Zain grinned, holding out his arms.

She rolled her eyes at the mischievous glint in his eyes.

"Of course I did." She squealed when he wrapped her up in his arms.

He was sweaty, smelled of the outdoors with a slight hint of musk. She should have been grossed out, but interestingly enough, she was aroused by it. Or maybe just the memories of his performance out there. He laughed and dropped a kiss on her lips.

"Not only did I notice you," she said, "but so did your fan club back there."

"I don't care what they think." He chuckled. He wrapped an arm around her waist and kissed the top of her head.

She didn't miss the fact that he didn't even look in the direction of the women. His eyes were only on her. A sliver of satisfaction slid through her at the notion that she was his focus.

"You're the only one I'm trying to impress."

He just knew all the right things to say.

She'd have to reward him.

"Oh, I'm impressed all right." She sighed, a smile

playing on her lips. She leaned into him, loving the feeling of his hard muscles against her. She rose on her tiptoes, trying to whisper in his ear.

He bent down for her.

"I'll show you just how much later."

"Promise?"

"Count on it."

"Jason, let's roll. Come on, Momma." Zain's hand landed a sound smack on her bottom.

She jerked, grinning like a fool. The meat of her ass stung from the swat.

Jesus.

The man could literally do anything to her and her panties became drenched.

Her core clenched as she watched him snatch Jason up and toss him on his shoulder. Her son squealed with laughter while holding on for dear life.

Zain turned around and walked backwards toward the parking lot with his infamous crazy grin on his lips. "You better hurry. We're starving."

Omara shook her head and followed her two crazy guys. It had been a long day, and she would have to admit she was famished, too. She couldn't help but glance over her shoulder.

Yup, the peanut gallery was eyeballing her. They

weren't even trying to hide that they were staring at her.

She tossed them a smile before heading to catch up with Zain and Jason.

Eat your hearts out, ladies.

He's mine.

20

Zain sat back and took Omara and Jason in. Today had to be one of the best days in his life. In just a short span of time, he had started bonding with Jason. The kid was easy to like, and Zain was already making plans for future outings for them. Everything between them seemed natural. Jason had a passion for football. Even Luca had picked up on it. The kid was like a sponge. Anything anyone suggested, he was able to do within minutes. He was a natural, and it would do him some good to play sports and expel some of that energy.

On the way back to Omara's, they'd stopped and grabbed dinner. After Omara's third yawn in the truck, he knew she would be too tired to cook. He, himself, wasn't the best cook, so it only made sense for him to volunteer to pick them something up. Omara had appeared relieved when he'd suggested it.

"If you are done, Jason, Mommy wants you to go get in the shower." Omaha wiped her mouth with her napkin.

The night was beautiful, and they had decided to eat on the small patio in the backyard. It wasn't quite dark yet, the sky a multitude of colors while the sun was almost down.

"Aw, Mom. I was going to ask Zain if we could toss the football around." Jason raised the football Luca had given him.

Zain wouldn't be opposed, but it was betting late, and the kid had school tomorrow. Zain remembered the days of begging his parents to allow him and Luca to stay up late. There had been many nights he and his brother would be out in the yard playing.

"Jason, what did I just say?" Omara's voice lowered slightly in her Mom tone.

Zain bit back a grin.

This tone she used may be to rear her child, but for Zain it was stimulating, and his cock was taking notice. He loved this side of her.

"Just ten minutes?" Jason was really pushing it. His eyes widened, and he poked out his lip. "I'll clean my room tomorrow when I get home from school."

The kid was smooth. Eight years old and already bargaining with his mother.

She glanced over at Zain. He shrugged. He didn't care about tossing around the old pigskin with the kid.

"Five minutes, and that room better be spotless tomorrow."

"Yes!" Jason flew out of his seat.

Zain stood and pushed back from the table. He eyed their trash on the table, about to help clean it.

"I got it. His clock is ticking." Omara chuckled. She stood and gathered their empty containers and napkins.

"Catch." Jason thew the ball to him the second he stepped onto the grass.

Zain smiled and caught the ball.

"Great throw. Who taught you how to throw the ball like that?" Zain asked. It almost had a perfect spiral to it. He was impressed.

"My gym teacher," he said.

Zain frowned. For a kid who loved football as

much as he did, he was shocked he hadn't said his father had taught him.

"You don't do this with your father?" Zain asked.

He sent the ball back to Jason who had to run a little, but he caught it.

"Nah. He's too busy. He usually takes me to my gran's house so I can visit her and my cousins."

So the fucker didn't even spend time with his child when he had him on his weekend? Just dropped Jason off and went about his life? What kind of father did that? What father wouldn't want to take the time to spend with his son? Bond with his son? Zain was extremely close with his father. There was never a doubt in Luca's or Zain's minds that their father loved them. He showed it to them by not only words but actions as well.

"Did your dad play football with you and Luca?" Jason asked. The kid sent the ball flying toward Zain.

Zain jogged over, and thankfully, with his long arms, he kept the ball from going over the fence into the neighbor's yard.

The report Brodie had pulled up was still ingrained in his mind. Zain had basically memorized every time Omara had to call the cops on Derrick.

Or the many emergency room visits he'd sent her to. Why would she hide his behaviors from her family?

And how could a man like Derrick produce a child like Jason?

Any real man would be proud to call Jason son and teach him how to be a man.

Zain certainly would.

"Yeah, he did. He would take us fishing, to the gun range, football and basketball games. We did a lot together." Zain saw the yearning in Jason's eyes.

This kid was starving for his father's attention. Zain held back on his fury when throwing the ball back to him. Derrick didn't deserve a young innocent boy like Jason.

"Do you think Luca would let me come back to watch the practices?" he asked.

"Of course. As long as your mom okays it, your homework is done, and room is clean, I don't see why not."

"You sound like Mom." Jason rolled his eyes.

"Well, she makes sense." Zain laughed. There was no way he was going to fall for Jason's games. He wasn't going to get Zain put in the doghouse. Whatever rules Omara set, that's what they were going to go by.

A few minutes rolled by with them talking and

tossing the ball. Zain glanced at the house. The hairs on the back of his neck stood up. Omara should have been back out by now. He was quite certain five minutes had passed.

"I think it's time to go inside, buddy," Zain said. He threw the ball one last time with Jason catching it. Zain had to hold back a laugh at the way the boy's shoulders slumped.

"Okay. My mom said my pits smell like onions," the kid muttered.

Zain shook his head and clapped him on the shoulder. They walked toward the house. Zain tried to remain normal, not wanting to alarm the kid.

"It'll be okay. We'll have plenty more days to toss the ball around." Zain entered the house first, keeping Jason behind him. He didn't hear Omara.

"Where's Mom?" Jason asked.

"I don't know. Let's look in the front. Maybe someone rang the doorbell."

They walked through the kitchen and made their way to the front. The door was open, and Omara stood on the porch.

She was tense.

Something was wrong, and Zain already had an inkling on who would be causing her distress.

"Stay behind me," Zain ordered. He'd guess the

authoritative sound in his voice told Jason to not argue.

The kid stayed behind him.

Zain approached the door, his gaze narrowing on the figure of the man whose picture and rap sheet he had memorized.

"Look, I can come see my son when I want. You can't stop me," Derrick growled.

"What's going on out here?" Zain asked. A dead calm overcame him. The same one that took control of him when he was out on a SWAT call.

"Who the fuck you got in this house with my son?" Derrick swung his gaze to Zain. His scowl grew as he sized Zain up. He had yet to recognize him.

"You need to lower your voice," Zain warned. He stepped out onto the porch and placed himself between Omara and Derrick. He met Derrick's eyes head-on with a frosty glare of his own. It was taking everything he had to not slam his fist into his face. Jason didn't need to witness such violence.

"Mom—"

"Go back in the house, Jason," Omara said.

"My boy can come greet his father," Derrick barked.

Jason froze in the doorway. Zain could almost

feel the young boy's confusion. It was a shame he'd spent his whole life with this idiot as a father.

"Go back inside, Jason," Zain said softly. He refused to take his eyes off Derrick. He didn't trust the man for nothing.

"Who the fuck is this, Omara?" Derrick stepped to the side, but Zain moved with him. The door slammed shut, footsteps growing distant in the house. "Didn't I tell you that I didn't want no other man around my son?"

"This is none of your business, Derrick," Omara snapped.

"I'm standing right here. Why don't you ask me who I am?" Zain took a step closer to him. He pushed Omara back behind him. She didn't need to answer anything.

"Back up, my man. Get out of my face—"

"Or what? You like picking on women but not face a man?" Zain bit out through clenched teeth.

The muscle in Derrick's jaw ticked away. He tried to step around Zain again, but this time Zain held his hand out, shoving him back. Like most men who abused women, he wouldn't look another man in the eye. He preyed on the weak.

"What you looking at her for?" Zain said. "Don't look at her."

"Get your hand off me." Derrick batted his hand away. A cynical smile grace his lips. He stepped back, holding his hands up. "Fine. You want me to address you. How is she? A good fuck, huh? I taught her everything she knows."

Zain shot his fist out, and it careened into Derrick's jaw. Omara's cry filled the air. Derrick fell back against the building. He pushed off, rubbing his jaw.

"Her pussy is going to get you in fucking trouble," Derrick hollered, his eyes going wild. "You don't know me, fool."

He gave Zain a shove, but Zain was braced and ready. He grabbed Derrick's arm, twisting it around behind his back. He slammed Derrick against the house.

"Derrick, just go!" Omara cried out.

She raced to their side, but Zain was too far gone. The ass wouldn't even address him. He was no man. He'd hurt Omara, the woman he loved.

"What the fuck, man!" Derrick shouted. He turned his head and glared at Zain. "Have you lost your fucking mind? Over this bitch?"

Had he?

Fuck, yeah.

Not only had he come to the realization that he

loved Omara, he knew he would go to any lengths to make sure she and Jason were safe.

Derrick tried to buck him off, but Zain leaned his full weight on him.

"You haven't even begun to see how crazy I can get," Zain snapped.

Derrick stared at him. His eyes widened, recognition setting in, and Zain nodded.

The fucker remembered him.

"Wait a damn minute. You're that cop," Derrick wheezed. He turned toward Omara. "You're fucking a cop?"

"So you remember me now. Didn't I tell you not to look at her?" Zain growled. "Had I known who you were at that time, I would have run you in that day."

His gut had been to take him in anyway, even though the woman swore she didn't want to press charges. Had he and Jones arrested him that day, they may have been able to prevent him from going back to that house and putting that poor woman in the hospital.

"What is he talking about? You've met before?" Omara gasped. She rested a hand on Zain's arm and tried to pull him off Derrick. "Let him go."

"You're going to break my arm," Derrick howled.

Zain twisted it more, wanting to hear the snap. For all the pain Derrick had caused Omara, it would be no less than he deserved.

"Why should I? You didn't care about all the times you hit on Omara, sent her to the emergency room. She's the mother of your fucking child, and that's how you treat her? That's how you treat all women?"

He shoved Derrick's arm higher, eliciting a scream from him.

"Zain." Omara yanked on him harder. Tears rolling down her face. "Please stop. People are looking."

Zain released him. It was only because of Omara that he did. He took a step back away from Derrick who turned around, cradling his arm.

"Get the fuck out of here," Zain growled. His chest rose and fell. Adrenaline raced through him. His hands were balled into fists he wanted to pound in Derrick's face. That calmness he always depended on was gone. Now, he felt like a savage, ready to tear into Derrick.

"You're fucking crazy," Derrick muttered. He brushed passed Zain and took the stairs. He stopped in the middle of the yard and spun around, still cradling the arm.

Omara moved to Zain's side. He slid a possessive arm around her, holding her close. She leaned into him, resting her hand on his abdomen.

"You're going to pay for this! You can't keep me from my son, bitch," Derrick shouted, walking backward.

Zain released Omara with a growl and took a step down the first stair.

"Call her a bitch one more time," Zain snarled.

Omara snatched his arm, tugging him back. A few neighbors were out on their porches openly watching the fiasco. Derrick jogged over to his black sedan and got in. The engine roared to life, the tires squealing as he put it in reverse. Zain stared at the car until it was out of sight.

He ignored the neighbors' stares and went back onto the porch. Unable to resist, he pulled her to him. He cupped her face, wiping the tears from her cheeks. The urge to follow Derrick and beat him to a pulp was strong for him putting tears on her face.

"Are you okay?" he asked.

She nodded and took his hand in hers.

"Let's go back inside. I'm not sure what Jason saw and heard." She sniffed, turning and guiding them into the house.

There was no sign of Jason. Zain shut the door,

releasing her hand as she jogged through the house and disappeared down the hall.

Zain scraped a hand along his face, trying to get his emotions together. He didn't want Jason to see him in this state. He took a seat on the couch, sitting forward to rest his forearms on his legs. He blew out a deep breath, hating for Omara to see him like that, but the urge to defend her had been strong. Footsteps padded their way to him. He glanced up. Omara guided Jason into the room.

"Zain, are you okay?" Jason asked, dashing toward him.

Zain stood and caught the kid in his arms. Jason's small arms wrapped around his waist.

"Of course I am, bud." Zain ran a hand down Jason's back. He flicked his gaze to Omara who was brushing tears from her face.

"I don't like when my dad is mean and yelling," Jason mumbled. He lifted his head, and Zain's heart cracked. "I don't like when he makes Mommy cry or hurts her."

Omara covered her hand with her mouth, squeezing her eyes shut. She fell against the wall, her body shaking from the soundless cries. Zain rested a hand on Jason's shoulder and looked him in the eye.

"Your father will never make your mommy cry

or hurt her again. I promise." This was one promise Zain was going to keep for certain.

Omara disappeared down the hall again, he was sure to get herself composed.

"I'm here and I will keep her safe," Zain said.

Jason studied him and nodded. He threw his arms around Zain again and squeezed.

"I wish you could be my dad."

Zain had to lock his knees together. The air escaped his lungs. He squeezed his own eyes shut, feeling a burn. He tightened his hold around Jason. He didn't know when, but the kid had crawled into his heart right along with his mother.

"Jason, honey. Mommy started your shower." Omara returned. Her eyes were puffy and red, but she was no longer crying.

"Okay." Jason slipped from Zain's hold and ran off down the hall, leaving Zain to stare off after him.

He blinked and looked at Omara. He held his arms open, and she flew across the room into them. They held each other for what seemed like eternity.

"Are you okay?" Zain murmured, his lips brushing her hair.

"Yeah. I'm sorry you're being dragged into this mess."

"Don't be. You belong to me, and I protect what's mine. That goes for you and Jason."

She lifted her head and stared at him. She blinked a few times. A small smile graced Zain's lips.

He ran a hand along her cheek. "You two are a package, and I accept that. He's great kid with an unfortunate ass for a father."

He leaned down and kissed her. Her lips parted for him. The kiss was soft but full of passion. They broke apart, her hands clutching his shirt.

"Will you stay with us tonight?" Her lips, swollen from the kiss, drew him back to them.

He pressed a small kiss to them. "Of course."

Her eyes closed, and she leaned her forehead on his chest. He rubbed her back, dropping a kiss to the top of her head.

"I don't know what to do. He's supposed to pick Jason up this Friday for his weekend."

"Do you have to let him go with him?"

"Yeah. He can file a contempt of court if I don't." She looked torn on what to do.

Zain didn't like the feeling of helplessness that filled him.

"But what happens if he doesn't show?" he asked.

"I let it go, because I just don't care if he misses

his time with Jason." She shrugged. "Maybe I should have done the same thing and filed with the courts, but honestly, I just want to be left alone. I don't want to give him a reason to come after me."

Zain gathered her close, resting his chin on top of her head.

"If he hasn't hurt Jason before then he's right. We can't keep him from his son, but I will be here when he comes to pick him up."

Omara's body relaxed at his offer. There was no way he was letting her face Derrick alone again.

21

Omara finished tidying up her area at the shop. Her last client had recently left. Since Derrick was picking Jason up tomorrow for his weekend, she wanted to spend a little extra time with Jason before he left. She always cut her Thursday's short for this exact purpose. Normally, she'd let him pick a fast-food restaurant for dinner, get ice cream, then go watch a movie or show of his choice.

She looked forward to these days. Zain was working the evening shift, so he wouldn't be joining them. He and Jordan had been busy at work. They'd gone out on multiple calls this week, but today, he was riding patrol.

She smiled thinking of how quick Jason had

taken to Zain. It wasn't a surprise. Zain was a great guy, and she would have to admit she had feelings for him already.

Their relationship hadn't started off in the traditional manner, but it had blossomed into so much.

A ridiculous grin played on her lips.

The night after Derrick had left, Zain had made love to her. It had been different. They both had an urgency to them that had been explosive. More so than it normally was. There were no bad dreams that night. She'd fallen into a rest-filled sleep in the circle of his arms.

It was there she felt the safest.

Nothing could hurt her while Zain was there.

She'd been lulled to sleep by exhaustion and the sound of his steady heartbeat. She wished they could fall asleep like that every night.

She blew out a deep breath and bent down to sweep up the hair in the dustpan.

Was it too soon to mention moving in together?

She must be going crazy. They hadn't even been together that long, and here she was, thinking of their future.

"I want to know who is putting that silly smile on your face," Sadie asked. She rested a hand on her hip with a suspicious look.

Omara froze in place. Had she been that obvious?

"None of your business," Omara quipped.

"Oooohhhh! So there is someone." Sadie cackled. She faced the salon. "Y'all hear that. There is someone!"

"Pay up, ladies," Alicia spun in a circle, holding her hand out.

Groans went around the room.

"Excuse me?" Omara chuckled. She glanced at everyone grinning. Had they been talking about her behind her back?

"Wait. We don't pay up yet. The bet was who it was," Kelsey shouted from the wash station where she was working on a client.

Omara's mouth dropped open, and she stared at her intern.

Kelsey saw her look and mouthed, "I'm sorry."

"Seriously, ladies." Omara cracked up. What was she going to do with these girls?

"Hey, we notice things, and you have been glowing." Shannon snickered. Her pink hair was pulled up into a high messy bun. She was in the midst of flat-ironing her customer's hair. "My money is on that sexy-ass cop who took her to the back that day."

The salon went into an uproar with laughter

and theories. Omara giggled and went over to discard the trash she had swept up. She put up the broom and dustpan before heading back to her station.

"Well, I will say this," Omara began.

The room fell quiet with all eyes on her.

She grinned. "I don't kiss and tell."

"It was the cop," they echoed.

Omara shook her head. Her back pocket vibrated. She pulled her phone out and saw it was Jason's school calling.

"I'll be back. I've got to take this." She spun on her heel and jogged into her office. She swiped her finger across the screen to answer. "Hello?"

"Hello, this is Principal Coleman from Rosemond Elementary. Is this Ms. Knight?"

"Yes, this is she." Omara took a seat in her chair. She frowned, unsure why the principal was calling. She hoped Jason hadn't got into trouble at school. Most times when the school called, it was his teacher notifying her of his excessive talking. The last time it happened, he had been banned from his video game for three days.

He didn't get out of school for another hour, but since it was the principal calling, she was a little worried.

"How can I help you, Mrs. Coleman?" Omara asked.

"I'm sorry to bother you, but I wanted to touch base with you. Mr. Allen showed up at the school and picked Jason up early."

Omara froze. Derrick did what?

"Um, okay." Omara was at a loss for words. This was unusual for Derrick. She would have to call him.

"When Mr. Allen was here, we had informed him that since you were the primary parent and hadn't notified us that he was coming to pick Jason up, we wanted to call you first to confirm. Mr. Allen became belligerent and very inappropriate."

"I'm so sorry, Mrs. Coleman. Jason's father can be very difficult to work with." Omara was growing more worried by the moment. What was Derrick thinking? He should have called her first to discuss, but who was she kidding? Derrick did what he wanted.

"I hated to let Jason go with him with the way he was crying—"

"Say again?" Omaha interjected.

"Jason kept saying he didn't want to go with his father. We called school security on him, but they were unable to detain him. Ms. Knight, I'm not sure of Mr. Allen's mindset. I'm worried—"

"Wait a minute. If you were questioning if my son would be safe with his father, you still let him go with him?" Her voice ended in a shriek. She stood and paced her office.

"I was thinking of calling the police but wanted to speak with you first."

"You know what? I'll call Derrick myself, ma'am," Omara said.

"Okay. If you need anything from us, please let us know," Mrs. Coleman offered.

Omara didn't respond but disconnected the call.

Blowing out a deep breath, she pulled up Derrick's number and hit dial. It rang and rang with no answer. Her hands shook as she hung up and tried him again.

Nothing.

Omara snagged her purse from her desk and flew out of the room. She stopped to lock the door before rushing back out into the salon. She walked over to Sadie who was scheduled to stay late to lock up since Omara was leaving early.

"Hey, Sadie. I'm leaving now."

"Everything good?" Sadie asked. She must have seen the look in Omara's eyes. Her smile disappeared, and genuine concern appeared. She paused working on her client's hair and faced her.

"I'm not sure. Derrick picked Jason up today. The school called, concerned, and he's not answering his phone."

"Go. The shop will be fine." Sadie waved her away.

"Thanks." Omara spun on her heel and made her way down the back hall where the door that led to the rear parking lot was. She stepped outside and quickly arrived at her car.

She drove home, repeatedly calling Derrick. By the time she arrived at her house, he still hadn't answered. She raced into her home, her body trembling.

Dropping her purse on the couch, she called Derrick one more time.

"What the fuck do you want?" Derrick's harsh tone greeted her.

"What is going on?" she screamed into the phone. "You're not supposed to get him until—"

"Watch your tone, Omara. You got yourself a cop between your thighs and you think you can talk to me any kind of way?"

"Derrick, where are you?" She was trying not to panic. Why did he care who she was sleeping with? He had fucked around on her with so many women it shouldn't even matter.

But Derrick was a jealous man and always had been.

"That's none of your business. I've told you I don't want other men around my son, and you've been sleeping with that cop in the same house as my son. Whoring yourself out for anyone."

"What I do is none of—"

"You aren't fit to be a mother," Derrick snarled.

Ice filled Omara's veins. Her heart all but leaped into her throat.

"You know that's not true," she whispered.

"You never learn, Omara. Looks like I'm going to have to teach you a lesson. I'm keeping the boy."

"You can't do that," Omara cried out. She swallowed around the lump in her throat, shaking her head. Her vision blurred from the unshed tears that threatened to fall. She would alert the courts on what he was doing. "The judge will hold—"

"You think a piece of paper will keep me from my son?" he snarled.

Jason's tiny voice was in the background. He sounded scared and worried. Her heart ached for her son. She hated when he had to see his father lose it.

"Don't worry about my son," Derrick said. "He's mine."

The line went dead.

She fell to her knees, a loud wailing filling her ears. It wasn't until she inhaled that she realized it was coming from her. She stared down at her phone in disbelief. She hit Derrick's number again, desperate to do anything to get her child back. This just wasn't happening. He had no right to take her child away.

"Come on, answer, dammit!" She screamed. The call went straight to voicemail. She hung up and repeated. Over and over again, but the call didn't go through.

Warm tears streaked her face.

She scrubbed it with the back of her hand. She stared at her cell, needing to phone for help.

Who should she call?

Jordan or Zain?

ZAIN STROLLED out of the oversized garage where he parked the BEAR. SWAT had been called out to serve a search warrant. It was a simple job that hadn't taken long. It definitely beat riding around in a patrol car.

He followed his team out of the garage. Conversations were light, a few jokes being cast. No one had got injured, no bad guys had to be shot. Just a few arrests and confiscating some drugs was all in a day's work.

"Next Wednesday, I scheduled our team training. At that time, Dec and I will complete evaluations. You'll be assigned one peer evaluation to complete," Mac said.

Zain groaned along with everyone else. Peer reviews sucked. No one liked having to evaluate one of their coworkers. To Zain, it was stupid. If he had a problem with the way someone did something, he'd tell them then so it could be corrected. He'd expect the same from anyone else if he was doing something wrong.

"Give me Zain. I'll write up a very colorful evaluation." Iker slapped him on the back.

"I don't know if I trust what you would say." Zain snickered.

"You don't get a say. Who you will get will be drawn randomly," Mac said. He pushed his shades to the top of his head. "Good job today, men."

"Excuse me?" Jordan interjected.

"Team," Mac corrected, giving her a nod.

Zain's pocket buzzed. He ignored the call, promising to look at it when they were done here. He was sure Omara and Jason were on their mother-son date. She was a little apprehensive about Jason going with Derrick this weekend. After the other day, Zain didn't want Jason to go either, but he had to. His phone went silent, and he focused back on the topic being discussed.

"The conference room is reserved. The one with the big table in the middle," Brodie said. "I can have the hearing up on the television screens in there for us to watch."

Zain's phone vibrated again. He frowned and dug his phone out. He glanced down at the screen and saw Omara's name flash on the screen.

He slid his finger across the glass to answer. He put the phone up to his ear and, spinning around, took a few steps away.

"Hey, babe. What's up?" he asked.

"Zain."

Omara's voice sent a dead chill through him. He gripped his phone, her pain hitting him.

"What's wrong?" He turned and was met with Jordan's gaze.

As if sensing something was wrong, she beelined to him.

"Jason," Omara hiccuped.

The pit of his stomach gave way. She was openly

sobbing, and he had a hard time making out her words.

"Baby, slow down. What's wrong with Jason?" Now he had the entire squad's attention. All eyes were on him.

Jordan stood in front of him, her lips pressed into a thin line.

Omara quieted. A sniff was all he heard.

"He took Jason."

He didn't even have to ask who the "he" was that she spoke of.

She brought him up to date on what had happened. His hand tightened on his phone. The son of a bitch was going to pay.

"I'm on my way," he growled.

"We're on our way," Jordan snapped.

"What's going on?" Mac demanded.

"Derrick went and picked Jason up from school today. He's not giving him back." Zain snatched off his helmet and slid a hand through his hair. He should have broken that fucker's arm.

"That son of a bitch." Jordan turned to him. "Who's driving?"

"I will." Zain spun around and headed toward the employee parking lot with Jordan at his side.

"Roman! Knight!"

They paused and spun around at Mac's shout.

The sergeant scowled at them, folding his arms. "You weren't dismissed yet," Mac said.

"Permission to be dismissed, sir?" Zain raised an eyebrow. He didn't have time for this shit. Omara needed him.

Mac walked over to them, eyeing them with his cold, hard glare.

"You think we're letting you go alone?" Mac's voice dropped eerily low. He narrowed his eyes on them. "What's Omara's address?"

Zain relaxed slightly. Of course his team would jump in for support.

"Yeah, if there is going to be some ass-kicking, we're in." Iker arrived at Mac's side.

His friend gave him a nod, and that was all Zain needed to see. The rest of the team stood behind them with determined expressions. Zain gave them an appreciative nod.

"I'll text it to you," Jordan said.

"Let's roll." Zain backed away before spinning on his heel. He couldn't afford any more delays. His woman needed him.

ZAIN STALKED up the stairs to Omara's house. The door flew open before he got onto the porch. Omara flew out of the house and into his arms. Her body trembled as the sobs overtook her. Zain's arms folded around her.

"I'm here," he murmured, his lips brushing her hair.

Jordan arrived at his side, her murderous expression matching his mood. The sounds of doors slamming echoed behind them. Omara lifted her head, and he cupped her cheek.

"I want my baby back." Her voice broke.

Her eyes were bloodshot, and his rage festered. He would get Jason back, and Derrick would pay. This would be the last time he brought tears to Omara's eyes. This was one promise Zain was going to keep. Her tears were breaking him.

"Please, I need him back with me. I need to feel him in my arms."

"We're going to get him back, sis." Jordan rested a hand on Omara's shoulder.

"Please," Omara whispered, leaning her head on his chest.

Zain kept his arm around her, turning to see his team standing at the edge of her walkway. They hadn't changed from their gear they had worn out on the call. They made a formidable picture, and they all meant business.

Omara glanced over at them, her eyes widening.

"What are they doing here?" she asked.

"We're here to help," Mac announced. He stepped forward and motioned to the house. "Let's go inside so we can talk."

Zain leaned over and opened the door, guiding Omara in. They went into the living room with everyone crowding around. Zain sat next to Omara on the couch, while Jordan perched on the coffee table in front of her.

"I know this will be hard, but tell us exactly what happened," Zain said softly.

"I was at work and got a call from the principal," she began.

The room was eerily quiet as she shared her conversation with a Mrs. Coleman. Zain's jaw clenched, hearing how Jason had been crying, not wanting to go with his father. She went on to the conversation with Derrick.

Zain had to hold back a growl.

Her hand reached out for Zain's. He took it and cradled it between both of his.

"Call it in." Mac glanced over at Declan. "We'll go ahead and have them issue an amber alert now. It sounds like Derrick isn't stable." His face softened slightly. "We're going to get him back, Omara. None of us will rest until your son is back home."

Confirmation from the group went around the room.

"I need Derrick's cell phone number, and if you can give me the description of his car and license plate number. I want to cross-reference it with what is in the system," Brodie said. He pulled his laptop out of his duffle bag.

Mac motioned for Zain.

"I'll be right back. Give Brodie as much information as you can. He's a whiz at finding anything," Zain murmured. He kissed her on the cheek and followed Mac into the kitchen.

Iker joined them, leaning against the doorjamb.

"Do you think this Derrick character will hurt his son?" Mac asked. He rested back on the counter.

"Honestly, I can't answer that. You know the type of shit we've seen." Zain blew out a deep breath. Being a cop exposed them all to some fucked-up shit. He prayed Derrick really loved his son and wouldn't hurt him. "But he's put his hands on Omara one too many times. There's no telling what he will do. He's pissed at her. He was here the other day and—" He paused.

"And what happened?" Iker asked.

"There was an altercation." Zain had put it lightly.

"I hope that means you beat the shit out of him." Iker arched an eyebrow.

Mac grunted.

"Close. I should have broken his fucking arm." Zain jammed a hand through his hair. If only he had listened to his gut and not Omara. He would have had some satisfaction in knowing he'd done some damage. "He made some threats, and I should have taken them more seriously."

"Well now, he's got our attention, and there will be no pulling back this time." Mac scowled. He pushed off the counter. "We're going to hunt this motherfucker down."

22

Omara felt as if she watched her life from the outside. She was numb, cold, and empty. She needed to feel Jason in her arms. She wanted to nuzzle him and tickle him until he screamed with laughter. She even wanted to smell his funky armpits.

She just wanted her baby back.

There were so many people in her home. Declan had called in the cavalry. She'd spoken with a few detectives and given her statements multiple times. Her gaze landed on Zain in the dining room with Brodie and some other people she didn't know.

It was completely overwhelming. She sat on couch, unable to believe all of this was happening. How had her life turned upside down?

"Here, you need to drink something."

She looked up. Jordan held out a hot mug with steam rising from it.

"I'm not thirsty." Omara sniffed.

"I'm not asking." Jordan forced it into her hands.

Her sister flopped down on the couch next to her. She'd finally taken off her ballistics vest and gear. It wasn't often Omara saw Jordan in her full SWAT getup. Omara did have to admit, she was impressed to see her sister in her official uniform. Now Jordan was more relaxed, but she'd kept her badge on the chain around her neck, and her gun holster was still on her hip.

Omara took a sip of the drink and grimaced. "What is this?"

"My version of a hot toddy," Jordan replied. She rubbed Omara's knee.

"I can't drink this. I need to keep a level head."

"Drink it." Jordan hit her with a hard gaze.

Omara stared at her before taking another sip. It was strong, and there was plenty of alcohol in the mug.

"I'm afraid," Omara murmured, holding the mug to her lips. She stared down at it, unable to look Jordan in the eyes. She felt so weak, so defeated. She wished she was as strong as Jordan and was able to stand up to Derrick. Had she had any type of backbone, Derrick wouldn't treat her the way he did.

"I am, too." Jordan scooted closer to her and took her hand in hers.

They entwined their fingers together.

"This is a total different ball park," Jordan said. "Even I'm shocked Derrick would go this far, but we don't know the state of mind he's in. We have to stay positive."

Omara nodded. She understood what her sister was trying to say. Derrick was unraveling, and there was no telling where his mind was. She just prayed that he loved his son and would never do anything to harm him.

"I've never heard you mention that you were scared of something before," Omara said softly. She squeezed Jordan's hand.

"There's been plenty of times I've been afraid," Jordan admitted.

"Yeah? Like when?" Omara asked.

Curiosity was getting the best of her. Jordan always met her battles head-on. Her entire life she'd been the "kick ass first, take names later" type of girl.

"Well, the first time was when my little sister moved out of the state to go with some dude she was seeing." Jordan glanced over at her.

Omara's breath stalled. She remembered Jordan trying to talk her out of it. She hadn't liked Derrick then, but Omara was "in love" and needed to be with him.

"I think the most scared I've ever been was when I began to suspect he was putting his hands on you. I didn't want you to become a statistic."

"Oh, Jordan." Omara sighed. She leaned forward, resting her head against Jordan's. "I'm so sorry."

"There's nothing you have to apologize for. This is not your fault at all." Jordan squeezed her hand tight.

Omara felt the love of her older sibling seeping into her pores.

"You are the strongest person I know," Jordan said, "and I don't know how you lived through what you have." She lifted her head. A lone tear slipped down her cheek.

"Me?" Omara's voice squeaked. She glanced around. No one was paying them any attention.

"Yeah. You. I'm a fighter, but you are a survivor. It takes more balls to survive and persevere." Jordan reached up and wiped her face. "And I now I'm scared that my nephew is in the hands of that lunatic."

"Should I call Derrick's mother?" Omara wondered aloud. She hadn't spoken with Mrs. Allen in a while, and they were on good terms. The woman always teased her, stating that Derrick had let her get away. The only problem Omara had with her was that she turned a blind eye to what her son did to Omara.

"I believe the guys are a step ahead of you. They were going to send patrol cars to all of his known hangouts, family members' homes, and friends."

Omara nodded, glad they were all over it. She didn't feel as if she was doing anything. Her son was out there. He needed her. Her heart broke again at the thought of Jason crying because he didn't want to go with his father. Had he been crying for her?

"I feel like I should be doing more than just sitting here drinking." She glanced down at the mug still in her hand.

"Take another sip." Jordan pointed to the mug. "We have everything covered."

Omara grimaced again once she took another taste. Warmth spread through her. It did help her feel slightly better. Her body had been so cold, and it was helping thaw her out.

She glanced over at Zain who was bent over looking at something on Brodie's computer. As if sensing her eyes on him, he glanced up. Their gazes held for a moment.

"He really likes you," Jordan murmured.

"I really like him, too." Omara smiled. She took another sip of her drink, feeling herself relax a little more. "He makes me happy."

"He'd better." Jordan's attention was caught by Ash's. She stood and patted Omara on the knee. "I'll be right back."

Omara nodded, then tilted back the cup and drank more of it. The warmth spread throughout her body. Maybe Jordan was right and she needed this. Unable to sit any longer, she stood and made her way over to Zain.

"You okay, baby?" he asked, a frown forming on his face.

The room tilted slightly, but she righted herself.

"Yeah. I think my sister is trying to get me drunk so I won't worry," she muttered.

He took the cup from her and sniffed it. He jerked his head back from it.

"You don't need this." He sat it on the table and brought her into his side. "I'm glad you came over here. We are trying to track Derrick's phone. Right now, it has to be off, but the second he turns it on, we'll be able to track him down."

"Okay. I just mentioned to Jordan, but what about his mom? Maybe I should go over there and speak with her?" she offered. Hope filled her. This would give her something to do.

"We've already dispatched a car over there. I want you to stay here and make sure that we're ready for Jason to come home." He rubbed her shoulder and dropped a kiss to her head.

"Zain, she'll talk to me. She's not going to give Derrick up." She shook her head.

The woman wouldn't rat her son out to the police, but she would speak with Omara. If she could make the woman see that Jason may be in danger, she would talk. That woman loved her grandson.

"No, we can't. Let the police do their jobs. This is an official investigation, and we need you to remain home for Jason." His voice softened.

Omara pressed her lips together, wanting to argue. She should be out there looking for her son.

"We are going bring him home," he said.

"I trust you," she whispered.

She glanced around the table at Brodie and Myles who were sitting next to each other. Mac and Declan were speaking with a couple of cops she didn't know in the foyer. Iker, Jordan, and Ash were in the kitchen talking.

Her house had once been a cozy, homey place of comfort. Now it was a base of operations for a SWAT mission. The scene was out of a movie. Computers, equipment, plans being discussed and drawn up, men with big guns on their hips—even her man. Zain had taken his bulletproof SWAT vest off, but he still had his weapons and utility belt on. His dark curly hair was tousled from him running his fingers through it. The intensity in his eyes took her breath away.

Had it been any other circumstance, she would have joked about how sexy he looked in uniform and tried to seduce him in her room.

"What have you found so far?" she asked.

"Plenty on your ex that we are sure you had no idea about," Brodie muttered. He typed out a few commands on his computer. "For starters, he was just put on unpaid leave from the company he works for due to his most recent arrest. It would seem he's been arrested quite a few times this year."

"What?" Omara grew tense. She hadn't heard of any of that. Anytime he cancelled his weekend with Jason, he never shared with her why until the last time when he'd mentioned moving. She honestly wasn't surprised. There was nothing special about her to make her the only woman he'd put his hands on. That was just the type of man he was. He loved having power over a small female and causing pain.

"He's in gambling debt and owes some bad people money, apparently has a drinking problem, some outstanding tickets he hasn't paid, and he hasn't filed his taxes in the last four years." Brodie glanced up at her.

"And you can tell all of that by searching the internet?" Omara asked, amazed. Why wasn't any of that brought up during their court hearings for custody?

"Let's just say Brodie has friends in high places who get him toys and access the common cop won't have." Zain chuckled. He tightened his hold on her and glanced down at her. "Has he been paying his child support?"

"Yeah, he's never missed a payment," she said.

That was the only good quality about Derrick. He went to work, and his child support was paid on time. Not that it was much, but every little bit she got from him helped. She never complained. She just made it work. She had worked hard to make her shop a success. Derrick may gripe and moan about the payments, threaten her with it, but it never failed to deposit into her bank account.

"Listen up," Mac announced. His deep voice was authoritative, and the room instantly died down.

Omara glanced around. Each man—and Jordan —had a look of respect in their eyes when addressing the sergeant.

The rest of the team joined them in her small dining room.

"I just got off the phone with the captain. He actually thanked me for notifying him of our current mission ahead of time."

Chuckles went around the room. Omara wasn't sure why that was funny. Didn't the captain know everything his SWAT team was involved in?

"I think this might be the first," Iker muttered, leaning back against the wall.

"Anyway, he gives his full support and access to all resources. We are to keep him up to date on the events." Mac's gaze landed on Omara. "We have the full backing of the CPD. There is now a full-blown manhunt for Derrick. We will find him."

OMARA JERKED awake at the feeling of warm arms encircling her, hefting her into the air.

"What—" She blinked and was met by familiar hazel eyes, unruly hair, and a matching beard.

"Come on, babe. Go to bed." Zain carried her out of the living room.

"No. I was up. I was just resting my eyes for a moment," she argued. Her eyes had only been closed for a mere second. She had been watching the local news. Word had broken about Derrick taking Jason. The amber alert had gone out around the state. It was only a matter of time until someone saw something and reported it. Omara was growing hopeful that there was a good Samaritan out there.

"Baby, you were doing that little snore thing you do when you're sleep." He nudged her bedroom door open with his foot.

"I need to be awake. If you are, then so am I. What if you leave to go after Derrick?" she asked. Fear crept into her. She didn't want to miss anything.

"Then I'll wake you. We aren't going to leave you alone." He lowered her onto the bed.

She slid around to rest her feet on the floor.

"Zain, I need to feel like I'm doing something. I

feel helpless right now. My child is out there some-where, needing me. What if he's hurt? What if he—"

"Shhh..." Zain rested a finger on her lips. He knelt on the floor before her and guided her head to his. He leaned his forehead against hers. "It's going to be all right. We are going find him and bring Jason back to you. But I need you to be fully rested so that when he comes home, you will have energy to take care of him. It won't do Jason any good if you can barely keep your eyes open."

She pulled back and stared at him. He reached up and cupped her face. He popped a soft kiss on her lips.

"Do you trust me?" His voice lowered.

She gave a nod. He knew she did.

Her body melted against him. Zain's embrace was all she needed. She slid her arms around his neck and held on tight.

"I just want my baby back. I want us to all be together again."

"I want that, too. I need both you and Jason in my life," Zain admitted. He cupped her face in his hands. The intensity in his eyes burned bright. "I wasn't truly living until the both of you entered my world."

"Oh, Zain." She tugged him to her, offering her

lips to him.

The kiss was slow, sensual, and full of heat. Her fingers threaded themselves in his soft curls she loved so much. A slight protest escaped her when he backed away from her.

He stood and went over to her dresser and found a comfortable nightshirt for her. He helped her out of her clothes. Tears formed in her eyes at the delicate way he was caring for her. Her big, bad SWAT officer was gentle and loving. She was soon dressed in her nightshirt and tucked away in the bed.

"Will you lie with me?" she asked, brushing her hair away from her face. Omara couldn't care less that her hair wasn't wrapped. It was the least of her worries at the moment. She was already feeling the pull of sleep. Exhaustion was overtaking her. She'd been up early that day since she had wanted to leave work early.

"Of course." Zain kicked his boots off and climbed on top of the blankets.

He turned on his side, allowing her to crawl into the cradle of his arms. She snuggled close, burying her face into the crook of his neck. She inhaled sharply and loved the faint scent of his cologne that remained, and the slight hint of musk that signaled he was all man. His strong arms comforted her.

As always, she felt safe when he held her.

"How about when this all is over, I take you and Jason away for a weekend. We can drive down to the beach. Just the three of us." His warm breath brushed her forehead.

Zain's fingers trailed along her back, sending a shiver through her.

She heard his unspoken words.

As a family.

"That sounds good. Jason loves the ocean," she murmured. Her eyes fluttered closed. Images of sandy beaches and the bright-blue ocean came to mind. It had been a while since she'd taken him to the coast where they could have some time to relax. That sounded wonderful. She would need to purchase herself a new bathing suit. Maybe they could rent a house on the beach. Breakfast out on a veranda overlooking the waves crashing against the coast was a dream way to spend a lazy morning.

A weekend away would be perfect.

She inhaled sharply, her body relaxing. She allowed sleep to take a hold of her.

The last image she saw was Zain and Jason tossing a football on the beach. A smile formed on her lips.

Her son would love that.

23

Zain paced the living room. He couldn't let morning come and they had no answer for Omara. The woman was tortured by the fact that her son was with his deranged father. There was no telling if Derrick was high on drugs or what was going through his mind when he'd decided to take the boy.

Zain's hand clenched into a fist. He was going to take great pleasure crashing it into the jerk's face again. Only this time, he wasn't going to stop.

"Bingo," Brodie announced. "That didn't take long."

Zain swung around and stalked over to the dining table.

"What have you got?" Zain asked.

The group converged into the dining room. Only SWAT was left in the house. Two patrol cars sat out on the street in front to ward off the media. They were only fed what was needed to get the story out into the public. A few camera crews sat outside, wanting an interview with Omara, but Zain wasn't having that. She had already been through too much.

"Derrick has turned his cell phone on." Brodie grinned. His fingers flew across the keyboard.

Zain watched a blip appear on a map.

"Is that him?" Zain jerked his head in a nod.

"Yup, and he's not near any of his known locations. He was at least smart in that aspect." Brodie chuckled. A minute later, and he sat back from the table. "Voila. Now that's how you track someone down."

"Where?" Mac demanded.

"This must have been a job site he was working on. It's a brand-new subdivision of homes. They aren't complete yet. It looks as if his company had won the lead contract to build. I can't zero in on which house he's in, but he's there."

The doorbell sounded. The room froze.

"It has to be my parents. I called them hours ago. I didn't want them to catch word of Jason missing on the news," Jordan said. She jogged out of the dining room.

Zain hated he hadn't thought about Omara calling her parents.

He hated that the first time he would get to meet them would be under these circumstances.

Frantic voices came from the foyer with Jordan's lower one trying to calm them down.

"Go, Zain. We'll devise a plan then catch you and Jordan up," Declan said.

Zain didn't wait twice to be told. He flew out of the room and headed in the direction of the voices. He came upon a handsome couple. Mrs. Knight was the exact replication of what Omara would look like in about twenty years. She was a refined woman, her salt-and-pepper hair pulled back into a low bun. Her big brown eyes were the mirror of Omara and Jordan. Mr. Knight was tall, fit for a man his age, and his eyes narrowed in on Zain as he approached them.

"Mom and Dad, this is Zain. He's one of my partners on SWAT." Jordan quickly made the introductions. "And he's Omara's boyfriend."

Their eyes widened. Mr. Knight eyed him with a different light in his eyes.

"Is that so?" Mr. Knight said. He offered his

hand to Zain who took it in a firm shake. "Well then, you can call me Cecil."

"And I'm Irene." The older woman shook his hand, a small smile on her lips.

"I'm so sorry we have to meet under these circumstances," Zain said. He made a promise for when this was over to have them and his parents over for dinner so the two families could meet under pleasant circumstances. Omara would love to have their families together.

"I've sort of heard about you." Mrs. Knight sniffed. She stood to her full height, which was the same as Omara's. That smirk was definitely Omara's. It was eerie how much her daughters resembled her.

"Oh?" he asked, raising his eyebrow.

"Just ask Omara how she has you listed in her phone." The woman brushed past him. She went into the living room with Jordan and Mr. Knight right behind her.

Zain was completely confused by her comment.

What the hell did that mean?

Jordan introduced the entire team to the Knights before they disappeared into Omara's bedroom. She had been asleep for a few hours. Even though she had fought it at first, her eyes had closed pretty fast when Zain had held her. He had wanted to stay in the bed with her and just keep her near him, but he had to return out there with the others in the search for Jason.

Zain marched to the dining room where the plans were underway.

"There are a total of four hours so far, but only two of them that are almost completed. The other two are only framed. We don't want to alert him that we're coming," Mac said. "There is nothing but woods surrounding the location. We don't want to turn this into a wild goose chase through the woods. Let's do what we do best. I'm calling in the K9s to assist on this."

"K9? You think we'll really need them?" Declan asked.

"On the off chance we have to go into the woods, I'd rather have them there already," Mac said. "Officers Rhys and Honor will be on site for assistance."

"I'm pulling up the blueprints of the homes. They are pretty standard," Brodie said.

Zain smoothed a hand along his face. What kind of man would kidnap his son then go hole up in an unfinished home that probably didn't even have running water or electricity?

"Why didn't he leave the city? Why stay and

hole up in a house on the outskirts of town?" Myles asked as if reading Zain's thoughts.

"Who knows. The only thing I can think of was he got wind of the amber alert and decided to lie low until it blows over," Ash said. "When these alerts go out, their information is plastered everywhere."

"Let's pack up and be ready to roll in ten," Mac announced.

Nods went around. Mac motioned for Zain to follow him. They stepped into the living room.

"The patrols will stay here with Omara. I already know Jordan is not going to sit this one out."

"You might as well not even ask her," Zain agreed.

"Between her parents being here and the officers outside, they should be fine. I doubt Allen will bring himself here."

"I'll go update them on what's going on." Zain slapped Mac on the shoulder and hurried down the hall toward Omara's bedroom. He gave a warning knock then opened the door. "May I come in?"

"Of course you may, dear." Mrs. Knight waved him in.

He stepped inside then closed the door behind him. Omara was awake, sitting on the side of her bed next to her mother while Jordan and Mr. Knight stood across the room.

"Any news?" Omara's face turned hopeful.

"Yeah. We've pinpointed an area where we think Derrick may be," he declared.

Omara flew from the bed and into his arms. Her body slammed into him hard. He closed her into his embrace and held her while she shook. She turned her red-rimmed eyes up to him. His heart stuttered at the tortured expression. He cupped her face, wiping the warm trail of tears from her cheeks.

"We're going to get him. I promise."

"Just be safe, okay?" she whispered.

"It's not me who you have to worry about." In that moment, he forgot they had an audience. All that mattered to him was that Omara was safe and that he would be hand-delivering her son back to her. He didn't ever want to see this look on her face ever again. The woman only deserved happiness. "Did you get any rest?"

"As much as I could, but I didn't sleep well. I kept imagining—"

"Stop." He pressed a finger to her lips.

Panic flashed in her eyes.

"Jason is like you," he said. "He's stronger than he looks."

Page 374 —

She jerked her head in a nod. She glanced down at his t-shirt, brushing off an invisible piece of lint. She fisted his shirt, holding on to it.

"Did you mean what you said earlier? About the weekend?"

He nodded. Her face softened slightly, her lips curled up in the corners. Zain would be willing to do whatever he needed to in order to keep her smiling.

"Willing to make it a week?" she asked.

"Anything you want." He popped a kiss on her lips. "Keep your phone on you. If Allen reaches out to you, I want you to alert the patrolmen who will be staying here. They will know how to get hold of me."

She nodded, her grip tightening on his shirt. He flicked his gaze to Jordan and jerked his head in a nod.

"Time to roll, Knight."

OMARA EMERGED FROM HER BEDROOM, once again dressed. Her mother had forced her to take a shower, and she would have to admit, she did feel better. Fresh clothes on, and she almost felt like a new woman.

Now she just needed her man, sister, and son to

return to her safely and she would be a happy person.

"Are you hungry?" Irene asked.

"Not really, but I'll take some coffee." Omara walked into the kitchen. It would be daylight shortly, and she prayed Zain would return with her son soon. Dropping her cell on the counter, she moved over to the single-brew coffee machine.

"You need to eat something. It won't do you any good to be weak when Jason returns," Irene snapped. She went over to the fridge and opened the door. "I'll make you something simple. Make your father a cup of coffee, too. I don't want him to get more ornery than he already is. A few hours in the car with that man is enough to drive me insane."

"Yes, ma'am." Omara smiled, knowing she wasn't going to win any fight with her mother. The woman was the queen of stubborn. She quickly made her and her father's coffee. She just prayed she'd made it the way he liked it. She carried their steaming mugs into the living room.

"Thanks, baby," Cecil murmured. He took a sip and closed his eyes briefly. "Almost as good as your momma makes it."

"Thanks, Daddy." It was a compliment. Anything her mother made was flawless, and it was hard to try to imitate the woman's perfection. Omara took a seat next to him and tucked her feet underneath her.

"Zain appears to be a good man, my dear," her father said.

Omara glanced down into her mug. She knew what was coming.

"Why haven't you told us about him?"

Omara shrugged.

"I guess it was too new, and honestly, we hadn't told anyone. Jordan only just found out," she admitted.

"And how did she take it, seeing that she works with him?" Her father chuckled. He sipped his coffee, his eyes filled with merriment. He knew how his oldest daughter was, and Omara shouldn't even have to tell him.

"She was pissed." Omara sighed. She tried to make light of the situation. "She introduced us. Apparently, there was a bet at the precinct, and he lost to her, and the punishment was a haircut."

"I'm glad to see that he puts a smile on your face." He suddenly sobered. He patted her on her knee. "I know there are some things you and your sister have kept from me and your mother."

She stiffened and hid behind drinking her coffee.

She didn't want to have this conversation now with him. Since she'd seen how they were dealing with this situation, it wasn't that she didn't think they could handle it, it was that she was ashamed of how her life had turned out.

"Daddy," she started, but he held up his hand.

"For whatever reason, unbeknownst to us, we don't know why you would ever hold something back from us. And if tonight is a just a small sliver of what you have been living through, I'm sorry, baby girl."

Tears formed in her eyes. She sniffed, holding the back of her hand to her mouth.

"There is nothing for you to apologize for," she whispered, her throat raw. She fought back the sobs. She didn't think she had any more tears left in her to cry.

"I'm sorry that you've been in pain." His voice shook.

Omara's eyes widened. She had never seen her father get this emotional before. He had always been the hard-nosed father who demanded she and her sister make the most out of life. He'd raised them to be strong, independent women.

"Do you think we didn't notice the change in you all those years? That you came around less? You pushed us away, and we thought it was something we had done."

Omara felt the shame fill her. That hadn't been the reason. She shook her head and took his hand in hers.

"No, Daddy. It wasn't anything you had done. I felt as if I had let you down. I wasn't that strong woman who you raised me to be. I became a victim and had lost myself. It was Jordan who came and saved me. I was too ashamed that I failed as a woman, a mother to my son—"

"Oh, baby." He gathered her to him.

She bit back the tears, refusing to give in and cry.

"There is nothing that you could have done that would have been a disappointment to me or your mother."

"He's right, you know." Her mother came into the room carrying a plate. She stopped in front of Omara and took the mug from her, sitting it on the coffee table.

Omara took the plate. Irene had found all the fixings for an omelet and had made her two pieces of toast with butter.

"It is me who should apologize," Omara said. She sat back and dug into her food. Her stomach grumbled in appreciation. She guessed she was hungry.

"We are not going to worry about that now. We are going to pray that our grandson will be brought back to us safe and sound." Irene sat on the loveseat next to them. Her lips were pressed together in a firm line. "And as for Derrick Allen, I hope the jail has room underneath it for what he's putting us through."

Omara agreed with her mother. This was the lowest of lows for Derrick. He knew he didn't want to be a full-time father. This was his way of getting back at her because he couldn't control her like he used to. He was intimidated by Zain who she was with. So in order to hurt her, he would take away the one thing that meant the world to her.

Their son.

"I wonder if the police officers need some coffee." Irene stood and walked over to the front window. She peered out of it. "And why do you not have a regular coffee pot? What is that thing in there?"

"It's a single-serve machine, Mom." Omara chuckled. She reached up and tucked her hair behind her ear. She sat her empty plate on the table and picked up her mug. She took a healthy sip. "I'm the only one in the house who drinks coffee. Jason sure doesn't."

"Well, I know what I'm buying you for Christmas. You need an adult machine. What if you are hosting guests? Is each person supposed to wait on their individual cup? What if they need more than one cup?" Irene was truly bothered by Omara's machine.

Omara rolled her eyes at her mother.

"Mom, it's fine," she said.

"Well, I'm going outside and see if they need some." Irene headed toward the foyer. The sound of the door opening and shutting echoed through the house.

"Let her be," Cecil murmured. He shook his head. "When that woman gets on a roll, just move out of her way."

"I figured." Omara blew out a deep breath. It wasn't truly the coffee pot that got Irene up in a roar. Omara was sure it was her mother's way of trying to stay busy under the stress of waiting.

Omara slid her phone from her pocket and put it on the table next to her plate. Would Derrick call her? She would think he was aware that what he was doing was against the law. He'd have to know the amber alert had been issued. The alarm went out to all cell phones and electronic devices. There was no way he couldn't know.

"Now, tell me about Zain," her father said. He sat his empty mug down and turned his attention to her. "He looks as if he really cares for you."

"He does." She smiled softly. "He and Jason get along so well."

She settled back and began to tell her father about her new relationship. Talking would help keep her mind off things that could go wrong. She just prayed Derrick and Jason would be found safe and sound.

24

Z ain pulled the BEAR to the opening of the subdivision. He hit the lights, basking them in darkness. The sun would be up soon. The skies were a multitude of colors. He glanced at it, wishing he was sitting with Omara, watching the sunrise.

He killed the engine and jumped out of the vehicle. The back door opened with the team spilling out. Behind them were additional patrol cars.

They moved to the side of the vehicle, opening the compartment doors. Zain snatched his semiautomatic rifle. This wasn't a shoot-to-kill mission. It was a secure and retrieve. Zain checked this weapon and ensured it was ready for use. His other teammates were doing the same. One look, and it would appear they were about to go off to war.

They always went in preparing for the worst.

"Gather around," Mac ordered.

They circled around Mac, awaiting his orders. The air was thick with tension. Zain stood next to Jordan who had a grim look on her face. Their eyes connected for a brief moment. He gave her a nod.

"I hope I'm not late to the party," a deep Southern drawl broke the silence. Officer Rhys Newman, and his K9 partner, Honor, walked up to join them. He was decked out in dark camouflage uniform, a black CPD baseball cap, and his ballistic vest with K9 splashed across the front. Honor, his German Shepherd, sat at his feet, waiting for her orders.

"You're just in time." Mac gave him a nod.

"To bring you up to speed, Officer Newman. The suspect is one Derrick Allen, forty-year-old black male who yesterday picked up his child unauthorized and has taken him. This is officially a kidnapping, and the Feds are on standby if we need them. His phone was recently pinged in this area, what is known as a job site he's worked in. We have reason to believe he's holing up with his eight-year-old son, Jason Allen. Jason is the nephew to Officer

Jordan Knight. We are to use extreme caution since there is a child involved."

Rhys's head snapped toward Jordan. "Sorry to hear, Officer Knight."

His gaze hardened, and he turned back to face Mac. They had worked with the K9 units before. They were a very effective team. The dogs were amazing to work with and were very valuable to the police department.

The air around them went silent.

"Also to be transparent, I need to share that Officer Roman and the suspect have a history of a recent confrontation where the suspect made threats toward Omara Knight, Jordan's sister. We are to treat him as a dangerous suspect," Mac continued.

"There are two houses we suspect they may be in," Declan said. The focus shifted to him. "Because of time sensitivity, we are going to split into two groups."

He went into further detail on their approach to the home. Zain would be teamed up with Declan, Iker, and Brodie. They would be approaching the second home, while Mac and the others would infiltrate the first house. This would be no different than any of their practices. They functioned as a well-oiled machine.

"Rhys, you and Honor can tag along with my team," Mac said.

"We'd be flattered," Rhys drawled.

Honor gave a bark, standing to her feet.

"Sync up your communicators," Mac ordered.

Zain hit the tiny device in his ear. Anticipation rose inside him. Jason wasn't his son, but he was damn sure going to be in his life. With the way things were going with Omara, he'd just be the kid's stepfather.

Zain paused.

Was he truly considering settling down again?

Marriage the first time hadn't panned out so well for him, but it hadn't been all his fault. Omara was nothing like Freya. She truly cared for him, wanted him, laughed with him.

She was everything he needed in a life partner. Deep down, he knew he wasn't going to ever let her go.

The love he had for her ran deep.

"You good?" Iker slapped him on the back, breaking him out of his thoughts.

"Yeah. Let's go get this fucker," he muttered. He pulled his mask up on his face and adjusted his helmet. He was ready to put an end to this. Derrick would be captured and arrested. He wouldn't be able to hurt Omara anymore.

"SWAT," Mac called out.

The tension was thick in the air. The two teams divided and ready. Zain's muscles tensed.

Mac slowly looked around and met their gazes. "Let's hunt."

Zain gripped his semiautomatic rifle tight, falling into formation with his team. They ran along the road that led into the housing development. Mac and the others ran along the opposite side. At the corner of the road, they would then split.

Up ahead was the three-way stop. The first house they approached was one of the framed structures that were currently being worked on. One could see completely through to the backyard. The house they would target was a few lots away.

Declan motioned for them to cut right and head toward their building. It was eerily quiet. The hairs on the back of Zain's neck stood to attention. He didn't like this setup. It was too damn quiet. With the sun set to rise soon, they lost the cover of darkness. Zain scanned the area and didn't see any vehicles as they advanced. The attached garage was open and empty.

They arrived at the front door. Brodie stalked to

the front of the line with his portable battering ram, making light work of the flimsy door. They flew into the home, arriving in the foyer. Declan went right, into the dining room. Iker went left into the living room. Brodie headed past the staircase toward the back of the house. They were nice-sized structures that didn't have basements they'd have to worry about, according to the plans.

"Clear," echoed through the comm device in Zain's ear as they searched the first level. He automatically took the stairs, going to the second level. As soon as they cleared that level, someone would join him.

Zain arrived on the second level. It was open, all of the rooms on the left-hand side facing the high-vaulted ceilings. The floor was carpeted, softening his footsteps. The wooden hand railing that traveled the length of the stairwell continued on down the hall, ending at the wall.

Zain opened the first door, finding a small empty bedroom with a standard closet. "First bedroom, clear," he announced. He stepped out and repeated his action with the next door.

A bathroom.

Zain swept the area and took it in. Nothing. He backed out but then paused in the doorway.

"Hall bathroom cleared," he murmured.

A sound caught his attention. He glanced down the hall and moved to the next room. According to the plans, there were two bedrooms on the second floor and a master suite. He arrived at the next door and pushed it open.

Same as the first room.

"Clear," Zain said.

He lifted his rifle and aimed it true as he went into the room that had to be the master bedroom. Zain took slow careful steps toward it. He reached for the door and turned the handle, pushing it open.

He took a step in, his eyes zeroing in on the air mattress and a few fast-food bags scattered on the floor. He swung around, a body rushing toward him out of the walk-in closet that was positioned near the entrance of the suite.

The bat connected with his shoulder. The hold on his rifle lessened, but he didn't drop it.

Zain grunted from the pain and tried to straighten. It landed on the side of his head. He went down on his knee, reaching his hand out to brace him, to keep him from falling.

"Go, Jason. Run to the balcony," Derrick snapped.

"Daddy, I'm scared," Jason hiccupped.

"Now!" Derrick pushed the boy toward the set of glass doors that led out to a veranda.

The sky was light, sunrays beginning to shine inside the home. Derrick brought the bat down on top of Zain's head, forcing him to fall completely to the floor.

"You son of a bitches think to keep me from my boy."

He spun around on his heel and gathered Jason to him, opening the doors. Zain lifted his head, ignoring the piercing pain. His eyes connected with Jason's. He reached up and removed his mask from his face. He pushed himself up off the floor.

"Zain!" Jason shouted. He spun, trying to run back to him, but Derrick scooped him up into his arms. He screamed and kicked, trying to break free.

"Oh, hell naw." Derrick turned and disappeared from sight.

The sound of Jason's screams echoed through the air.

The room tilted to the side, but Zain was able to right himself. He left the rifle and pulled his Glock out of his thigh sheath and followed them.

"Allen and the kid are headed down the stairs from the veranda off the master bedroom," Zain shouted into his comm. He blinked, seeing double.

He held on to the railing and took the stairs. He was halfway down them, and his vision blurred again with his balance going to shit. He tumbled forward, sliding on them on his ass.

He cursed, pain exploding in his glute muscles. He lifted himself and took in Derrick trying to make a run for the woods carrying a wiggling Jason.

"We see him," Iker's voice came in.

"I got eyes on him, too," Ash said.

Zain pushed off and dug deep. He took off running after Derrick. Sweat beaded his skin as he pumped his arms faster. Jason broke loose, falling to the ground. Derrick rotated, and Zain leaped on him, crashing into him.

"Get the fuck off me," Derrick hollered.

Zain pulled back his fist and slammed it into Derrick's mouth. Derrick rolled them over, landing a punch of his own before he pushed up to run. Zain tackled him by his legs, sending him to the ground.

Zain growled, seeing double from the pain in his head. Derrick kicked out his foot, narrowly missing Zain's face. Zain gained the upper hand and landed another punch to the side of his face. They went down, exchanging blows.

"Stay down," Zain ordered.

"Fuck you," Derrick snarled. He brought up a knee, hitting Zain in the thigh.

Zain rolled to the side as Derrick tried to get up. He took one step, but the growl of a dog had him pausing.

"Shit!"

Instead of staying still, he chose to run.

Bad choice.

Derrick raced across the yard but was no match for Honor.

Zain found Jason kneeling on the grass, tears running down his face.

"Jason." Zain pushed off the ground. The pain exploded in his head, and stars filled his sight. He stood and held his arms open.

Jason raced to him, slamming into Zain. He wrapped his arms around the little guy who was sobbing.

"It's okay, buddy. I'm here. I got you."

"Jason!" Jordan came barreling around the corner. She rushed toward them, stopping in front of Zain. She grabbed Jason's shoulders and spun him around. "Are you okay?"

"Yes, Auntie. Zain saved me."

She folded him into her arms, tears spilling down her face. Zain had never seen the woman cry, but this was her nephew. Her blood. Zain's eyes grew scratchy. This could have ended in a different manner. He was just glad Jason was safe.

Rhys handcuffed Derrick with Honor hovering over them ensuring Derrick didn't try anything with her handler. Declan stood by and helped Rhys lift Derrick to his feet.

"Honor. Heel," Rhys commanded.

The dog immediately ceased her growling.

Myles and Ash went over with Declan and took over for Rhys. They escorted Derrick past them. Jason moved back to Zain, hiding his face in Zain's stomach.

"I bet you're happy about this, bitch," Derrick shouted at Jordan. He jerked to try to jump at her, but he was pushed back by Myles.

Jordan held her head up high, not batting an eye at the idiot.

"Watch it. You attack her, you're going to deal with all of us," the big man growled. He grabbed Derrick's arm and dragged him toward the front of the house.

"Can we go home now, Zain?" Jason looked up at him.

"We sure can. Your mom is waiting on you. She's

so worried," Zain said softly. He blinked a few times and tried to steady himself.

"You good, Roman?" Jordan asked, staring at him.

Zain felt like shit. His nose was bleeding, his head was killing him, and he was now seeing two of Jordan. There was no way the world could deal with two of her.

"Of course I'm good. Why don't both of you help me get him to a patrol car." Zain swayed in place.

"There's two of me? What the hell?" She rushed to his side and pulled out her flashlight.

He grimaced at the bright light. Did he admit he was seeing two of her?

Fuck.

"My dad hit him on the head with the bat. Twice," Jason said.

Jordan cursed. "We need a medic!"

"I'm okay, buddy. I promise." Zain smiled.

Jason moved to his side as if to help steady him. Jordan went to his other arm and lifted it around her.

"Stop being so damn stubborn. How the hell did you run him down like that? You probably have a concussion," Jordan said.

"Here, I've got him." Iker appeared. He gently

moved Jason so he could take the brunt of Zain's weight. "Jason, stay with us. Okay?"

They walked toward the front of the house with Zain complaining. He wasn't weak. It was just a couple of hits to the head. He had his helmet on. He would be fine, but no one listened to him.

The yard was now crawling with investigators and patrolmen. An ambulance was parked in front of the house.

"I don't need a hospital," Zain grumbled. He had to get back to Omara. He had to take her son to her so she would know he was safe. He had made her a promise and he was going to live up to it.

"You need to get checked out," Iker said gruffly.

"Omara." Zain's eyes fluttered closed, but his legs held him up. He didn't want to do anything but go back to her and hold her. Let her know that her nightmare was over.

"Medics first." Iker's voice was firm.

They arrived at the ambulance. The EMTs hopped down and came over to him.

"What do we have?" they asked. They brought the stretcher out and lowered it on the ground.

"He's been hit in the head with a baseball bat a few times," Jordan announced.

They helped Zain take a seat on the cart.

Jordan motioned for Jason. "Come on, Jason. Let's have them look him over."

"I don't want to leave Zain," he cried out. He broke away from her and threw himself at Zain.

Zain closed his eyes and hugged the little body pressed against him.

"I'm okay. I promise," Zain said. He tried to make light of the situation. "I have a really hard head, and it would take more than a bat to put me down."

Jason lifted his head, and the sight of his tears streaking down his cheeks sent a ripple of pain through Zain's heart. This little boy cared for him. He ran a hand over the top of his head.

"You promise?" Jason asked, wiping his face with the back of his hand.

"As soon as they are done, we'll head home to your mother, okay?"

Jason gave a nod and stepped back to allow the EMTs to get near Zain.

***

"WATCH how you're taking them corners!" Zain banged on the partition.

He sat in the back of the BEAR while Iker

drove them. Declan sat in the passenger seat up front with him. The EMTs had finished their assessment of him. Besides a few bruises and being put on a concussion watch protocol, he was allowed to leave.

He glanced down at Jason was who sitting between him and Jordan. The kid had been so excited when Zain had suggested they get a ride in the truck. He was unable to drive it, so they could just drop him off at Omara's.

"This is so cool. Wait until I tell Ricky and all the guys I got to ride with SWAT," Jason muttered.

Chuckles went around the air. Little did Jason know, he had just been adopted by his new uncles.

"I thought you were already cool, since your auntie is a cop." Jordan squeezed his cheeks.

"Auntie," Jason groaned.

She plopped a big kiss on his cheek.

"You know I love you," she said, dropping another one on top of his head.

"I love you, too." He smiled. He leaned into her, allowing her to hug him.

Jordan's eyes met Zain's, and she offered a smile to him. Words didn't have to be exchanged between them. He knew how much she loved her nephew.

"Can I hold your gun?" Jason asked her.

Zain snorted at the question. Of course the kid wanted to hold a gun. Look who his aunt was.

"Hell no. You trying to get me in real trouble with your momma?" Jordan laughed. She pulled back and grinned at him. "Maybe when you're older we can take you to the gun range and officially teach you gun safety."

"Zain, would you be there, too?" Jason asked.

Zain felt all eyes were on him. His teammates went quiet waiting for the answer as well. He hadn't really updated them on the progression of his relationship with Omara. He wasn't ready yet. He loved his ready-made family and wanted to do everything right this time.

His lips tilted up in the corner, him thinking of the future that was waiting for them. He wasn't going anywhere. As long as Omara wanted him, he would be around.

"Of course, bud," he said.

Jason relaxed, as if it was the answer he had been hoping for.

"We're here," Iker announced.

The vehicle drew to a halt. Mac stood and opened the back door. He jumped out with Myles, Ash, and Brodie following.

"Come on, big man. Let's get you back to your

mom." Zain stood from his seat. His balance was still off. He braced his hands along the side as he staggered to the door.

"Do I need to help you down?" Myles grinned.

"You do, and I'll put a slug in your kneecap," Zain muttered. He paused and allowed Jordan to hop down.

She turned and helped Jason. Once he was on the ground, he waited for Zain.

Inhaling first, Zain made his way out of the truck. It wasn't graceful at all, but he did it on his own without managing to pass out or vomit. He turned and took Jason's hand. They walked around the truck. The front door flew open, and Omara came barreling out of the door.

"Jason!" she cried out.

"Mom!" Jason took off toward his mother. He flew into her open arms and hugged her tight.

Sobs racked Omara while she held Jason in her embrace.

Zain and Jordan went over to them. Her eyes opened, and her gaze landed on Zain.

"What happened to you?" she cried out.

Jason moved to her side, not letting her go. She reached out and cupped Zain's cheek. His head was killing him. The medication the EMTs had given him was wearing off. He was going to be bruised and sore for a few days.

"It's nothing," Zain said gruffly. He pulled her and Jason into his arms. This felt right.

This was what he'd been missing his entire life.

"Thank you." Omara lifted her head and sniffed. She turned to her sister and left his arms to hug her.

Jordan's eyes were mysteriously red again. Tears fell from them while she held Omara tight.

"Love you, sis," Jordan whispered.

"I love you, too." Omara stepped back and waved to the entire team. "I don't know what I can do to thank you all for bringing my baby back to me."

"You don't have to do anything. We're just glad we were able to bring him back safe and sound," Mac said. He ambled over and stood in front of them. "The EMTs checked little Jason out but didn't find anything wrong with him. He's as healthy as a horse."

The front door opened, and Omara's parents stepped out onto the porch. Jason turned and saw them. He beelined it to them. Zain brought Omara to his side, needing to feel her against him.

"Now this one you need to watch." Declan pointed to Zain. He arrived at Mac's side. "He's under concussion protocol for taking a few hits from a bat to the head."

"What?" Omara gasped.

"Derrick got the drop on me, but I promise you, it won't ever happen again." He rolled his eyes. He was still pissed that Derrick had caught him off guard. Hiding in the closet was a cowardly move.

"He's on light duty until he gets cleared to be back in the field," Mac said. He leveled Omara with his gaze. "He wanted to be left in your company, but if you don't want him, we can find somewhere else for him—"

"He can stay here. I'll take responsibility for him and make sure he gets rest." Omara turned those big brown eyes to him.

He bit back the grin that threatened to spill across his face. He couldn't wait to see how she was going to help him rest.

"Well, good. If he's any trouble at all, call any of us, and we'll come straighten him out." Mac gave her a nod.

"Oh, don't worry. He'll behave."

25

T wo whole days since her baby had been returned to her. Omara closed Jason's bedroom door and sighed. She leaned her forehead against it, thankful her son was safe and home. Derrick had been arrested on parental kidnapping charges. She was still unable to grasp that he had tried to go this far to hurt her. Had Zain, Jordan, and the SWAT team not had access to things most police didn't have, she would have lost her child.

At his little hideout, there was evidence that Derrick was planning to cross state lines with Jason. He'd had a fake Texas ID made for himself and had signed a six-month lease for an apartment in Dallas under the fake ID's name. There were also plane tickets leaving Monday morning for two to Dallas.

Omara shuddered to think what would have happened if they had been late. That monster would have taken her baby. Now he was residing in jail, waiting for his first hearing.

Zain had been right. Her baby was so strong. There had been so many detectives and police stopping by to speak with them. Even the FBI was involved. Jason was calm as he answered all of their questions. Zain and Omara did not leave his side. He was so strong and resilient, she didn't know where he got it from. She, on the other hand, had been a mess.

Zain had been her rock along with her family. Her parents had finally left a few hours ago to drive back to Atlanta. Now that everything had calmed down, they wanted to return home but promised they would be back later this week.

"Everything okay?" Zain's voice sounded behind her.

She glanced over at him and smiled. He was shirtless and had a pair of pajama pants riding low on his waist. His dark hair was tousled from him running his fingers through it. He was downright sexy, and he was all hers. He rested against the doorjamb to her bedroom, his intense hazel eyes locked on her.

"You, sir, are supposed to be resting." She pushed off the door and went to him.

He drew her into his arms and kissed her. She leaned into him, welcoming his tongue inside her mouth. She slid her arms around his neck and returned the kiss. It grew heated, his hands sliding down from the small of her waist to her amble bottom. He gripped her ass tight, holding her to him.

"This is not resting," she murmured, her lips brushing his.

"But I've missed you." He buried his face in the crook of her neck.

She bit back a moan, remembering they were outside Jason's door. His tongue skated along the column of her neck. He nipped her gently before making his way to her ear. He nibbled on it, pressing his hard member against her stomach. Her core clenched at the feel of his massive length, hard and ready.

"Zain," she whispered. She tried to put some distance between them, but moving him was like trying to move a mountain. "You just saw me. What are you talking about?"

She laughed. This man was going to drive her

crazy, but in the good way. He took her hand and pulled her into the master bedroom. He'd stayed with her since he had returned with Jason. Having him in the house helped calm Jason down. He still had nightmares from his father taking him.

Zain shut the door and flicked the lock. Her back was pressed against it with Zain covering her front.

"I'm missing you." He raised his eyebrows and glanced down at bulge underneath his pants.

"Oh." She bit her lip.

He was not supposed to be engaging in anything strenuous since he was being monitored for a concussion. Thank goodness for his helmet he wore out on missions. She didn't want to think what would have happened if Derrick had hit him without it.

"That's all you have to say?" He took her hand and placed it over his cock.

She groaned feeling the warm, wide girth of him beneath his cotton pants. He captured her lips again, this time in a kiss that took her breath away. His hand came up to grip her hair at the base of her neck. He drew back and gazed into her eyes.

"I need you, Omara."

"Zain," she breathed.

They couldn't. They'd advised against any activities that could potentially cause his blood pressure to go up. The man had literally seen double the first night he'd stayed with her.

"I need to be inside you."

She stroked him. Holding him fed the fire that blazed inside her. Her core was pulsating, her panties already growing damp. She was fighting the need.

What if she hurt him?

"Zain, what if you get hurt?" she asked.

His deep chuckle rumbled in his chest. He reached up and pushed his pants down, allowing his cock to spring free. Her gaze locked on it while her hand came up to continue its motion. She skated her hand from his base to the tip. A tiny bead of his salty liquid appeared on the tip. She licked her lips, very familiar with what he tasted like.

"Then I will gladly go to the hospital and tell them my woman fucked the life out of me." He grinned, puffing his chest out slightly.

He would do something like that, too. She believed him.

"Zain." She rolled her eyes, a groan escaping her. Only he could make a joke out of something so serious.

He slid a hand underneath her soft cotton nightshirt. His fingers pushed her panties aside, and a strangled groan escaped him the second he was met with the proof of her desire for him.

"Fuck." He shuddered. He bent down and scooped her up and carried her over to the bed.

"You shouldn't be—"

"Shut it, woman," he grumbled.

Omara was flat on her back, holding back a laugh. The feral look in his eyes faded her smile. He tugged her gown over her head and tossed it behind him. Her panties and his pants disappeared.

Zain covered her with his body, his mouth taking hers. It had been a few days since they had made love. Omara cried out when he tore his mouth from hers. He lifted her breasts in both of his hands, his eyes locked on her dark nipples.

"Your breasts are so fucking perfect." He captured one with his mouth, his tongue teasing her hard nipple.

Omara's head dropped back on the bed, and she turned herself over to him. She could no longer resist him.

His hot length rested on her thigh. Her channel clenched; she needed to feel him sink into her. She panted as he moved to the next breast. She tugged on his hair, chanting his name. His eyes flicked to hers while he suckled her mound.

"Zain. Now. I need you inside me," she gasped.

He released her, grinning.

"Oh, but when I say it—"

"Now," she whimpered, widening her legs.

He reached between them and took hold of his cock. He ran the tip through her slick slit, his smile disappearing.

"Jesus, Omara."

He rolled them over to where she landed on top of him. He moved them higher on the bed to where he rested back against the pillows. His eyes darkened when he took in her naked form. Anytime this man looked at her had her feeling perfect and beautiful. His feral gaze ran along her breasts and down her to her pussy.

"Hop on, pretty lady."

Omara didn't hesitate to lift to allow him to align the blunt tip of his cock to her opening. She impaled herself, holding back the cry that threatened to spill from her. They had pretty much mastered the art of silent sex since her son's bedroom was next door.

"Fuck," Zain breathed through clenched teeth.

She was seated fully on him. Omara closed her eyes, loving the sensation of him deep within her.

She rested her hands on his chest while her walls worked to acclimate to him.

"Oh God," she whispered.

Omara rotated her hips, eliciting a moan from Zain. She arched her body, riding him as he commanded. Zain's hips thrust up, sending him even farther inside of her. Their bodies moved as one.

Pleasure rocked her down to her core. Omara glanced down to find Zain's eyes on her. She held his gaze, unable to look away. The love she felt for this man scared her. She had never felt anything like this before. Tears blurred her vision with her thinking of all the ways he'd taken care of her and her son. He owned her heart and her soul.

"Zain," she sobbed, the tears falling.

She had to tell him. They had never spoken the words, but she knew deep in her heart that their feelings were mutual.

His hands gripped her waist as he guided her down on him harder.

"What is it, baby. What's wrong?" He paused, his breaths coming in pants.

He was lodged so deep inside her, she never wanted him to leave.

"Am I hurting you?" he asked.

She shook her head, reaching up to brush the tears away.

"I love you," she whispered.

He froze in place, and it even looked as if he had stopped breathing.

"Say it again," Zain breathed. He studied her face as if he couldn't believe what she'd said. He guided her face down to him. The new position angled his cock deeper inside her.

"I love you."

"Oh God. I love you, too." He crushed her mouth to his. He rolled them over to where he was on top and thrust even harder.

Omara wrapped her arms around his shoulders and held on for dear life.

Her core clenched at his growl.

"That's it. Squeeze me harder," he whispered in her ear.

She did it again and was rewarded with his sexy groan. Omara teetered on the brink of her release.

Zain must have sensed it. He slipped a hand between them and strummed her slit. She cried out, unable to control herself.

"That's it, Omara. I want you to come on my dick," he whispered in her ear.

She closed her eyes and couldn't hold back any

longer. She threw her head back, and the waves of her release slammed into her. Her muscles tensed, and her body shook.

Zain gasped, pumping a few more times before he joined her in ecstasy. He froze in place, burying his face into the pillow as he reached his release. His warm seed filled her, bathing her walls.

His body dropped down on to her. She wrapped her arms around him and basked in the feel of him on her.

"I love you and Jason so much, Omara," Zain said after a few moments. He lifted his head and peered down at her. He turned onto his side and brought her into the cradle of his arms. "I want you forever, babe."

Omara leaned up on her elbows and smiled.

"Then I'm all yours."

EPILOGUE

Omara smiled as she finished putting the finishing touches to Zain's gift. She inhaled sharply and loved the smell of the fresh flowers sitting on the master bedroom dresser of the home they were renting on Tybee Island. The scent of the ocean surrounded her. This was the happiest she had been in a long while. Zain had kept his promise and had taken her and Jason away. Two weeks in a mini paradise was more than she would have imagined.

Tucking the tissue paper in the bag, she padded over to the double doors that led out onto the veranda. She didn't see Zain or Jason out by the private pool the home boasted.

It was a gorgeous warm day with the sun shining down on them. It couldn't get more perfect than this.

Derrick had been released from jail on bond after his arrest. He was looking at a hefty fine and up to a couple of years in prison for taking Jason. As he wasn't the primary parent, he had no right to take Jason outside of his scheduled time. The prosecutor definitely didn't like the evidence that he had planned to take Jason across state lines without her permission.

Lately, the man barely showed for his court-supervised visits. He was allowed two per month and had only made one in the past few months.

Times flies when you're having fun.

She grinned, glancing down at the beautiful ring adorning her finger. The day Zain had proposed to her had been the craziest of her life. But, of course, why wouldn't it be when it came to that man.

He'd blown right into her life and showed her everything she had been missing—him.

They had moved in with each other a month after the fiasco with Derrick. Omara packed up her and Jason's belongings and moved in with Zain. Her home had sold within a week of being put on the market. She had worried Jason wouldn't be able to adjust, but that son of hers proved her wrong.

Jason and Zain had grown close. In a way, she saw how her son sensed he was safe with Zain and that Zain really cared for him. Zain had been more of a father figure to him in the short while they'd been together than his father had been his entire life.

Together they had planned a family gathering, inviting both sides and his extended SWAT family. She should have been alerted that something was amiss with how nervous Zain had been.

After almost catching the back patio on fire, he'd released a curse, grabbed her in front of everyone, and got down on one knee. Omara had burst out crying and accepted.

How could that man think I'd turn him down?

Shaking her head, she decided to go find the men who owned her heart. Snagging Zain's present, she walked through the cottage and went outside. Laughter floated through the air.

Of course they would be on the beach. Jason loved the ocean and building sandcastles. She snagged one of the large towels hanging off the back of the patio chair and rested it on her shoulder.

She made her way around the pool and exited the private yard through a short gate that led down to the beach. Her toes sank into the warm sand and felt so good.

Jason and Zain were right where she knew they would be. Wading in the water tossing a football back and forth. Jason threw a long shot, and Zain had to jump up but fell into the powerful waves that hit him on the waist.

Omara laughed at the sight of him, but the smile slowly faded away. He stood, the water dripping off his toned physique. It didn't matter how many times she'd seen this man naked or without a shirt on, her mouth still went dry, and her body always reacted strongly.

"Slow down, you little hussy," she muttered to herself. Her core clenched, alerting her that it, too, had taken notice of Zain.

He ran his hand through his hair, and she just about climaxed watching him.

Clearing her throat, she called out to them.

"Hey, guys!" She waved her hands. She found a spot and spread the towel down then took a seat.

Jason ran over to her, wet and covered in sand. A large grin was plastered on his face.

"Hey, Ma!" He fell to the ground next to her and lay across the towel.

She'd found it at a local shop that boasted the towel was for one family.

"Having fun?" she asked, already knowing the answer.

"The best." He flipped over onto his stomach and stared out at the water.

Zain ambled over, cradling the football in his hand.

"Finally returned to the land of the living." Zain chuckled.

She rolled her eyes at his joke.

"When do I ever take naps?" she scoffed. The answer was, she normally didn't. But when in a little piece of paradise, it would be foolish not to. It wasn't many days she got lie around and do nothing.

Zain took a seat next to her. His playful grin widened.

"I'm just playing. You deserve it." He leaned over and kissed her waiting lips. His eyes dropped to the gift bag in her hand. He jerked his head toward it. "What's in the bag?"

"A little something for you. Since you got me this wonderful gift." She held up her hand and admired the ring.

"You are all the gift I need." He chuckled. He pushed it away when she tried to hand it to him.

"Don't be like that. I searched hard to find the right gift for you. I didn't cost me that much, and I just want to show a little appreciation for all of this." She waved a hand around at the area.

He couldn't have booked a better trip for them. Sun, sand, and water were the perfect retreat for their little family.

He eyed her for a moment before finally taking the bag from her. Jason turned his curious eyes to them. He sat up and moved over to her. She smiled at him and blew a kiss.

"What is it?" Jason asked.

Zain took the tissue paper out of the bag and paused. His head cocked to the side. His smile disappeared while he reached inside and pulled out the gift.

"Is this what I think it is?" Zain asked softly. He took out the three pregnancy tests she had taken yesterday.

All of them were positive.

His eyes flew to her, shining bright with unshed tears.

Omara bit her lip and nodded.

Zain jumped to his feet and took a few steps away. He leaned down, resting his hands on his knees. Omara chuckled and stood.

"What are these, Momma?" Jason bent down

and picked the tests up. He stared at them then turned to her.

"Mommy's going to have a baby," she said.

"We're going to have three babies?" Jason hopped up and down, grinning.

Oh my goodness.

"No, silly. Just one. I took three tests to make sure the first one was right." She couldn't hold back her laughter at her son's excitement.

She took a step toward Zain who rotated, tears running down his face. He stalked to her and scooped her up in his arms. She squealed, holding on tight as he spun them in a circle.

He sat her down, allowing her to slide along his body. Omara bit back a moan. The feeling of him against her always pushed the right buttons for her. Too bad she couldn't escort him back to their master suite in the cottage and celebrate privately.

"You're pregnant?" His eyes were awestruck as he looked upon her. His hands cupped her face, his thumbs caressing her cheeks.

"I'm very sure." It had been extremely hard not the shout and scream when she'd seen the results. She had been suspicious for a while, and when her breasts became tender, she was certain. She had made up an excuse to stop at the grocery store and purchased the tests. When she really thought about it, she had been so busy with everything going on that she hadn't realized she'd missed a few monthly visits from Aunt Flo.

"You know that I love you and Jason." He waved Jason over to them.

They opened their arms and brought Jason into the group hug. This was her family, and soon they would be expanding by one more.

"Are you excited? You're going to be a big brother," Omara said.

"Can it be a boy? Please? Girls are so stupid." Jason rolled his eyes.

"Jason!" She tried to use her Mom voice, but her lips still cracked into a smile. "I'm a girl. Auntie Jordan is a girl."

"Y'all are cool girls." He shrugged.

Omara tightened her grip on him, kissing him on the cheek. He hollered and dashed away from them, heading back to the towel.

Zain brought her back flush to him with his arms around her waist.

"You don't know how happy this makes me," he said. He leaned down and buried his face into the crook of her neck. He placed a small kiss to the column of her throat. "Thank you."

"What are you thanking me for? You participated in creating this baby." She giggled. Her arms tightened around him; she understood this was a lot for him to take in. He had basically given up the thought of fatherhood.

"For giving me you. Giving me Jason and now this. I can't ask for anything else. I have everything a man would ever want in life."

Omara's heart stuttered. He lifted his head and gazed down at her with so much love in his eyes it took her breath away. She reached up and guided his face to hers and chastely kissed his lips.

"Zain Roman, we are just getting started."

ZAIN STARED AT THE CEILING, unable to believe how his life had taken a turn. He glanced down at Omara who was slumbering naked next to him. Her soft, curvy frame was nestled against him. Their bodies always fit perfectly with one another. Once Jason had fallen asleep, Zain had carried Omara back to their room and showed her just how much he appreciated the gift she had bestowed upon him.

His heart still raced at the thought of the life

they had created together. Those three pregnancy tests sat on the nightstand beside their bed. For so long he had wanted to be able to bring a child into the world but had been denied that opportunity. After the divorce from Freya, he had put aside the thoughts of a family.

Maybe being a family man wasn't for him. With the dangerous job he had, maybe having a family wasn't in the stars for him. He had accepted it. At least he'd tried to convince himself of that.

Then Omara had come into his life. With her sexy smile, talented hands, and a body that hardened his cock with one look.

There was no doubt this woman was for him.

But now, not only did he have a ready-made family in Omara and Jason, who he loved like his own flesh and blood, now they would be expanding.

Zain reached down and placed a hand over Omara's little pouch of a stomach. He smiled, remembering her complaining that her favorite jeans didn't fit. She had cursed and pouted, refusing to even think of going out to purchase new ones.

Now they knew why.

A shudder rippled through him. He stared at the woman who he loved more than life itself. Soon, she'd have his last name, and they would be spending the rest of their lives together.

The realization hit Zain, snatching all of the air from his lungs. Tears blurred his vision. He wiped them away before they had a chance to fall. He settled back on the bed and brought Omara into his embrace. She snuggled closer to him, draping an arm across his stomach. He smiled, kissing the top of her head.

The life he had always wanted was finally his.

A NOTE FROM THE AUTHOR

Dear reader,

Thank you for your love and support of my SWAT series. It has meant so much to me over the years. I hope you enjoyed Zain and Omara's story. They were a joy to write about and I'm glad they got their happy ever after.

For all of you who have asked, yes, Jordan will get her own book! She will end the SWAT series. So stay tuned, I'll be sharing more about her book soon.

Happy reading,
Peyton

P.S. Don't forget to leave a review of this book! This helps other readers know what others thought.

P.S.S. And just to tease you a little...we will be coming back to Columbia in the future!

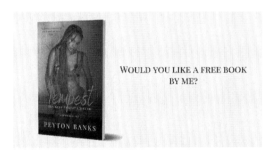

TRUST & HONOR SERIES
ANOTHER ROMANTIC SUSPENSE SERIES BY PEYTON BANKS!

Saving a damsel in distress was not in the description for these two first responders.

The Trust and Honor series is full of suspense, action, and plenty of steamy heat that will have readers devouring the pages well into the night.

If you love alpha males who will fight to save the women they love, then download this collection now!

Book One: Dallas

It wasn't his job to protect her, but there's no way he's leaving her side.

Book Two: Dalton

Putting out fires was his life's work. This new flame, there's no way he's extinguishing it.

Click HERE to download this complete series today! Love audiobooks? Snag it HERE on Audible!

The Trust and Honor series is a steamy, contemporary BWWM romance. It is reserved for mature readers over 18 years of age.

ABOUT THE AUTHOR

USA TODAY bestselling author, Peyton Banks is the alter ego of a city girl who is a romantic at heart. Her mornings consist of coffee and daydreaming up the next steamy romance book ideas. She loves spinning romantic tales of hot alpha males and the women they love. Make sure you check her out!

Sign up for Peyton's Newsletter to find out the latest releases, giveaways and news! Click HERE to sign up or visit her website www.peytonbanks.com!

Want to know the latest about Peyton Banks? Follow her online:

Current Free Short Story

Summer Escape

Blazing Eagle Ranch Series

Back in the Saddle

Knockin' the Boots

Roping a Cowboy

Country at Heart

Cowboy, Take Me Away

Hard to Forget

Special Weapons & Tactics Series

Dirty Tactics (Special Weapons & Tactics 1)

Dirty Ballistics (Special Weapons & Tactics 2)

Dirty Operations (Special Weapons & Tactics 3)

Dirty Alliance (Special Weapons & Tactics 4)

Dirty Justice (Special Weapons & Tactics 5)

Dirty Trust (Special Weapons & Tactics 6)

Dirty Secrets (Special Weapons & Tactics 7)

Dirty Ultimatum (Special Weapons & Tactics 8)

Trust & Honor Series (BWWM)

Dallas

Dalton

Interracial Romances (BWWM)

Pieces of Me

Hard Love

Retain Me

Silent Deception

The Christmas Secret

Mr. Hotness

African American Romance

Breaking The Rules

Mafia Romance Series

Unexpected Allies (The Tokhan Bratva 1)

Unexpected Chaos (The Tokhan Bratva 2) TBD

Unexpected Hero (The Tokhan Bratva 3) TBD

Made in the USA
Columbia, SC
15 March 2025